Fatal

T.A. BROCK

OMNIFIC PUBLISHING

LOS ANGELES

Omnific Publishing
1901 Avenue of the Stars, 2nd floor
Los Angeles, CA 90067
www.omnificpublishing.com

First Omnific eBook edition, March 2014
First Omnific trade paperback edition, March 2014

The characters and events in this book are fictitious.
Any similarity to real persons, living or dead,
is coincidental and not intended by the author.

Library of Congress Cataloguing-in-Publication Data

Brock, T.A.
   Fatal / T.A. Brock – 1st ed.
   ISBN: 978-1-623421-05-2
   1. Young Adult — Romance. 2. Zombies — Fiction.
   3. High School — Fiction. 4. Supernatural — Fiction. I. Title

10 9 8 7 6 5 4 3 2 1

Cover Design by Micha Stone and Amy Brokaw
Interior Book Design by Coreen Montagna

Printed in the United States of America

Prologue

RISING

An infected human dies immediately. True, but what they don't tell you is how long they stay dead. Perhaps that's because there's no real way to answer that. Ask a zombie whether or not they're dead, and they'll tell you without hesitation, yes. Ask a human whether or not a zombie is alive. They'll tell you, with the teensiest amount of hesitation and a question mark at the end, yes?

That's why it's better the humans don't know about us. Easier.

We get what we want that way: anonymity.

To them we are simply more of what they are: human. Nothing creepy, nothing scary. Nothing toxic.

Living in secret isn't as hard as you think; I promise. No castle on a hill to hole up in or anything like that. We live among them. The best hiding place is in plain sight.

There is only one thing you must remember: the water. Always remember what I told you about the water.

Let's see…I think I covered everything. Any questions?

No? Good.

Welcome to our tribe.

Chapter 1

A Great Day to Be a Zombie

Grayson Patch didn't need an alarm clock. His brother, Leiv's, habit of blaring eighties era Poison and Whitesnake on the surround sound in the living room usually did the trick. Leiv was what you would call a morning person. On a normal day Grayson would despise him for it, for depriving him of the privilege of hitting the snooze button. But not today.

Today was a great day.

Grayson rolled out of bed and stretched. With surprise, he realized he was smiling. And maybe there was a little hop in his step as he went into the bathroom. Looking in the mirror, he actually considered what to do with his hair. The thick black locks normally stood out from his scalp in total disarray because he just didn't care to fix them. Leiv had once said his hair made him look like a rock star.

Grayson guessed that was probably a compliment.

Today though, he used a little bit of that gel stuff Raina had bought for him — his sister was always muttering for him to fix his hair. But even with the gel, it stuck out every which way. It was rebellious. Like him. So he let it do its thing. After all…

It was a great day.

Grayson's mood only got better as he pulled on his jeans and a black T-shirt. His accessories consisted of a huge ugly ring that he wore on his middle finger, a length of chain, and a leather strap. Although these things went with his look, they weren't for decoration. They were simply the only kind of weapons he could carry in high school. And he definitely needed weapons.

Grayson was a…well, a zombie. A riser, to be exact. One who wasn't a disintegrating mess.

So were Leiv and Raina.

None of them had reached the Age of Deterioration yet, so in many ways they were normal. And in many ways, they were not.

Unlike his adopted brother and sister, Grayson spent a lot of time hating who he was. Hating that he was dead. Hating the things he had to do to survive.

Not today though.

He went into the kitchen where his brother was bobbing his head to "Here I Go Again." The only thing keeping the guy from singing at the top of his lungs was the gallon jug of water he was about to chug.

"Oh, hey, bro," Leiv said and then began gulping.

The water did its job, quickly filling in the parts of Leiv's face that had sunken in and turned gray overnight. Grayson started in on his own jug as Raina breezed into the room, her long black hair flowing behind her. Clearly she'd already hydrated since she didn't look like death warmed over.

"Today's the big day," she announced as if any of them needed a reminder. "How you feeling, Gray?"

"Fine," he mumbled.

"Oh, come on. You're better than fine." Her perusing eyes settled on his head. "Is that gel in your hair?"

Grayson shrugged. He didn't want the two of them to know how excited he was. For them it was already too late. For Grayson however…there was still a chance. But that's all it was. A chance. He wished they wouldn't make such a huge deal about it. The three of them were placing a lot of hope on something that could very well not work. After all, it hadn't worked for his brother and sister. Now they were stuck like this. Until they became rotters.

Still, this was *his* chance.

Today he would meet *her*. The one and only person who could free him of his zombie curse. For each of his kind there was but one in the world — one human — who could help them reverse the plague that made them into living dead. It wasn't easy though. No one had figured out how to do it yet. All they knew was that the cure would bring death to the human.

That was the part Grayson was choosing to ignore.

Because that was the part that would finally make him a monster.

Leiv had told him there were tests a *Save* had to pass before they died. Tests given by the Oracles. Tests that were apparently impossible. But even still, passing the tests didn't matter if you couldn't finish the deal. The dying part was the biggest mystery. You couldn't just outright kill a *Save*.

Zombies had tried that tactic. And failed.

Grayson shivered. He hated the idea of murdering a human, as he'd been murdered. Since rising, he couldn't remember any of his true family, but he was fresh enough that whoever they were, they were likely still alive. What if one of them were *Save* to a zombie, were killed for a mere chance at reversing the rising?

He shook his head. This had to happen. It was the only way for him to be human again. The guilt, he would deal with later.

Grayson grabbed his backpack and headed for the door. As he was leaving, he caught his reflection in the mirror by the entrance. His eyes were dark, shadowed, haunted. What would they be like when he was no longer a zombie?

The same, he thought. *They would be the same.*

He shoved the depressing thought from his mind because today was a great day to be a zombie.

Chapter 2

A Horrible Day to Be Human

As Cori Abbott trudged toward the daunting double doors of Westland Heights High, she was filled with pure dread. Starting a new school at sixteen years old was hard. Starting a new school in this dreary, watery, hopelessly tiny town was even harder. But they needed a brand new start, her mother had said. And she was right. Cori could admit it.

After her father's sudden death there'd been too many memories in Indiana. Around every corner, a face that held pity. Around every bend, a place that brought a recollection of happier times. And so they'd moved halfway across the continent to the Pacific Northwest and a cute-as-a-button place called Asher, Oregon.

Maybe it would've been harder to pick up and leave if Cori'd had more friends. But the truth was, she was only leaving one behind. Although Asia had been her best friend, things had been a little bumpy between the two of them lately. It was Cori's fault. She'd pushed Asia away after her dad's accident. Even still, she wished Asia was here now.

Because this was a horrible day.

Cori was shy and backward and the thought of talking to people she didn't know made her feel nauseated. People just didn't get her. No one did except maybe Asia. And her daddy. He'd gotten her. She'd taken after him. His shy, quiet ways were hers. Hadn't Mom always said they were cut from the same cloth?

"Corinne, you are a mini-Norman," she'd say with a huff. "Now, I adore your daddy, but you need to be more outgoing. Give people a reason to like you."

On the other hand, Daddy always told her, "Be yourself, Cori. It's reason enough for people to like you."

She didn't know which one of them was right, but at least her dad had known what it meant to be loved for *who* he was, not *what* he was. She'd admired that about him.

This was her chance though. No one knew she was quiet and backward and in mourning. No one knew anything about her. She could fake it. She could fake being normal…at least for a little while. She just had to force herself to be outgoing. Look people in the eye. Be the first to speak. And smile. Her mom was always reminding her to smile.

As soon as she'd passed through the doors of the school she felt eyes on her. Apparently staring wasn't considered rude here in Asher. Maybe that was just part of living in a small town.

Luckily, she already had her class schedule and the school was small enough for her to easily find her way around. Her locker was difficult to get to because of all the people standing around it. But they stopped talking and parted for her when she got close.

Like Moses and the Red Sea, she thought.

They kept up the staring as she deposited her backpack. Still, no one said anything.

Be the first to talk.

After a deep breath of courage, she turned to the girl closest to her. With dark rimmed glasses taking up most of her roundish face and her hair stuffed up in a beanie, the girl seemed approachable. Normal even. "Hi, I'm Cori," she told her.

The girl, frowning, looked her up and down once before finally answering, "I'm Rachel."

Umm…okay. *Say something!*

"It's my first day," Cori blurted.

Rachel rolled her eyes as she slammed her locker. "Yeah, I got that."

Cori cringed inside. It was a horrible day.

She watched, dumbstruck, as a beefed up guy wearing a green and white letter jacket pushed Rachel up against the locker and dove in for her lips. Whoa. She knew she should look away, but it was like a train wreck. Or like a Hot Wheel colliding with a Mack truck. There should be some resulting damage.

A whistle blew and they pulled apart, Rachel giggling. "No PDA, Evans. Last warning." Cori looked away in time to see an older man in warm-ups, carrying a clipboard, pass by.

Rachel's boy toy grinned. "Yes, Coach."

When he was gone, Cori was still staring at the couple.

"What are you looking at?" Rachel hissed, and then the two melted into the crowd of students.

"Don't mind her," a voice said from behind. Cori turned around to see who the voice belonged to and had to look up quite a ways until she saw the curly redhead with startling green eyes. "She's just snooty," the girl continued.

Snooty? By appearances, she just seemed so average. What did she have to be snooty about? Besides the hunk that was obviously very much into her.

"I'm Peg."

"Cori."

She nodded. "What's your first class?"

Cori glanced at her schedule. "Uh, English with Mr. Peters."

"It's next door to mine. I'll take you there if you want."

Cori tried to smile. "Yeah, thanks."

Peg was tall and graceful like a dancer and her stride was long so Cori had to really work to keep up with her. She talked a lot too, but it wasn't the kind of conversation where you had to do much answering, so that was good. She knew she should be listening to what the girl was saying, but her rattled nerves were a distraction.

And so were Peg's clothes.

The girl was colorful, from head to toe, starting with her bright red hair. She wore a lemon yellow T-shirt that was a little too tight, an orange scarf draped around her shoulders, and a black denim mini-skirt with hot pink leggings. It should have made her look like a toddler but somehow she pulled it off. Maybe it was the three-inch cork-soled sandals that did it.

As they passed people in the hall, Peg smiled or nodded. And people smiled back. Genuinely. Not that saccharine smile that some people their age had perfected to get them through high school politics. That told Cori one thing: people liked Peg.

"All right, here we are. Mr. Peter's class. Who do you have next?"

Cori looked again at her schedule. "Mrs. Simon."

Peg screwed up her face. "Eww, Mrs. Simon. She smells like fish. You'll find her class down at the end of this hall, on the right."

"Okay. Thanks."

"Do you have lunch A or B?"

"Uh, B. I think."

Peg smiled, showing a perfect set of straight teeth — except for the slightly chipped one in the front. "Good! Me too. If you want, you can sit with us."

Us. That meant meeting more people. But then, that was exactly what she was going to be doing. Meeting new people. She had no choice. Well, she could drop out of school, maybe…but that was stupid.

"Yeah, that would be great," Cori answered.

"Okay. I'll see you then."

Peg hurried through the door on the opposite side of the hall and Cori turned to face the one she was supposed to go through. The hallway was mostly empty now with the last stragglers slipping into their appointed classes and a few who clearly didn't care if they were tardy. She had to force her feet to move forward.

The bell ringing startled her. Great. Now she was late.

A guy with drumsticks stuffed in his back pocket — and not the cool kind; the ones with the big pads on the ends — brushed past her, stepping on her toes. A whimper escaped as his boots crushed her smallest digit.

It was a horrible, awful day.

And then she was in the room. Just as she'd suspected, everyone stared. Some yawned, still trying to shake the morning fog. Some sat at attention, clearly interested. But all stared — except for the one in the back who seemed to be asleep. Even the teacher just looked at her like maybe she was lost. He was the *teacher*. Wasn't he expecting her?

She moved to his desk and handed him her schedule.

"Ah, yes." He nodded. "Class, we have a new student. Corinne Abbott."

"Cori," she corrected.

"All right, Cori. Let's see, I think there's an open desk over there in the corner. Take a seat and I'll get you a textbook."

Carefully, she made her way between the crowded row of students until she found the first empty seat. Next to drummer boy.

A couple latecomers slipped in while Mr. Peters rummaged through a cabinet.

He'd just handed over a thick book when all of a sudden, Cori's vision got blurry and dizziness swamped her. She squeezed her eyes shut, hoping it would go away, hoping nobody noticed. She was already the center of attention. Fainting would make that ten times worse.

When she opened her eyes again, she was relieved that the dizziness was gone and the lesson had started.

Bonus lesson: it's a bad idea to skip breakfast.

Cori made it through her first two classes with minimal interaction. She was pretty sure she forgot to smile most of the time. No one really talked to her, but that was more of a relief than a disappointment.

In her next class, she was horrified when the blurry vision returned — this time with a crippling headache. She pushed her palms into her eye sockets to try to ease the sudden sharp pain. It didn't let up though. It was fire and nails and a million kinds of blades. She tried opening her eyes and immediately had to close them. The light seemed too bright, too intense. Like the sun was perching on the shoulders of the girl in front of her, sticking his fiery tongue out in mockery.

With both hands gripping her head, she tried to think of what to do, but it was impossible. The pain was too much.

And then as sudden as it came, it went. In its place was the strangest sensation, like a pulling force of some sort. Almost like she was a magnet being drawn toward metal. It wasn't uncomfortable; it was just really intense. Compared to the headache, it was heavenly.

She looked toward the door. Through the window, she saw *him*. Tall and dark, with crazy messy black hair. And gorgeous. He was *gorgeous*. He looked so out of place there that she wondered if he was even a student.

Then he looked at her. Directly at her. As if he was looking *for* her.

Chills raced up her spine at his expression. He looked so very angry. Why?

Cori was held spellbound by this stranger's shrewd gaze, unable to look away.

A moment later, he was gone. Weird.

Surely his anger wasn't for her. But still, could things get worse?

This was a horrible, wretched day.

Would it never end?

Chapter 3

A Nothing-Special Human

Grayson didn't know who she was, but he knew she would be there today, at school. He'd known the exact date for years. He also knew that finding her would be a cinch. They were meant to meet. They would each feel the connection, the pull. It would be undeniable.

What he didn't know was what to do once he found her. But he would get to that later. First things, first.

As he stalked toward the doors of the school, he kept up his usual glare — couldn't risk anybody thinking he was in a good mood. He spared a glance at the moist, colorless sky. His pale grayish skin fit right in with his surroundings. A morbid chameleon. Anywhere else in the world, the natural skin tone of a zombie would stand out. But not here in the upper northwest corner of the United States. Some of the humans here could almost be mistaken for a zombie just because of their coloring. The lack of sun did much to help his kind blend in.

He pushed through the doors and immediately began scanning the crowd. He couldn't feel her yet, but he wasn't alarmed. Somewhere in this place there was a new girl…he just had to follow all the awkward stares until he found her — or got close enough to feel her.

As he meandered through the halls, people stayed out of his way. As they always did. It was good because he was all purpose right then. It'd be extremely annoying if some twiggy freshman got in his way.

There it was. The pull. Like an invisible bungee cord that connected him to her. It had been stretched too tight for so long, linking them across distances, that it'd been almost nonexistent. But now that they were in each other's vicinity, the band was snapping back, contracting with a force neither of them would be able to ignore.

Grayson stopped walking and let his senses take over. Yes, it was her. She was here. And nearby.

He was shocked to realize he almost felt alive again — the hair on his arms stood up; a chill ran down his back; he could breathe easier, think clearer. He knew both zombie and *Save* would experience unique physical reactions when in close proximity to one another, but Leiv and Raina hadn't told him he would feel like *this*. He really couldn't remember what it felt like to be alive…but this was as close as he could imagine.

He noticed some students looking at him strangely. When he went to glare at them, he was horrified to realize he was smiling. *Smiling*. Great. Just great.

Whatever.

He continued down the hall, following the pull. Almost…he was almost there. Just a little closer…riiight…there.

Grayson stopped short when he saw her.

This was a mistake. Had to be. He looked around for someone else. But no, she was the only person he didn't recognize.

With narrowed eyes, he examined her. She wasn't what he'd expected. Not. At. All. He'd imagined someone much like his sister: statuesque and strong, with an attitude to match. Someone who could make a valid attempt at passing the Oracles' tests. Someone who could actually succeed. What was before his eyes was…shrimpy.

He watched from a distance as the girl put her backpack in her locker. She was tiny, barely five feet tall, and plain as vanilla ice cream. Straight brown hair hung down her back. He couldn't see much of her face, but from what he could tell, it wasn't anything to look twice at. She was dressed simply in jeans and a long sleeved shirt. There was nothing special about this human.

Nothing at all.

How was this depressingly average girl supposed to save him? She looked like she could barely carry her books down the hall.

Anger and frustration filled him until all he could see was shades of sepia. That's when he knew his eyes had turned. Quickly, he ducked into the restroom and shut himself in one of the stalls. He forced himself to calm down. Leiv had taught him a lot about taming his temper, and he was glad for it in moments like these. Because if anyone got a look at his eyes right now…these eyes weren't human, weren't alive.

A minute later the door opened and he heard two voices.

"You see the new girl?"

"Yeah. Nothing special."

His thoughts exactly. Grayson rolled his eyes.

"I heard she was from New York or something."

"No, man, Tennessee."

"Oh, yeah. I guess that's it. Whatever."

Finally they were gone. Grayson came out of the stall and examined his reflection in the mirror. His eyes were back to their normal green-brown color. His reflection looked mad. He *was* mad.

So long, he'd waited for this day for so long, only to find that his savior was a miniature human from Tennessee.

Good thing he hadn't hung his hopes on her…yeah, good thing.

He left the bathroom but decided to skip his first class. Instead, he spent the whole hour in the parking lot, staring out his windshield and wondering what he should do now.

Maybe he shouldn't discard her yet. Just because she looked inadequate didn't necessarily mean she was. Maybe she knew something that could help him. Maybe she was super smart or something, a genius. Sometimes brains could be better than brawn. Sometimes. Mostly never.

He decided that he should talk to her. Then he would know for sure if she could help him.

Grayson couldn't make himself sit through class yet, so he spent all of second hour planning out what he would tell his brother and sister. There had to be a way to let them down easy. In his mind he'd already failed. There was nothing this girl could do for him. But at least he would be sure before he went home to his family.

He couldn't find her in the hall before third hour, so fifteen minutes into class he asked to be excused to the restroom. It didn't take long for him to locate her. Once he could feel himself being drawn in her direction, it took only minutes to reach the classroom she was in. As he walked past, he glanced through the window.

And he became angry all over again.

Sure enough. There she was, his shrimpy little savior.

He still couldn't see her face very well. He'd have to get a better look at her at lunch. Hopefully she had lunch B.

When he was almost back to class, the unexpected happened.

Grayson was overcome by a gut clenching pain. It wasn't the first and it wouldn't be the last. But it was damn sure inconvenient. In the zombie world this pain was known as a water cramp, and it occurred when they were under-hydrated. Zombies had to have water. Lots of it. They had to drink it, live it, breathe it, and dream it. It was the only way their bodies could function. The cells had to be consistently hydrated and rehydrated. It was their one crutch and there was no avoiding it. They could go longer between feedings, days even, but water was a constant need.

He glanced around. No water fountains in sight. But the bathroom wasn't too far away.

Grayson was in pure agony as his internal organs refused to work. As quickly as he could, he scooted—or as he liked to think of it, zombie-walked—toward the bathroom. With his joints refusing to move right, it really did resemble Hollywood's version of the ghoulish undead.

Once he'd made it there, he lunged for a sink and, lowering his head, drank directly from the faucet. He drank and drank but still the pain didn't ease. A full five minutes later he finally felt close to normal. He turned off the tap. Dried his hands. Looked in the mirror. He could recall it as if it had happened just yesterday instead of fifteen years ago…

He awoke that morning to Raina's nearly unbearable excitement. She was bustling around the house, fixing things up and humming (off key) while she did it.

"What's up with her?" he asked Leiv.

Not meeting Grayson's eyes, he said, "We'll be having a visitor this evening. Someone special."

"A visitor? Human or zombie?"

"Zombie," Leiv answered.

Grayson was astonished at the idea. He'd never seen another zombie besides Leiv and Raina.

"An Oracle," Leiv added, making Grayson's jaw drop in wonder.

The Oracles were revered by all of the Dead Walking. They themselves were of the risen dead, however, they were special…they had made it past the Age of Deterioration without losing their minds, without their bodies withering, without becoming contagious. And so they were allowed to live. Forever, it seemed, since none had ever had reason to be euthanized. There were few of them but they were the oldest and wisest among all zombies. The Old Ones, they were called. They guided the species in the proper ways, their leadership necessary in order to maintain balance between the zombies and the humans.

But there was rarely a reason for one of them to visit a tribe.

"An Oracle? But why?"

"She's coming to see you, dude," his brother answered as he picked the newspaper off the table.

Grayson's jaw couldn't have gotten any closer to the floor. "Me?"

"Yes," Leiv said, still not looking at him. "Today you will learn everything you need to know about your Save."

Grayson was wrong; his jaw, amazingly enough, dropped farther.

This was something he'd been waiting for. From the moment he'd risen, all he could think about was being human again. Either that or dying again—but without the rising.

Grayson walked around in a fog for the rest of the day, not sure whether to believe his good fortune or not. But when the doorbell rang ten minutes after sunset, he knew Leiv had been right. He watched with a strange detachment as Raina rushed to the door to let their visitor in. She had filled goblets with icy water and set them out in the living room where he and Leiv were waiting. There was also a tray full of thinly sliced raw beef, pork, and veal.

All of it was forgotten though, as a small white-haired woman dressed in all white pranced delicately into the room. She didn't appear old even with the white hair—and even though she actually was. Perhaps it was the absence of wrinkles. She was petite from her short, pointy nose to her inevitably tiny toes. One might think her powerless, especially going *by the expression on her heart-shaped face. It was guileless, angelic. She almost seemed like a child.*

He couldn't believe it really. This was one of their renowned leaders?

She gave a single nod to Leiv before taking a seat. Once she was comfortable, her eyes honed in on Grayson and it was then that he knew he'd terribly misjudged her. Those eyes were the strangest color of brown he'd ever seen—sort of a mocha color mixed with ash—and they were shrewd. He had to force himself not to shiver. When she spoke, he was even more certain his first impressions were wrong.

In an unexpectedly deep voice she said, "You are Grayson." It was the voice of a smoker who'd swallowed velvet.

There was no question mark after she spoke, but he nodded anyway.

"I am Hannah. I assume you know what I am." Again no question mark. And again, he nodded. She gave him a once-over, pursing her dainty lips in a way that made him want to squirm. "I have seen that you've been unhappy with your lot, quite nearly from the day of your rising."

"You've seen?" He hadn't meant to say it out loud.

Her expression became even sharper. "Of course I have seen; I am a seer."

"Yes, ma'am— "

"As I was saying, we've not seen another of the Dead Walking who is quite as unhappy as you. It puzzles us—and believe me when I say, there is not much in the world that succeeds in puzzling us. When you are as knowledgeable as we are, it is almost a joy to discover something that has the power to mystify." She sighed heavily, almost dramatically. "As thrilling as it is, however, we are not entirely cruel-hearted." She glanced quickly at Leiv and then back. "No matter what some might think. So. The time has come for you to begin the journey that will lead to your inevitable happiness. Are you ready to hear of your Save?"

Grayson knew his eyes were wide. He would need water soon; he could practically hear the fluid as it pumped wildly in his veins. Never had he been so excited. Finally he nodded.

"You will meet your Save for the first time in your nineteenth year after rising. You will meet her at the high school you will begin attending in your sixteenth year, in a town not far from here called Asher." Grayson nodded. He knew where Asher was; he'd been there plenty of times. "She will come on the one hundred and ninth day of school. She alone has the

ability to save you from the reality that you hate so badly, but know that it will come at a price: her life for your happiness. If you are willing to accept that, then you will have what you desire." Hannah stopped and stared at him, appraising.

Grayson nodded like the price required was his favorite comic book and not someone's life. He reacted like a zombie.

He was a zombie.

And maybe inside he always would be.

Chapter 4

A BUMP IN THE NIGHT...ER, DAY

By the time the bell rang for lunch, Grayson was completely out of patience. In the hall, he tried to feel the pull…and then it was there. He followed it until the shrimp was in his sights. She was struggling down the hall, carrying a stack of books almost as tall as she was. It was clear that she couldn't see where she was going.

Suddenly, he had an idea.

As casually as he could, he sauntered toward her, watching her stumble along. When he was close, he stepped in front of her.

Perfect.

The tiny wonder smacked right into him and all her books went flying in the air. With a gasp, she dropped to the ground to pick them up.

Up close he could see that it was just as he'd suspected: she was plain as the dickens, flighty and weak. He was about to walk away without saying anything to her. But then she peered up at him.

It was the first good look he'd gotten of her face. And it was sorta like a punch in the gut. A much deserved punch since he'd just purposely tripped her up.

It was her eyes. They had him riveted. They were ice-blue, but not at all cold. And they sparkled like tiny crystal orbs, but they weren't delicate. It was more like they contained electricity. Like tapping into them could easily support the power grid of a good-sized city.

These eyes didn't belong on a human. They were…otherworldly. They were…they were…so not average. Not plain. And not weak. He wondered whether, if he stared at them directly, he would be burned or something — they were that powerful, that intense. Like staring at the sun. But with a blue flame.

Then she spoke.

"I'm so sorry. I wasn't watching where I was going and I was in a hurry. I guess I just…"

He wasn't paying any attention to the words coming out of her mouth. Not at all. He was way too distracted by her voice. It was like music. But not the hair-metal stuff Leiv listened to or the femme-rock that Raina liked or even the indie-rock that he often jammed out to. No, it was like the stuff the angels played in heaven. Grayson didn't believe in heaven — or angels — but maybe…maybe she was one? She couldn't be human. Couldn't be. No way.

"…anyway, I'm sorry."

She waited for him to say something but he didn't. So she went back to picking up the books. He watched her. He should've helped, but he was too busy being astonished.

When she was done, she awkwardly stood up. This close, he could see that she wasn't even as tall as his shoulders.

He noticed she missed a book, so he bent to retrieve it. When he handed it to her, they locked eyes again. Hers were cool and sweet like a drink of ice water in the desert. He wanted to ask her what she was, but he couldn't make those words come out. Probably a good thing.

"What's your name?" he asked instead. His voice sounded rough, cruel. But she didn't seem to care.

"Corinne. But people call me Cori." She hesitated. "What's yours?"

He didn't want her to know his name. He didn't want anything to do with her. She was strange — possibly even more than he was. He wanted to forget her, forget this whole day, forget what her eyes looked like, forget how her voice made him feel like he was human again. He wanted to go back to thinking she was plain and dull and useless.

"Next time watch where you're going," he growled and then turned and stalked away.

Cori stared after him, apparently stricken paralyzed. Because moving was just out of the question. Who *was* that guy? He was so rude. And oh my, why was he so utterly gorgeous? She'd never been attracted to the bad-boy type before. But this guy—

There was *something* about him.

Of course, he could be less of a jerk. Would it have hurt him to help pick up her books?

When he was out of sight, Cori continued to her locker and shoved the giant stack of texts inside. Making her way to the cafeteria, she kept an eye out for Peg. She found her at a table smack in the center of the room. Only one other person was sitting with her, and Cori let out a relieved breath.

After going through the line at the salad bar, she wove through the crowd toward Peg's table.

"Oh good! You made it," Peg said with a smile.

Cori put her tray down and realized she was shaking a little. The run-in with the mystery guy had only made her nerves worse.

"This is Rex," Peg told her, pointing to the only other person at the table.

Cori tried to smile at the guy. He was the gangly type with almost too-big ears. His face, she noticed, was incredibly symmetrical, giving him a distinct quality different from what might normally be considered attractive. Thin wire glasses sat upon his perfectly pointed nose, and his hair—maybe his best physical trait—was a gold-blond layer of spiky perfection. It seemed that his name was meant for someone different. Almost as if his parents had chosen it with wishful thinking. It was like naming a kitten Tiger.

"A pleasure to meet you, Cori," he spoke with such eloquence. "I'm told you are from the great state of Tennessee?"

She grinned. "Uh, no. I'm from Indianapolis."

He semi-glared at Peg, and she shrugged. "Someone told me Tennessee. So kill me."

He returned his attention to Cori. "How are you liking the tiny town of Asher?"

Not wanting to offend him, she said, "It's nice."

He surprised her by rolling his eyes. "Hardly. But at least it's not hot here. I detest the heat." His pointy nose crinkled.

She had to smile. He was just so strange, but in a way that she could still appreciate.

Before she could answer, her weird headache came back, followed by that odd pulling sensation. Her attention was drawn to the back of the cafeteria. The guy she'd smacked into was there, by himself at a table, with just a bottle of water. He wasn't looking at her—or anything else for that matter. Instead, his brow was drawn tight and he was glaring at the table as if it had offended him. Every little while, he would gulp the water.

Someone cleared their throat. It was Peg.

"Grayson Patch," she said, inclining her head toward him as she bit into her sandwich.

Cori was still staring at him.

"He's bad news," Peg continued. "Unless, of course, you're into the bad boys. Then he'd be right up your alley. But I get the feeling he's not really into high school girls."

"Or girls at all," Rex added.

"Or people, period."

"What do you mean?" Cori asked, distracted.

"He's what you would call a loner," Rex explained. "A recluse. As antisocial as one can be while in high school. It's quite possible that he hates everyone and everything. Including himself."

Well at least it isn't just me, Cori thought.

"I, uh, bumped into him in the hallway."

Peg's eyes got wide. "Really. And you still have your head?"

"Yeah. Barely." Cori laughed nervously. "Do you think I should try to apologize again?"

Peg and Rex exchanged a pitying look.

"Doll, it wouldn't matter if you apologized seventy times seven. He still would hate you—as he does everyone else," Rex told her.

Cori pressed her lips together.

"Aw, don't worry about it," Peg said, patting her on the back. "He'll hate someone else by the end of lunch."

Cori sighed. She didn't want him to hate her.

"Maybe he's just misunderstood," she tried.

There was a pause. "Oh, good. You're an optimist. We needed one of those around here," Rex said with a grin that managed to be both friendly and sarcastic at the same time.

Peg turned to glare at him. "What are you talking about? *I'm* an optimist."

"No, Peggy, *you* are a realist."

Peg's face transformed into a scary mask between one blink and the next. "If you *ever* call me Peggy again, there will be hell to pay… *Rexy*."

Rex turned white. "Point taken."

Peg shifted to Cori again, her face returning to normal. "We've been friends since we were in diapers. Sometimes the names slip out."

Cori nodded. So they were friends and not more. Good to know. But she wondered if there was a story there.

"Listen, it's real sweet of you to think of Grayson like that…but he really is just a meanie, Cori. You'll see."

Cori let it go and finished her salad.

She decided she really liked Peg and Rex. They were different, like she was, and they were fun. But she couldn't get Grayson Patch out of her head. She knew people like him only acted hateful because they were miserable. It was a way of coping. So what was his problem? His *real* problem. Why was he so unhappy? Maybe she could help him somehow. It was just her way to try to fix things — especially the things that seemed unfixable.

"I think…I think I'm gonna try to talk to him," she mumbled.

"Um, okay." Peg seemed truly puzzled.

Cori stood. "I'll catch you guys later."

After she dumped her tray, she wandered over to Grayson's table. He didn't look up when she approached.

She cleared her throat, more for courage than to get his attention. "Um, hi." He glanced up and then back at the table. And whether it was his action or that she needed more to eat, vertigo hit her hard. She steadied herself with one hand on a chair. "I just wanted to say sorry again for running into you in the hall, and make sure you came through unscathed. No textbook injuries, right?"

He didn't answer.

"Those things can be dangerous. I swear one of them weighs ten pounds." She laughed nervously.

He remained silent.

"Uh…you're Grayson, right?"

Slowly, he lifted his head and stared up at her through slitted eyes.

"Y-You never told me your name," she sputtered.

"I never told you because I didn't want you to know it." He spit his words as if they were weapons. Darts. Her face, the bull's-eye.

"Oh. Um, well…Peg told me."

"Did she? How precious," he sneered. "Do me a favor, shortcake. Go away and leave me alone."

Cori remained right where she was. She wasn't sure why. Maybe because she refused to be ordered around by a stranger. Or maybe because she didn't think he really wanted to be left alone.

"Are you deaf as well as clumsy?"

She shook her head.

"I said. Go. Away." His face was cruel, which made it so much more disturbing that it was also beautiful.

"Okay," she said softly. She hated sounding so timid, but that's exactly what she was. The fact that she'd found it so easy to walk over here and initiate a conversation was a complete mystery. But now her courage was gone and she felt like crawling under a rock.

Cori walked away as fast as she could and didn't look back.

Chapter 5

USING THE USELESS

Grayson watched Cori go and he was more frustrated than ever. He didn't have much time to think about it, though, because Peg Matthews was beelining it for his table.

"What did you do?" she hissed.

He just looked at her. He didn't owe her any explanations.

"What did you say, huh?"

Still he didn't respond. Why bother?

"You listen here, Patch, that girl is sweeter than sugar. She's probably in the bathroom now, crying her eyes out. What's your problem anyway? Someone piss in your Cheerios this morning?"

He didn't eat Cheerios. Couldn't. Meat only. And raw. But someone should invent zombie cereal. Meat chunks in a bowl with water. It could work.

Peg threw up her hands in a frustrated gesture. "Just…be nice. She's used to nice. I can tell."

With that, she stomped off in the same direction as Cori.

What she really meant was Cori was timid and fragile. Fragile like most humans. And she was right. She probably was off crying somewhere. Which was just fine with him. She should toughen up. The world didn't get any easier from here on out.

Part of him though, a tiny, miniscule part, hoped she wasn't crying because of him. After all, she hadn't done anything wrong. Yes, she was a disappointment, but that wasn't her fault. She didn't know that he had practically bet his life on her — sight unseen. That was all on him. His fault. And now, at least she would get to live.

The way he figured it, that was a good thing because those eyes weren't meant to see the inside of a coffin. Hearts and flowers and butterflies maybe. But never a grave.

Grayson dreaded going home after school. So he didn't. Instead, he went to his favorite place: the cemetery, known to the locals as Stonehenge. He liked it there because it was peaceful. Something about the dead staying dead comforted him — to rest in death was only an figment of the imagination for him and his kind.

His favorite place of all was beyond the rows of headstones. A thick strip of trees lined the outer edge of the farthest lawn, and if you walked through them you could find your way to the river.

It was solitude.

Quiet.

And best of all, wet.

Glancing around to make sure he was really alone, Grayson stripped down to his shorts and jumped into the cool water. Immediate relief, as if his skin cells were drinking through a straw. He floated on his back, everything except his eyes, nose, and mouth covered in cool liquid bliss.

As he stared at the overcast sky, his mind was finally calm enough to think rationally about the events of the day.

He wished things could be different.

Like, he wished he hadn't been so mean to Cori. And he wished he could've just looked at her and known the answers to becoming human again. He wished that nobody had to die to get him there. Most of all, he wished he didn't hate being a zombie so much. Maybe then he could just live out his existence like Leiv and Raina, more or

less happy. If only he could be satisfied with the life he'd been given…
if you could even call it a life.

His thoughts drifted to Cori.

Her eyes…they were so…what? Beautiful? No, he didn't want
to use that word. Intriguing? Yes, but that wasn't enough. Stunning?
Again, yes. But still not adequate. Magical? Yeah. That was it. They
were…magical.

Grayson didn't believe in magic either—he didn't believe in
much—but Cori's eyes were magical in some way. Mysterious and
puzzling and altogether unsettling.

But so what? So there was one spectacular thing about her. Everything else was painfully normal. Well, she also had that tinkly
musical voice.

But still.

How was she supposed to help him? Pretty sure none of the
Oracles' trials involved singing or eye modeling.

When darkness fell, he climbed out of the water and dressed.
He was quick and he went through the woods so he was home in
record time. Just as he feared, his brother and sister were waiting
barely inside the door.

"How was it?" Leiv asked at the same time Raina said, "Did you
talk to her?"

Grayson went past them and into the kitchen where he started
in on a jug of water. They both followed.

"Gray? Was she there? Did you meet her?"

"Yep."

Leiv's whole face lit up. "Awesome, bro! What do you think?"

He forced himself to look his brother in the eye. "She can't help
me."

He hated the way Leiv's face suddenly became a shadow. And
he couldn't even look at Raina.

"What do you mean?" she asked, her voice sounding broken.

"I mean just what I said."

"Well, describe her." Raina's expression was one of confusion, her
perfectly plucked eyebrows dipping low.

Grayson swallowed more water and it rebelled going down.

When he could speak, he said, "She's a tiny little thing, timid and frail. She's shy, quiet. She isn't strong enough to deal with zombies, let alone save one. She's just…weak."

Leiv and Raina were stone quiet. And then his sister's eyes got all misty and a sad little smile found her lips. "She is perfect for you, Gray," she whispered. "She could make you happy, I know it."

Perfect for him?

He looked at her like she'd lost her mind. Anger welled up, and he was completely helpless to stop it. "What are you talking about, Raina? You act like she's supposed to be my girlfriend or something. I'm not looking for love. I'm looking for a way out. I hate living like this. Despise it!"

He was seeing sepia again. For the second time today his fury had turned his world sick shades of brown. He could feel the veins in his eyes constricting.

"Grayson, calm yourself!" Leiv had lost his normally jovial tone.

Grayson turned to the sink and braced his hands on the counter. His breathing was hard and a furious growl was rising in his chest. He just let it come because it was nearly painful to stop it. The gnarled, desperate sound thundered through the kitchen. When he was done, he hung his head and waited for the rage to leave his body.

It did. Eventually. What replaced it was a sinking sense of reality.

"She cannot save me. I am just as doomed as the both of you, and that's the truth of it. I'll be in my room."

He left them staring after him as he struggled to keep his temper in check.

In his room, he went straight for the bed, not bothering to kick off his boots first. He didn't even know who he was angry with, or why exactly. Or even where all the anger was coming from. But there was so much of it inside him, he felt like he could blow. He had to get a grip. Breathing was the key. In and out, steady.

He must have lain there for hours, staring at the ceiling. Eventually, there was a knock on the door. It was Leiv.

"Hey, bro. You hungry?"

Grayson sat up. "Yeah, a little."

Leiv was carrying a platter-sized plate of several different cuts of steak. Another plate held half a chicken and several pork chops.

All raw. The scent of the bloody flesh wafted over to him, and his stomach responded with a fierce growl.

They ate in silence, and when it was all gone, Leiv finally spoke. "You can't give up yet, brother. You're looking at this all wrong. Instead of hating yourself for *what* you are, try giving *who* you are a chance."

What did that even mean? Leiv was much, much older than Grayson. And wiser. He was ninety-four years from rising and nearing the Age of Deterioration, which, for most zombies, took place sometime around the hundred-year mark, give or take a few years. He still had some time. Grayson hated to think of what life would be like without him.

"Tell me about the girl," he said.

"I told you. She's basically useless."

Leiv gave him an awful look. "No being is useless, Gray," he admonished. "Now, you told me all the things that are wrong with her. Tell me something good about her."

Grayson didn't want to. Didn't want to think like that. It was a waste to.

"She's very…plain." *Liar.*

"Oh, really." Leiv raised a skeptical eyebrow. The pierced one. The stud glinted in the light, reflecting the blue walls of the room, and reminding him of Cori's eyes.

"Yeah." Big fat liar.

"But—"

"But nothing."

Leiv narrowed his eyes. "I can read you, little brother." Grayson stared at him with a blank expression. "Come on, stop trying to be tough. Tell me what you like about her. Or are you just looking for a reason to discard her?"

Suddenly he couldn't face his brother any more, so he got up and began pacing the area in front of his bed. There wasn't much room, but it was better than sitting under Leiv's scrutinizing gaze.

"What does it matter? I'm not supposed to *like* her. I'm supposed to *use* her. Isn't that how it works?" It made him sick inside to say it, but it was the truth. If by some chance he succeeded where no one else had, if Cori stood any chance of passing the tests, and if he discovered the secret to the life-for-life stipulation…he would no longer be a zombie, but he would certainly be a monster.

He couldn't stand to think about it, so he blurted, "She has these eyes—they're honest. Open. Like they don't have any secrets. They're just…they're clean, you know?"

He kept pacing.

Out of the corner of his eye he saw his brother nod and instantly wished he hadn't said anything.

"What else?"

"Nothing else. That's it."

Leiv was silent. Which was annoying.

"Oh, fine." He shouldn't say it. He shouldn't. "There's something… nice about her. She's just, you know…*nice*."

"Caring. You like that." Leiv made it a statement instead of a question, so Grayson didn't answer. He *did* like that. But he equally hated it. Despised everything about her, really, because she couldn't be nice or caring or pure and still save him.

His brother got right in his face. "Don't give up, yet. She can still help you. I know how miserable you are. I know because I was right where you are once. It is possible for you to be happy, little brother." His big hand landed on Grayson's shoulder. "You simply have to wait for it."

He really didn't understand his brother.

"Leiv, can the old ones be wrong?" Maybe this was a mistake and his *Save* was someone else. Someone more suitable.

"No. Never. She *is* the one who was meant to help you, Grayson."

When he was alone again, he sank down on the bed, exhausted. This day had really taken it out of him. He didn't want to think any more. He just wanted to sleep.

And so he did.

Chapter 6

THE NEWER NEW STUDENT

Cori rushed home after school, even knowing her mom wouldn't be there. She'd be working late, of course—it was her way of coping. Cori couldn't blame her really. She had a way of coping too: sleep. And besides, her mom didn't truly know how hard Cori was taking everything. She'd done well at hiding it.

Truth was she missed her dad like crazy. So bad it made her throat burn and her head pound with repressed grief. Everything reminded her of him. Movies they'd watched. *American Idol.* Fried chicken. The sound of a door closing. It made doing anything hard. Except sleeping.

Ready to ignore life, she went straight to her room and collapsed on the bed. Sleep was the great eraser of all things bad. She knew that if she could fall asleep, she could be numb for a while. Eight hours was what she was aiming for.

It took only a matter of minutes for her brain to shut down as she fell fast into a state of mindlessness that she was oh so thankful for.

But things didn't go exactly the way she'd hoped. The numbness didn't last.

She was dreaming—the kind where you know you're dreaming. It was as if she were reliving the day. She saw herself walking toward the doors of the school. Then she was inside. She was looking for someone. Who? Up and down the halls she went, searching. Suddenly, she felt that same strange pulling sensation she'd felt in class and again at lunch. She followed it, feeling excited and happy. Funny, but she couldn't remember feeling that way earlier. Finally, she came to a stop and looked around.

Icy fear came over her when she realized she was looking at herself through someone else's eyes. She watched as she dumped her backpack in her locker and turned to talk to the snobby girl. The train wreck kiss. Coach's whistle. She saw Peg standing off to the side and knew what was coming next.

But then she was overcome with heavy disappointment, a feeling of hopelessness. Whose eyes was she looking through? And why this feeling? The aching heaviness of it was nearly unbearable. She could only compare it to how she'd felt when she first learned of losing her dad. It was awful and ugly and she wanted to run away from it. But she couldn't. It was as if it was a part of her. As if the feeling had melded with her soul, never to be separated.

As she watched herself walk away with Peg, she realized *she* was the cause of the despair. Someone, whoever she was seeing through, was feeling hopeless and lost all because of her.

And how could that be? She didn't *know* anyone in Asher. She couldn't be the cause of anyone's sorrow.

It was a dream, she assured herself. That was all. Just a crazy, weird dream.

As quick as a blink, the dream ended and Cori came awake…to the daylight. She'd slept the whole night through and she was glad for it. Except now she had to go to school again. She had to face people again. She had to try to be normal again.

Ignoring the disturbing dream, she got ready for school and went downstairs. Her mom was already gone—no surprise there—but at least she'd made blueberry muffins and left them on the counter. Cori ate one, standing at the sink, and then forced herself out the door.

The second day of school had to be better than the first. It was like a rule or something. First day sucked; second day was better. First day: headache, epic book crash with hottie, mystery meat for lunch, and Mrs. Simon (she really did smell like fish). Second day: preventative action. No carrying huge stacks of books, stick to the salad bar, and keep her distance from Mrs. Simon.

Feeling a touch optimistic, she headed toward her first period class. She did the same pause-just-outside-the-door routine except she was early this time. Students brushed by, hurrying to class. But no squashed toes today, so second day was already better.

Deep breath. *Here goes part two.*

She entered the room and instantly felt that pulling sensation. She ignored it and scanned the room for an available seat.

Her heart sank. There were exactly four empty ones and they were all surrounding a particular student who'd been missing from class yesterday.

Grayson. Wonderful.

How was every desk already full? Was it a class of overachievers? Or did they sacrifice a few minutes of hallway social time in order to avoid the class grouch?

She glanced at Mr. Peters, but he was busy writing page numbers on the board. And it wasn't like she could ask him for a different seat option.

Drummer boy smirked at her from his seat one row away from Grayson.

She sighed.

The first empty desk was the second from the back, which meant she was forced to step over a lot of legs to get there. She also noticed that not every seat was actually occupied with a student. Books and jackets took up any extra openings. Saving seats should be against the law. Moments like this, it was akin to smothering kittens.

Eventually, Cori was able to slink down into the chair. Just before she did, she made the mistake of glancing at Grayson.

He was glaring at her with something close to hatred. But why? Because she'd bumped him in the hall? Was he crazy? A psycho maybe?

The bell rang and Mr. Peters started outlining appropriate research methods for their upcoming paper on Shakespeare. Minutes later, the door opened and another student entered. Or, Cori guessed he was a student. He was big—kind of huge, really. And dressed all wrong for such a wet climate. He wore jeans, a faded blue T-shirt that hugged his muscles, and flip-flops. Considering the constant drizzle that was Asher's calling card, the flip-flops were a bit much.

It was clear by the way everyone gawked that he wasn't a familiar face.

"Class, it seems we have another new addition to our student body." There were some snickers at the phrase *student body*. "Meet Aiken McGrath. Aiken is from…"

"Minnesota," Aiken said, coolly.

"All right, then. Aiken, you can take a seat next to Cori. She's new too. Cori, raise your hand."

Hesitantly, she slipped her hand up. Aiken's eyes danced around the room until they found hers and then locked on like a heat seeking missile. His were the strangest shade of gray-blue—more gray than blue. They bore into hers as if they were trying to see the back of her skull. He maneuvered through the aisle with an unearthly ease, his solid gaze never breaking from hers.

Just as he was about to sit, a throat cleared roughly behind her and Aiken's head snapped toward Grayson. Aiken froze, his slate eyes narrowed. Cori couldn't tell what Grayson looked like because he was behind her, but it felt like some kind of standoff. Did they know each other? The tension was a thick sludge.

Finally, Aiken took his seat.

Throughout the lesson, Cori snuck looks at him. He was pale, like most people in Asher (no matter the skin tone, there was a general lack-of-sun feel to everyone). However, it didn't take away from Aiken's looks. With his short wavy brown hair and those eyes, he easily put most guys to shame.

Most. But not all. She could name one, who happened to be sitting behind her, who could definitely hold his own against the new guy.

Just then, Aiken glanced over and caught her looking. Quickly, she ducked her head.

"You're new too. Where're you from?" he whispered.

When she glanced back at him, he was smiling. It was a friendly smile. A stunning smile. A take-your-breath-away smile. She found herself grinning back.

"Indiana."

He raised one bold eyebrow and nodded. "You like it here?"

"Not really."

"I get that. Why'd you move here?"

"Long story."

He leaned toward her, not caring that Mr. Peter's was still in full lecture mode. "Maybe you could tell me at lunch. You have A or B?"

"B."

He smiled that brilliant smile. "Me too. What do you say?"

She was a little surprised. Gorgeous guys didn't usually talk to her, much less want to eat lunch with her.

"Uh, sure."

He grinned wider. "Sweet."

As she turned her attention back to the teacher, she marveled at how her second day of being a new student was turning out so much better than her first.

Grayson scowled deeper as he listened to Cori and Aiken. In a matter of two minutes Aiken had managed to do what Grayson had never even thought to: learn about her. Apparently she wasn't from Tennessee.

But Aiken kept looking at her even after they'd finished talking. And for reasons he couldn't answer, that made Grayson angry.

Well, there was one reason — a big one: Aiken was a zombie.

Grayson could tell the minute the guy walked into the room. He could *smell* him. He smelled, well, dead. Humans couldn't register the scent, but other zombies sure could. Just like Grayson could tell Aiken was older than him. His scent was stronger. But not as strong as Leiv's and Raina's.

Just then, Grayson couldn't help himself. Leaning forward so he was only a few inches from Cori's hair, he breathed deep and closed his eyes. She smelled like rain and mint. Fresh. Not stagnant. Not dead. He loved her scent, loved how it drowned out the stench of zombie.

He hated his own. And Aiken's. Especially Aiken's.

The bell rang and he watched as she hurried out. The class emptied and still Grayson sat there. Aiken was the last to leave. He stood and stretched, acting all casual, as if he had no clue what Grayson was. His shirt came up in the front and Grayson noticed a purple tinged scar in the shape of teeth on his lower abs. A *skar.* More evidence that he was a zombie.

Grayson followed him out into the hall.

"Hey, you," he called. "Why are you here?"

Aiken turned slowly. His gaze skimmed over Grayson like he was some kind of organic sludge.

"Is your tribe local?" was all the guy said.

"Of course. Now answer my question. What are you doing here?"

"What's your name?" the zombie countered.

"It doesn't matter." Grayson scowled. "The quota is too high in Asher. You can't live here. How many are in your tribe?"

"I don't have a tribe. I'm here on business."

Oh, really. "What kind of business?"

Aiken stared at him eerily for several moments and then smirked. "That is for me to know and for you to guess at." He spun on his heel and sauntered away.

But Grayson wasn't done.

"Leave the girl alone," he said, his temper rising too quickly and threatening to take control.

Aiken turned and regarded him with one eyebrow cocked. "Why would I do that? She's stunning. And all work and no play makes Aiken a very dull boy."

Grayson felt a growl coming and had to bite his cheek to rein it in. "She's not a plaything."

Aiken smiled easily—too easily. "Don't worry, buddy. I won't hurt her. I'm not a monster." He winked before disappearing into a group of students.

Grayson stood there for a minute, his mind all whacked. He didn't want that zombie anywhere near Cori. He shouldn't care but… well, he didn't know a thing about him. What if Aiken was one of the bad ones? What if he hurt her? She was too vulnerable for that.

He went to his next class, determined to find a way to keep the guy away from her. Except, she was there. God, how many classes did they have together? He'd skipped a couple after lunch yesterday too. He wondered if they shared any of those.

Her being in the same room was nothing more than a distraction. And he needed to think. At least this time she was sitting all the way across the room from him.

A second later, Asher's newest zombie stepped through the door. And worse, he sat next to Cori again. Between breaks in the lesson, the two of them chattered. Lucky for them, Mrs. Simon ran an easygoing classroom. Normally he was glad for that. Now? Well, it would be a great time for her to start cracking down.

Grayson watched through slitted eyes as they exchanged smiles. A shy grin from her, a knowing one from the zombie. Rage became a slow burn inside Grayson's chest. Until the final straw was broken.

Aiken said something—Grayson couldn't hear what it was for the way his ears were pounding—and Cori laughed, a quiet bubbly happy sound. That was all it took for his vision to flip to russets. His skin felt tight and his throat burned. He would lose it if he watched a second longer.

Grayson lunged from his chair and ran from the room.

Chapter 7

OVER MY DEAD...WELL, YOU KNOW

A commotion caught Cori's attention, someone stumbling. She was shocked to see Grayson practically running for the door. He looked strange…sick.

"Mr. Patch, where are you going? Are you all right?" Mrs. Simon called after him, but he was already in the hall.

Cori glanced at Aiken. He had an odd look on his face. His eyes were narrowed…and was he sniffing the air? She didn't smell anything strange.

"What is it?" she asked. And just like that, the expression vanished and he was back to normal.

"Guy's weird," he said.

"He looked sick."

"Yeah, maybe. Anyway…what were you saying about your mom?"

She couldn't remember. All she could think about was Grayson. Should someone check on him?

"Uh…" She glanced at the door. At Mrs. Simon where she was helping a student work through an algebra problem. At her own paper. Back at the door.

She could sense that feeling again. The drawing. What was it? She wondered absently if she should see a doctor. Combined with the headaches, she supposed it was cause for concern. But then, she hadn't had a headache today. Just the foreign sensation of being drawn to something.

She raised her hand. "I need to use the restroom."

Mrs. Simon produced a hall pass, and Cori completely forgot about Aiken. Out in the corridor she stopped just long enough to get her bearings. She let the odd feeling be her guide. It was something like instinct. A sixth sense. It felt natural—even as it felt supernatural. She didn't understand it, but she followed it anyway, a sense of urgency propelling her.

Cori walked between the rows of lockers, winding through the school. After a little bit, she started to feel panicked, like she was running out of time. She gave up walking and started running. She forgot all about how ridiculous she must've looked, forgot about everything except getting to whatever was calling for her.

Rounding a corner, she stopped abruptly. Because the pulling had stopped. And because Grayson was up ahead. He was hunched over and stumbling as if he couldn't get his legs to move, scooting away from her. It was obvious something was very wrong. He needed help.

"Are you okay?" She ran to him.

He threw up his arm—even though he was clearly having trouble moving—as if to shield himself. From her?

"Do you need help?"

His face was partially covered by his arm and he was bent over, but she could tell he'd turned a pasty white. And he was trying to shake his head but was jerking it instead.

"Let me call someone—"

"No," he croaked. His voice was almost non-existent, airy and gravelly. "I'm…fine. I just…need…"

She came closer. She still couldn't see his face but he looked like he was suffering.

"What? What do you need? An inhaler or something? Where is it? I'll go get it."

He shuddered and gasped, still trying to shuffle away. Cori thought he might collapse at any moment.

"Come on. Talk to me. What's wrong with you?" Urgency made her voice hard.

"Water. I need…water."

"Water? Okay. The bathroom's not far. Here, lean on me."

He didn't move so she scooted close and tried to support his arm.

"No! Don't—don't touch me."

She couldn't believe he was going to be a jerk now. When he was in obvious pain and she was the only one around to help.

"Oh, shut up. Do you want my help or not?" she snapped.

He didn't so much answer as groan. So she took it as an invitation. Since he was a lot taller than her, it was easy to duck under his arm. She expected to struggle with his weight but found he wasn't all that heavy. She must've been experiencing an adrenaline rush.

Together they limped along. Cori was grateful that the men's room was empty since she wasn't technically supposed to be in there.

"The sink," he rasped.

She propped him up there, turned on the faucet, and backed away. That's when she got a good look at him. His skin was wispy thin, like tissue paper. His eyes were dark holes sunken into his face; the irises were mud brown, the whites yellow and veiny. His lips were blue, his cheeks hollow.

She squeezed her eyes closed as an unwanted memory of her dad nestled into a silk-lined coffin pounded at her brain like a fist.

Grayson looked similar—unbelievably close to death.

The thought terrified her. So much she couldn't move. Could barely breathe. Would he *die* right here in front of her?

She stood there in disbelief, watching him drink from the tap. She waited as he slurped, her hands balled and knuckles white, muscles both locked in place and poised to run.

When he finally rose from the sink, Cori could hardly believe her eyes. He was completely back to normal. The black eyes and sallow skin, gone as if they were never there. He was standing at his full height again and moving easily. The pain seemed to be…just gone.

Cori swallowed hard and met his eyes in the mirror—eyes that were green again. He didn't say a word, his expression blank. He only stared.

For so long, he stared.

"Are you okay?" Her voice came out so easy. So much more level than she actually felt.

He looked away, busying himself with washing his hands. "You should go before someone catches you in here."

She shook her head, trying to figure out what just happened. "Do you feel better? I mean, what…what was that?"

He dried his hands. "I'm fine." Then he walked out of the bathroom, leaving her staring after him.

Grayson was freaking out on the inside.

Freaking. The freak. Out.

Nobody'd ever witnessed him in the midst of a water cramp—well, nobody except his family.

He walked as quickly as he could away from the bathroom, away from Cori. But she was right behind him.

"Wait a second. Hold on. You should see the nurse. Or, or… something." She was practically running to keep up with him.

"I'm fine," he said again, with an edge this time.

"Yeah, *now*. But you…you looked like death."

She had no idea.

"Dehydration," he snipped. "It does that to people." Well, not people but zombies.

He looked straight ahead and kept his pace. But she wasn't done.

"Just, will you stop for a second?"

He did. Abruptly. But he couldn't look at her. "What?" he barked.

She was stone silent. What was she thinking? She must be freaked out, wondering what she'd seen. Maybe in shock. He finally glanced at her. She didn't *look* freaked out.

She stepped closer, eyes narrowed. "You're not all right. Not really."

She was reaching for his arm. She was going to touch him again? Was she crazy?

Fear and confusion had him jerking backward. "I said, I'm fine," he snapped. "Now, stay the hell away from me."

He stuck around only long enough to see her eyes flutter away and her face burn red with embarrassment. Good.

He was relieved when she didn't follow him. He needed to think. What would Leiv do in this situation? Obviously he would make sure she didn't suspect he was something other than human. But he couldn't make himself go there right now. Besides, she hadn't really seemed scared. Exactly how much had she seen?

Lunchtime was hell. He watched from afar as Aiken sat down at the table with Cori and her new friends. He watched Peg and Rex as they transitioned from curious to accepting. Peg seemed especially affected by the zombie. Aiken's obvious charm worked well because by the end of the hour, they were all laughing like they'd known him for years.

Grayson hated that laughter. Most especially, Cori's. It wasn't because it was ugly. No, it was lovely. More so than her voice. Grayson hated it because…because…because he wasn't the one making her do it.

And just why did that matter to him?

On the way to his next class, he stopped by the bathroom to wash his face and gulp some more H_2O. The bathroom was empty until Aiken slipped in. He stood in front of the door as if to block it.

"Whew! You stink, man. How old are you anyway?"

Grayson regarded the zombie with exaggerated patience. Truly, he had none. "I'm barely nineteen."

"In zombie years? Seriously?"

"Nineteen years from rising."

"Wow. You better rein in your temper or you'll never make it to a hundred. And drink more water, dude."

Grayson didn't want to do what the guy said, but he was feeling a little dry. When he'd finished drinking, the stranger was still there.

"What do you want," Grayson snapped.

"I could ask you the same question but I probably wouldn't get an answer. So, I'll ask another. What's the deal with you and Cori?"

Grayson ground his teeth together. "There's no deal. It's nothing."

"Really. Doesn't seem that way." He hesitated. "You like her?"

"Like her? No." *Liar.*

Aiken smirked. Crossed his too-big arms over his chest. "Good. 'Cause I do. And since she's nothing to you, I'm taking her out tonight."

If Grayson had blood instead of the watered down crap in his veins, it would have boiled. Taking her out? Over his already-dead dead body.

He took a fighter's stance, arms loose, legs apart. "You're not taking her out," he growled low.

Aiken stepped up, clearly ready to do some damage. "Says who?"

"I do. I'll kill you right here and now before I let you take her anywhere." He didn't trust the guy. Not an inch.

The other zombie's nostrils flared but his gaze was calculating.

"You would kill a fellow riser for a simple human girl?"

"She's not simple." Oh, so now you admit it.

"Fine, I take the challenge." Aiken's easy manner had changed into something cruel. "But first, you tell me, who should I deliver your body to? Because you *will* die today."

Grayson showed his teeth. "I'm not afraid of dying. I'm already dead, remember?" With that, he stepped up and threw the first punch. It landed squarely on Aiken's jaw, knocking his head back against the tiled wall. The hit was good, but the zombie seemed annoyingly unaffected.

And then he was furious.

He came at Grayson with a vengeance. A kick to the gut, followed by a righteous uppercut, sent him flying into one of the stalls. He scrambled to his feet, only to be met by more of Aiken's fists. But he did manage to kick the guy's feet out from under him, which gave him the upper hand.

For about five seconds.

He took advantage of it by pummeling Aiken's face until watery brown sludge started to leak from his wounds.

Then the roles were switched again and Grayson found himself flat on his back. Aiken was straddling him, the look of death upon his once-appealing face. Time seemed to stand still as Grayson realized a blade was being held to his neck. Of course, the only way to *really* kill a zombie…

But then he got a look at where the handle peeked out from Aiken's grip and he went limp. He felt his eyes turn and the color leach out of his surroundings once again.

"You're a Reaper," he hissed vehemently. A Reaper was trying to get close to innocent Cori…he really would die before he let that happen. Reapers were dangerous to humans, especially those who might find out about the zombie race. They were the law enforcers for the Dead Walking.

Strength came from somewhere, and he shoved Aiken off, ready to take him out. But he had barely enough time to stand before he was being pushed into the wall face first. Tiles rattled at the impact. And then the blade was pushed against his neck again — this time in the back.

"I won't let you touch her. Do you understand me? I'll return from the grave all over again if I have to." Grayson didn't know how, but he would find a way.

"Why? I thought you didn't care about her?" The Reaper's voice was distorted slightly as he tried to come down from his own rage. Grayson's was coming out in the same garbled manner.

"She's…she's my *Save*."

Instantly, the knife was gone and instead of being face-plastered to the wall, he found himself being spun around. Hate-filled eyes beamed into his, but the murderous glint was mysteriously gone.

"Your *Save?*"

Grayson nodded.

"Cori is your *Save?*" His tone was skeptical. Grayson knew how the guy felt. As far as *Saves* go, she was terribly unassuming.

"Yes. So either kill me or let me go. Your breath stinks."

Immediately he was released, but Aiken didn't step back and he wasn't done with the questions.

"If she's your *Save*, why…why are you just ignoring her? Why'd you tell me…?"

Grayson didn't want to have this conversation with a Reaper. Or anybody really. But if it would make the guy stay away from Cori then maybe it was worth it.

"You've seen her. She can't possibly help me. So why would I talk to her? Why would I risk her ever knowing about zombies?" His next words were so close to a growl. "So someone like you could come along later and kill her?"

Aiken looked puzzled. "We don't kill humans. Ever."

"Yeah, right." The world was still shades of brown even though he was trying to level out. *Breathe, breathe.*

Aiken shook his head. "What do you mean, she can't help you?"

Grayson rolled his eyes. "Does she look like the type who could deal with our world? She can't save me, even if I knew how to make it work."

Aiken narrowed his gaze. "You're giving up on your *Save* because she doesn't *look* like she can help you?"

"Oh, please. Have you ever seen a *Save* like her?"

He smirked. "She has some pretty amazing qualities if you ask me. Want me to name them?"

"Don't say that. Don't talk about her like that." Grayson hated the gleam in his eyes.

"What? You don't appreciate her, so I can't either. That it?"

Grayson glared at him.

"Well, too bad. Your loss," he said as he went over to the sink and drank from the faucet. Grayson wanted to bash the guy's head into the basin, but he needed water himself so he drank too.

When they were finished and their faces no longer looked like wet misshapen clay, he faced the Reaper once more. "So, you'll stay away from her." He wasn't asking. He was telling.

Aiken peered at him. "I won't take her out tonight. That's all I'm promising."

It wasn't enough.

"Reaper, stay away from Cori."

Aiken was already at the door. "First of all, my name is not 'Reaper.' Second, did you ever consider she might not want me to stay away from her?" He smirked and walked out, leaving Grayson staring after him with his mouth hanging open.

Chapter 8

PUSH BACK HARDER

Cori was the first to class after lunch so she picked a seat in the back corner, farthest from the door. She breathed a sigh of relief when the seats around her filled up and none of the people in them were Grayson. Maybe she'd actually be able to focus in this class.

Aiken walked in just before the last bell, Grayson right behind him. Neither of them had a smile on their face.

Another class with him, with both of them. That made three.

She thought a lot about the incident between her and Grayson and could come up with only one explanation for what she'd seen: he was suffering from an illness. Possibly something terminal. It explained so much. Why he was always angry. Why he distanced himself from people. She wondered if any of the teachers knew.

Her heart went out to him. What if he *was* dying? What a burden to carry. And too young. And with no friends to be there for him. Family? Surely he had family. Still, he needed someone, a friend. He could use somebody…like her.

But he was so cold. He pushed people away so hard. She'd been on the receiving end of that push twice already. And it sucked. But maybe she'd just have to try harder. Maybe if she pushed back.

The next day, she sat in front of him again in first period. Shoring up her courage, she turned in her seat to talk to him before class started.

"Hey," she said. He glanced at her and then back at his notebook where he was scribbling randomly on the cover. *Push back,* she thought. "Are you feeling better today?"

"Fine."

She could do this, she could. Just keep making conversation… "So…did you finish last night's homework?"

"Yeah."

Oookayyy. "Good. Me too." Uncomfortable silence, except for the thunder outside. Thunder. Rain! "Do you like the rain?" Dumb question but she couldn't think of anything else.

"Yeah."

That surprised her. Did he actually like rain, or was he just trying to get her to shut up?

"Really? You do?"

"Yep."

Okay, so he wanted her to shut up. Well, too bad. "I don't. I mean, a little bit is okay, but it's like a rainforest here. But without the heat. I might never get to wear flip-flops again. And that would be sad because I have this great shade of red nail polish I've been dying to use. But like, what's the point if I can't wear sandals? You know?"

He stopped doodling and grudgingly looked at her. "I wouldn't know."

His disregard for her made her want to keep going — if only to irritate him. "Well, that's true. I mean it's not like you paint your toenails or anything. Unless…" Good, he was still staring at her. "No? No, I didn't think so. But you can never really tell now, can you? Anyway, I guess I could use the red stuff on my fingers. But I usually avoid anything that bold above the waist." She pretended to be interested in examining her fingernails. When she glanced back up at him, she was surprised he was still watching her. With a totally careless expression, but still.

When she was about to continue babbling just to see where it would lead, Aiken strolled through the door. With a coolness that was in no way exaggerated, he came to sit in the seat next to her.

"Mornin'." He smiled that million-watt grin, and she returned it with one of her own.

"Hi." Now why couldn't Grayson be easy like this? She glanced at him again and noticed he was still looking at her. "Grayson and I were just discussing nail polish," she blurted.

Aiken cocked a perfect eyebrow. "Uh…" Then he gave Grayson a strange look.

"*She* was talking about nail polish. *I* was forced to listen."

She ignored the jab because at least he hadn't gone back to doodling. Time for a subject change.

"So, how come you eat lunch by yourself?"

Annnnddd…back to the doodling.

"Come on, answer me."

He didn't.

She didn't know what made her do it. Stupidity, probably. But she reached over and swiped the pencil from his hand.

He looked at her, part shock and part glare.

"Pencil's loud I guess. You probably couldn't hear me. How come you eat lunch by yourself?"

"I heard you just fine." His eyes were narrowed in an expression that was threatening, but she didn't dare look away.

"Hmm. Then I guess you're just rude." This wasn't like her. Being confrontational felt like wearing an itchy sweater. Totally uncomfortable.

Grayson smiled, but it was all shark-like, cruel. "Bingo. Someone give the girl a prize."

Like this, she could see that his eyes were spectacular — greenish brown, like moss. Not like they had been yesterday, more yellow.

She leaned closer so she could whisper. "You really shouldn't push people away just because you don't like what's happening to you." His eyes widened just slightly as she laid the pencil down on his notebook and turned to face front just in time for the teacher to take attendance.

She was horrified that she was shaking but didn't think anyone else noticed. It was more like she was shaking on the inside. Cori was never bold like that. Never. And even if it was uncomfortable, it felt…nice. Scratchy sweaters were still warm.

She risked a glance at Aiken. His brow furrowed, but he remained quiet as he opened his English book.

She didn't try to talk to Grayson in second period. Her stomach was still quaking from the first time. But she was determined to try again later.

At lunch, she sat with Peg and Rex again. Aiken joined them, much to the dismay of an obviously popular group of girls a few tables over. Cori couldn't help thinking that it was a little strange that a guy like him was interested in her and her new friends. Not that he shouldn't be, of course. They were awesome. It was just that he seemed out of place.

Unable to help it, her eyes were drawn to where Grayson was approaching an empty table with his usual bottle of water.

Rex sighed. "Doll, you might as well give that one up. He is insufferable."

"Agreed," Peg added.

"What? Oh." She'd been caught.

Aiken was peering over his shoulder at Grayson. "Nah, you can do better than that, Cori."

"No, it's…not like that. He just…I think he's sick," she sputtered. Surely her face was an embarrassing shade of crimson.

"Oh, indeed," Rex agreed. "The illness is called 'badattitude-itis.'" He swigged his bottle of Coke, completely satisfied with himself.

Peg giggled. "No, I think it's called 'Grouch-akemia.'"

"Or maybe 'Hater-itis.'"

"No, got it. 'Don't-get-in-my-way-or-I'll-bite-your-head-off-itis.'"

Cori knew they were just trying to be funny, but she still didn't like it.

"I'm serious, you guys."

Peg blinked. Rex sipped his Coke. Aiken cleared his throat.

"You think he's sick?" Peg finally asked, her look incredulous.

Cori nodded.

"I doubt it, hon. He's been this way as long as I can remember."

"What way? Moody? Edgy? Hateful?"

"All of the above," Rex muttered.

Cori stared at Grayson. His face was like stone, giving away nothing. He fingered the label on his water bottle. There was something up with him. The bathroom incident was enough of an indication.

"Do you know why my mom and I moved to Asher?" she asked absently.

No one said a thing.

"My dad died. Suddenly. Car accident. Do you know what I was like afterward?"

Still they were silent.

"I was mean. Horrible. To my mom, to my friends. I was angry and I didn't want to talk to anyone or see anyone or be near anyone. Asia, my best friend, I was even mean to her. But she was the only one who would put up with me. She just let me be angry." Cori pulled her eyes from the brooding Grayson and faced her friends. "I'm telling you guys, there's something wrong with Grayson. And I'm gonna figure out what it is."

They were all quiet for a moment before Peg spoke, concern layering her voice. "Maybe you're right. Just try not to get hurt in the process."

Rex nodded solemnly. Aiken was quiet.

She looked at Grayson again. Oh, she probably would get hurt. Scratch that—it was a sure thing. But then, she was already a great big ball of pain. A little more wouldn't make a difference. And at least trying to win him over would give her something to keep her mind busy.

When Cori arrived in class, Grayson and Aiken were already seated. There was just enough time before the bell rang for her to try talking to Grayson again. Before she could though, Aiken dropped a bomb.

"Hey, you wanna go see a movie or something tonight? We could check out what this Tinker-town has to offer?"

"Uh…okay. Should we ask Peg and Rex?"

His gaze became personal. "I think it would be more fun just the two of us."

She was confused. "Just the two of us?"

He leaned closer to her. "Yeah. You know, you and me. Spending time…alone."

Her jaw was hanging open. She could feel it, but she couldn't seem to do anything about it. He wanted to go out with her? Like on a date? Well, she'd never been asked before. So…

Before she could answer, a pencil rolled off the desk behind her—Grayson's desk—and landed on the floor by her feet. She bent over to retrieve it and handed it back to him.

"Thanks," he muttered.

It was such a little thing, but it shocked her as if she'd touched a live wire. She met his eyes and a grin spread across her face.

"You're welcome."

Their eyes stayed locked like that until Mrs. Wan starting speaking in Spanish and flailing her hands as if that would help them understand what she was teaching.

A crap ton of verb conjugations later, Aiken cleared his throat. "So, about tonight—"

"I spend lunch alone because there's no one else interesting enough to spend it with." Grayson forced the words out as if it pained him to let go of them. As if sharing the info cost him something. Maybe it did.

But her foot was in the door. Now she just had to nudge it further open.

"Hmm. How do you know? Have you tried?"

"Tried what?"

"Tried spending it with someone."

He stared at her, and for so long that she wasn't sure if he was going to answer.

"No," he said in a gruff way.

"Well, maybe you should."

"I don't think so."

She shrugged as if it didn't matter. "Your loss." And then she turned back to Aiken who was patiently awaiting her answer. "About tonight—"

"What's so great about having lunch with someone?" Grayson interrupted.

"What's so great about being alone?" she countered.

"Everything," was his immediate reply.

The air left her lungs on a sad sigh. She knew exactly how he felt. Exactly. Sometimes being alone was the only thing that didn't hurt, the only thing that felt right. It didn't make sense and she couldn't explain it, but…there were times when you just didn't want to drag anyone else down into the pit with you. You needed—and wanted—to be there by yourself.

She looked him squarely in the eyes. "You're right. I get it." To Aiken she said, "About tonight, I can't. My mom is expecting me home. But maybe another time."

He grinned uncomfortably, but still, it was stunning. "Sure. Definitely another time."

Cori had done enough pushing for one day. And going by the frowny-faced Mrs. Wan, she'd had enough of them talking in class.

Chapter 9

PEEPING ZOMBIE

Breathe. Just breathe. Grayson had come so close to losing it. There was no description for the feeling that had washed over him when he'd heard Aiken ask Cori out. It was sort of like taking a bath in acid. It was a real testament to his progress with temper management that he didn't try to rip the Reaper's head off. He hadn't even growled. Even when her eyes got all foggy at the prospect of being alone with Aiken, he'd managed to hold it in.

But the truth was, he didn't care if she liked Aiken or if she wanted to be with him. That was just too bad. He wasn't going to let Aiken get close to her. No way. Something inside him just revolted at the thought of the two of them together. And so, it wouldn't happen. He would see to it. The shrimp and the Reaper would never be.

He caught Aiken after class.

"What the hell was that," he ground out.

Aiken flicked his gaze over before he sighed dramatically. "That was you interfering with my night out on the town." He continued down the hall, Grayson trailing after him.

"We talked about this. She's not here for your entertainment."

Aiken cocked an eyebrow, which was apparently his trademark. "Maybe I'm here for hers. Ever thought of that?"

Grayson ground his teeth together. "Why exactly *are* you here?"

"Not like it's any of your business," the Reaper drawled, "but there was an incident with some rogues a couple hours north of here. Asher was a routine check along the way."

Rogues. Grayson flinched. It was so rare. Most zombies ate strictly animal flesh. Like normal people, they bought it from the grocery store. They just…didn't cook it.

But there were some who craved the living. Humans. Whether it was the taste or simply the power trip of being higher up on the food chain, he didn't know, but the idea that these beasts were out there made him sick. The idea that he shared any commonality with them at all made his skin crawl. Made him desperate to be different. Drove him to consider using his *Save.*

"Routine, huh? Then why are you enrolled in school?"

Aiken kept walking as if they were discussing the weather and not slavering zombies. "Duh. Because we decided to stick around for a while," was his cryptic answer.

"We?"

"Of course. I'm a 'teenager,' you know," he said sarcastically. "I have 'parents.'"

Grayson wanted to throttle him, but he wanted answers more. "Why are you 'sticking around'?"

He finally stopped walking and faced Grayson. "You ask too many questions." Another dramatic sigh. "There are some situations that need to be monitored here." He grinned widely. "Therefore, I am."

"What situations?" Couldn't he answer a damn question?

"None of your biz."

"Fine. Let's discuss what *is* my biz. Cori. Stay away from her. And this is my last warning." Grayson's voice was made hard by his determination.

"Are you threatening me?" Aiken asked coolly.

This time it was Grayson's turn to smile—even though it came out as something none too friendly. "Being a Reaper, you of all people should know what a threat sounds like."

The stiffening of Aiken's shoulders was the only indication that Grayson had gotten under his skin.

Aiken stepped up until they were eye to eye. "Being a civilian, you of all people should know better than to threaten a Reaper." His words, though calm, held a menace that Grayson, for some reason, had no trouble ignoring.

"Ask me if I'm scared."

Aiken stayed silent, his eyes telling of his restraint.

"I won't let you use her." Grayson meant it. Wholeheartedly.

"Funny," Aiken gritted out, his face so close to Grayson's their breath was mingling. "I was just thinking the same thing."

As the Reaper stormed off, Grayson realized what the guy meant: he knew if Grayson learned how to save himself, that was exactly what he was going to do to Cori, use her. Oh, how the irony stung.

Shaking off the unease he was feeling, he decided he'd save that worry for later. Right now, he had to make sure Cori didn't end up alone with a zombie — er, a zombie other than himself.

Following her home was easy once he rationalized that he should know where she lived in case Aiken tried to pull something. Luckily, she walked home, so it was nothing to stay hidden as he trailed her.

When Cori walked up to an average cottage-style house with an oversized front porch, he wasn't at all surprised. It was nothing like his own — zombies loved expensive accommodations, the lush and ritzy. Something about wanting to be as far away from the stereotypical dead as possible. It was one thing to chill out in a graveyard, but when it came to living…well, they wanted to live it up. High style ideals. It was especially important if you lived in a bigger city where the zombie quota was higher. According to his brother and sister, no respectable zombie was without money.

He waited until she was inside before he snuck around to peek in one of the windows. She was in the kitchen, staring into the open refrigerator. She stood there a while before finally closing the door and plucking a banana from the bowl on the counter. Grayson couldn't remember what a banana tasted like, but he could remember that he'd once liked them. And they smelled amazing.

Leaning against the counter, she ate. He watched, riveted, imagining what the fruit must taste like. And then an errant thought had him practically drooling: if he kissed her lips right now, would they taste like a banana? This led to other thoughts: what would her lips taste like? Feel like?

The spell was broken when she tossed the peel into the trashcan. Grayson scrambled to right his thoughts. He shouldn't think like that. He *couldn't* think like that.

Cori wandered out of the kitchen. Keeping to the bushes, Grayson went around to the side of the house to look in another window. This one opened up into the living room and he could see Cori sitting on the couch. From his vantage point, he could only see her in profile. She was just sitting there, stiffly, shoulders slumped, staring at the wall. How odd. There wasn't a picture there or anything else of interest—or anything at all. Then suddenly her face crumpled and her head dropped to her hands.

Sobbing. She was sobbing, her body shuddering with each breath.

The sight terrified him. But why? He had no idea. He, who was truly afraid of nothing.

Just days ago he might have shrugged it off, her crying. He'd thought her weak, frail, easily spooked. But something was different now. He'd noticed a vein of strength in her that put his earlier judgment to shame.

He didn't understand her. Not at all.

But why was she crying?

Grayson pushed away from the window. It wasn't any of his business.

But he didn't go home. What if Aiken showed up and convinced her to go somewhere with him? No, he would stick around until her mom returned.

Hours passed. So many that he'd had to go around back to find the garden hose for a drink. This part of the country got dark early so he spent a few hours in relative blackness before he checked his cell phone for the time. It was nine forty-five. Where was Cori's mother?

He had several text messages from Leiv and Raina so he sent one back: *Be home soon.*

At ten twenty he wandered back over to the window. It was pitch dark inside, but he could see fine. Stellar night vision. One of the few zombie benefits. Cori was still on the couch, but she was curled up, asleep. He guessed she'd been like that since he walked away earlier.

More time passed while he watched her sleep. She was peaceful, her face relaxed, one hand tucked under her cheek. Whatever had troubled her earlier was gone. Grayson was…glad. It surprised him that he cared.

With a scowl, he shook off the feeling and went to the back of the house for more water.

As he returned to the window, he heard a cry, the noise coming from inside the house. Cori was still asleep, but she stirred fitfully and moaned as if she were in pain. The longer it went on, the harder it became for him to remain where he was. He cringed with each tortured sound. Then she was sobbing again, full out, in her sleep.

Why would she cry like this? So many tears, and for what?

The thought occurred to him that he should help her. He should do something to make it stop.

Grayson stared through the darkness as Cori huddled tighter into a ball, shivering, tears streaking her cheeks. He couldn't stand it. She was clearly suffering, her dreams tormenting her in ways he didn't understand. She shouldn't suffer like this. He didn't like it. Whatever the reason for his sudden concern, he hated to see her like this.

Grayson went to the front door and tried the handle. He was shocked to find it unlocked. He frowned. She should take more care with her safety. Anyone could've easily walked right through the door.

Just as he was about to go inside, a flash of light caught his attention. Headlights, to be exact. A car was pulling into Cori's driveway.

Grayson jumped over the side railing of the porch and crouched down in the bushes. From there he could see that the vehicle was a tan SUV, but he couldn't see who was driving it. They parked and shut off the engine. A middle-aged woman wearing periwinkle scrubs and a tired expression emerged carrying a large flat box: pizza. This had to be Cori's mom.

For some reason he'd been holding his breath and now he let it out.

The woman went to open the door, pausing, frowning when she realized it was unlocked. After she went inside, Grayson moved back around to the living room window. He saw several lights get flipped on and then the woman came into the area where the couch was. She paused when she spotted her daughter. Cori had stopped crying, but telltale wetness lingered on her face. For so long, the woman just stared. Her face held a sorrow so deep Grayson knew something was terribly wrong. What was their story?

She blinked. Wiped her eyes. Then she pulled the throw from the back of the couch and draped it over her daughter. She stood there a while longer, watching Cori with her sad eyes. Then she flicked off the light and left the room. A faint glow came from the kitchen but then it was gone, followed by another one upstairs.

He waited until everything was dark again before peering one last time through the living room window. Cori was sleeping soundly, the lines that had creased her brow gone. With her eyes closed, the rest of her features weren't as painfully average as they normally were, and he could see that there was something quite beautiful about her.

Grayson pushed away from the window and headed home before the thought could take root in his mind.

When he got there, he was grateful that his siblings were already in bed. He didn't feel like trying to explain where he'd been.

He went to the refrigerator, snatched a hunk of beef, and went to his room. Sitting on his bed, he tore into the flesh, just realizing how hungry he'd become.

As he ate, he considered what he should do about Cori and how to keep her away from Aiken. The Reaper had already weaseled his way into her life with his oh-so-friendly demeanor and matching smile. For a moment Grayson thought maybe he could do the same thing. Charm her. But no, he wasn't smooth like that. And he didn't smile. The best he could do was distract her. Maybe if he kept her busy enough she'd stay away from Aiken. And maybe it could also help with whatever troubles she was dealing with at home.

After he finished eating, he showered and consumed enough water to last him through the night, then climbed into bed. He stared at the ceiling, trying to come up with a good enough plan to keep Cori distracted. Before he knew it, the sound of blaring Whitesnake informed him morning had come.

Chapter 10

Of Marshmallows and Golden Retrievers

Cori woke up annoyed to find herself on the couch. But at least it wasn't the middle of the night. No, the sun was blazing through the window, landing on her face. She sat up and rubbed at eyes that felt like they had wool eyelids. She'd slept awfully. Nightmares. And the crick in her neck might as well have been the cherry on top of a crap sundae.

Cori made her way to the kitchen, rolling her shoulders to get the kinks out. Mom was already gone, but she'd left a note on the counter. And she'd brought pizza home again. Cori was sick of pizza, but her stomach was making an almost constant growl, so she started in on a slice, the same way she ate most of her meals at home now — alone and standing at the counter.

As she chewed, she forced her mind to still. If she started thinking about things, she'd cry again and she didn't want to have cry-face for school.

When she was done, she went upstairs to get ready. She managed to shower, brush her teeth, and dress before random thoughts started tormenting her.

She'd decided she wouldn't try to talk to Grayson again. It was clear he didn't want to be bothered. And really, she didn't have the energy to keep it up. After all, she was just a fragile breath away from breaking herself. It was dumb to think she could somehow help him.

As for Aiken...well, she didn't have the energy for that either. Yeah, he was a total hottie and he was interested in her, but he couldn't possibly understand her, not to mention all she was going through, and she just didn't have it in her to make him understand.

At school she bypassed her locker in hopes of avoiding Peg. She didn't feel like putting up a shiny front. In class, she busied herself with her notebook. Probably pointless, but she hoped when Aiken got there he wouldn't try to talk to her.

Grayson walked in first, and she avoided looking at him. When he sat down behind her, she let out a relieved breath. At least she knew he wouldn't bother her—

"Hey." He said it as if he was trying to get her attention. Not like he was saying hi.

She ignored him. How the tables had turned. But she just wasn't in the mood for being nice today.

"Cori," he tried again a few minutes later.

She sighed. He'd get the hint.

Except he didn't. "Cori."

She was going to have to answer him. "Yeah," she said without turning around.

But he was silent again. Fine, whatever. Jerk.

It was only when class started that she realized Aiken was absent. For that, she was exceedingly thankful.

When the bell rang she hurried out of class and to her locker. Peg was there with a smile as bright as her neon yellow denim jacket.

"Missed you this morning," she said, eyes appraising. "You okay?"

Cori returned her friend's smile, but she was pretty sure it was more like a grimace. "Yeah, fine. Just had a rough night."

"Oh." They started walking. "Have you seen Aiken?" Peg asked.

Cori shook her head. "He wasn't in class."

Peg's crimson eyebrows furrowed. "So...last night? You didn't have fun? I mean, he seems..."

"What are you talking about?"

"Uh, well Aiken told Rex he was taking you out."

Cori ground her teeth together. "No, he *asked* me if he could take me out. I said no."

Peg's eyebrows went sky high and then came back down to register some other emotion. Something Cori couldn't name. "Um, okay. I just assumed, you know."

Cori shrugged. "It's no big deal." But it sorta was. Why would Peg just assume she'd said yes? Because he was cute? Well, yeah, that made sense. And Aiken…presumptuous much?

In class, Grayson didn't sit behind her as usual. This time, he sat in Aiken's desk. She pretended not to notice. At least until he started talking.

"I thought about what you said yesterday," he said abruptly.

She looked at him because it would be rude not to. And she wasn't rude. Unlike *somebody*.

He still had that shut-off expression but now he was willingly having a conversation with her. What was up with that? And really, did he have to sound so grumpy all the freaking time?

"About what?"

He hesitated. "About lunch."

"Oh."

"I mean, I want to try not having lunch alone." Each word was stilted, as if he had to force it out. As though she'd somehow coerced him. That got under her skin.

"Well, I guess you found someone interesting enough for you." He could just go suck an egg as far as she was concerned.

"Yeah. You."

"Me?" Her? Well, yeah…okay.

He nodded as if to say, *Duh*.

"I'm not that interesting," she said and picked up her pencil. She didn't feel up to playing games with him. And that was certainly what he was doing. Just yesterday, he couldn't stand her, and now this?

"Look, will you…will you…have lunch with me today?"

She stared at him. Was he serious? She couldn't tell. He was so frustrating.

"What about my friends? I sit with Peg and Rex and Aiken."

He glanced away. "What about them?"

"So, you just want me to blow them off and sit with you. Why would I do that?"

His jaw was clenched tight as if to keep him from spouting something off. Something rude probably.

"Why?" she asked again.

"Because I want you to."

Arrogant jerk. She was about to tell him no in a very creative way that involved a few colorful words. But then he added, "And because I asked you to."

True, he had asked. And he'd done it nicely, more or less, which for him was apparently no easy task.

It took her several moments before she could answer. And she was sure that nothing good could come of it, but…"Fine."

His features seemed to relax, and even though it was just a tiny bit, she was shocked by the severity of the change.

"Fine? Does that mean yes?"

She nodded and went back to her busy work. Grayson didn't say anything else to her for the rest of the class.

When the bell rang, Peg caught up with her in the hall.

"Hey, I'm sorry if I upset you earlier." Peg's smile was the halfway kind.

Cori stopped and faced her. "It wasn't you. I just woke up grumpy. Really."

Peg shuffled her feet. "I was under the assumption that you and Aiken were, well, you know."

Cori shook her head. "We aren't. I'm not looking for that right now. I'm…well, relationships aren't my thing. I'm bad at them."

"Aw, that can't be true. You seem like a pretty good friend. So far." Peg grinned, showing that chipped tooth, and chucked Cori's shoulder.

Cori smiled back because the girl was downright contagious—and she needed a bit of Peg's good mood to rub off on her. Especially if she was going to spend lunchtime with Grayson.

"Keep me around for a while and we'll see if you still think so."

Peg nodded and they continued walking, her bright red stilettos clicking on the tile. "Of course, I give all my friends a complimentary trial run before they are welcomed into true friend-dom."

"Awesome. Sixty days?"

Peg pursed her lips, pretended to think it over. "Ninety."

"Ninety? I'll never make it."

They were giggling and suddenly Cori wasn't having to pretend she felt better—she actually did.

"Oh yeah, I almost forgot. I won't be seeing you at lunch." When Peg gave her a strange look she hurried up with the explanation. "I'm, uh, going to sit with Grayson today."

Peg stopped walking so suddenly, her dangling silver hoop earrings swung with momentum. Her mouth was hanging in surprise.

Cori shifted awkwardly. "He asked me, so I couldn't really say no. You know how I've been trying to talk to him. I mean, I suggested he sit at our table, but he didn't like that idea." Peg was still gawking. "It's just for one day. No big deal, right?"

"Are you sure you want to do that? I could help you come up with an excuse."

Cori shrugged as they continue down the hall. "It's just for thirty minutes. I can handle it."

"Oh, I'm sure. It's just—why would you want to?"

Cori didn't have an answer.

By lunchtime, Aiken was still nowhere in sight. She guessed he was sick or something. In the cafeteria she went through the salad bar line and looked around for Grayson. She didn't see him, so she took her time as she got a Coke and paid for everything. But then he still wasn't there.

Now what?

So maybe this was all part of the game. Was he…standing her up? Her cheeks turned to fire at the thought. The tips of her ears burned. Of course he was. How could she have been so stupid? The sudden change of heart he'd had was not him trying. It was him pushing. Pushing back. And harder than she ever would have.

She started quickly toward her usual table. Hopefully Peg wouldn't ask in front of Rex. God, how humiliating.

"Where do you think you're going?" The voice came from behind her but it seemed to wrap all around her and even through her. Though it wasn't much more than a whisper, the intensity of it made the hair on the back of her neck stand up. Was it his voice or was it that pulling sensation she'd been experiencing? It was almost like the feeling you got when your blood pressure dropped. Or what it felt like to go fast down a big hill.

"I was going to sit with my friends since you weren't around," she managed to say.

He stepped in front of her. "I'm here now."

She nodded, annoyed by the idea that he might've stood her up and disturbed by the odd feeling that had come over her. "Lead the way."

They wound through the cluster of tables until they arrived at one in the far back corner. It was about as secluded as you could get in a crowded high school cafeteria. Cori put her tray down and slid into the empty chair. Grayson sat opposite her without a speck of food. He had water though, as usual. It was strange that he never ate. She could ask him about it but didn't feel like dragging the answer out of him today. She started in on her salad while Grayson wordlessly sipped his water — or rather gulped it.

The next ten minutes went without a word being spoken.

When she'd finished eating, she pushed her tray aside and sat back, crossing her arms. What now? She glanced at him but he wasn't looking at her. He was staring at her empty tray. She let her eyes travel around the cafeteria while she contemplated something to say.

"So, this is what it's like having lunch with someone else," he mused. "Huh. It's not that much different than being by myself." He was looking at her now, those greenish eyes so guarded.

It felt strange to be alone — well, sort of alone — with him. Cori wasn't a big conversation starter in normal situations, but put her with a rebel loner with a lack of social skills that rivaled her own and she was basically useless.

"Sorry," she muttered. Maybe if he was a little friendlier it wouldn't be so hard to talk to him.

Yesterday was a fluke, she decided. Whatever air of bravery had made her talk to him like she had was clearly gone today. She was back to her normal mousy self. It wouldn't be a surprise to her if she started speaking in squeaks.

He finished off the last of his water and capped the bottle before leaning forward in his chair so he was invading her personal space. Mouse or not, she was determined to not back down. She had a shred of pride left.

Eyes squinting, he said, "What's wrong with you? Yesterday you were annoying the hell out of me. Now, you won't say anything."

She gave him a dirty look. "I guess I don't feel like talking to you."

He was quiet, just staring at her. After a second, he glanced past her and she knew he was looking at Peg and Rex.

When he next spoke, his voice had changed, becoming eerily flat. Emotionless. "You can go sit with your friends if you don't want to be here." He didn't look at her any more. Instead, he started fiddling with the lid on the empty water bottle.

Here was her out. She could trade this super awkward situation for one that was only slightly awkward. She could just tell Peg and Rex that she was bored or something. But…

She sighed, long and loud. "No. I don't want to be there either."

"Why not?"

"I don't know." Frustration made her curt. "I just…I just don't."

Still he capped and uncapped the bottle. "Where exactly do you want to be?"

"I don't know. Somewhere else. Anywhere but here."

He grew quiet again. Screw cap on; take it off. "Do you want to leave? I know a place."

She didn't think she'd heard him right. "What?"

"I know a place. Where we can go." He shrugged. "If you want."

It was strange but sometimes when she looked at him, when their eyes clashed, he didn't seem quite so hard and distant. This was one of those times. And it was disarming.

But what was he asking?

"You mean leave, right now? Ditch class?"

"Yeah."

She'd never done that before. It was so not like her. And besides, she couldn't go anywhere with him. She didn't know a thing about him.

"I can't do that," she said, sounding way too appalled, like he'd asked her to strip or get his name tattooed on her arm.

His mouth quirked which made him seem almost playful. "Of course not. You're a *good* girl."

She frowned. "There's nothing wrong with being a good girl," she insisted.

"Very true." He said it with such conviction that she believed he meant it. Until he added, "If you're a golden retriever."

Cori leaned forward so that they were eye to eye. "Did you just call me a dog?"

"No. I called you a good girl." There was something in his eyes. Amusement? Did he think this was funny?

"I guess you think you know me," she mused. "Well, you know what I think? I think you're not as tough as you'd like everyone to believe."

"Oh, really?"

"Yeah." She reached across the table to poke one of his well-formed biceps. "I think you're a great—" *poke* "—big—" *poke* "—marshmallow." *Poke.*

His mouth was parted slightly as if no one had ever dared to call him such a thing. Well, look at that. She could be a trailblazer.

"I'm not a…marshmallow," he said indignantly.

Cori sat back and silently sipped her Coke, thoroughly happy with the way she'd handled that one.

"Well, suit yourself then," he mumbled. "I guess you'll just have to sit here with me and be miserable for the next ten minutes."

"I'm not miserable." Not any more. It was kind of fun when she was one-upping him.

"You're not?" Black eyebrow cocked. "Sure seemed like it a minute ago."

Cori lifted one shoulder in a shrug. "That was then."

He narrowed his eyes. "What's changed?"

She couldn't help snickering. "I don't know. I guess I figured out you're a marshmallow under that hard shell."

Now he scowled, dark brows furrowing deep over his pale eyes. Underneath it though, he seemed oddly…satisfied.

She laughed some more because, well, because it felt good. And it had been a while since it felt this good to laugh, felt real.

In an instant, his scowl went away, his expression becoming something more like awe. It surprised her, seeing such raw emotion written there in his features—features that were usually so tightly guarded—that the laughter faded.

"Don't stop," he said, his face still bright, foreign.

"W-What?"

And then everything was shut up again, locked tight, key tossed. She was about to say something, try to fix whatever had just happened. Except then she noticed he wasn't looking at her any more. He was looking behind her. Glancing over her shoulder, she saw Aiken. He was sitting at the table with Peg and Rex and he was glaring at Grayson. The phrase "if looks could kill" applied.

"Don't mind him." She turned to face Grayson again. "He might be a little mad at me."

"Mad at you?" he gritted out, clearly agitated. "For what?"

She shrugged. "You were there."

"Because you didn't go out with him?"

"Because I didn't go out with him and now I'm sitting with you."

Grayson glared back over her shoulder at the other guy and was about to say something when he was interrupted by the bell.

Dread hit her like a wrecking ball. Lunch was over and Aiken was here. She'd have to face him. And now he seemed to be angry. She wished he'd been here this morning so she could have talked to him about things. But then, maybe he wasn't as mad as he looked. Yeah, go optimism.

Wordlessly, she rose and dumped her tray. Grayson followed. In the hall, he didn't speak and neither did she. At her locker he was still with her.

"Don't you have to get your book?" she asked as she spun the combination on her lock.

"No."

Then Aiken was there, standing so close she had to crane her neck just to look at him.

"Hey," he said, completely ignoring the fact that Grayson was standing less than a foot away from him.

"Hey," she answered, carefully avoiding his gaze. "You weren't in class earlier." Stupid thing to say. But then, that was how she did things sometimes.

"Nah. I had an appointment."

"Doctor?"

"Something like that. So, Peg and Rex want to do something tonight. Just the *four* of us. You up for it?"

She saw this for what it was: a shameless set-up. Thanks, Peg.

Truth was, she just didn't want to go out and be with people. Yes, these people were her new friends but they didn't get how hard it was for her to cope, especially in public. Sometimes she felt like she was barely hanging on; it was all she could do to just get through the school day. Now they wanted more from her?

"Sounds fun, but I really can't. I'm supposed to meet my mom for dinner." Not exactly a lie. She *hoped* she would meet her mom for dinner. Okay, it was pretty much a lie.

But he wasn't deterred. "What time? I could pick you up afterward. I'm sure they wouldn't mind waiting."

He'd moved in so close she couldn't even tell if Grayson was still there. With Aiken looming over her like he was, she was almost afraid he might try to touch her. Oddly, the thought left her feeling uneasy.

"Uh, I don't know. We have dinner pretty late." Not a lie. *When* they had dinner it was always late.

This made him grin. "Well then we can get together earlier, like right after school. Problem solved."

She kind of hated how he'd manipulated the situation. She hated it enough that she wasn't going to back down. "Let me think about it."

His grin turned triumphant. "Okay. See you in class." Then he spun, nearly knocking into Grayson—he was still there, apparently—and strode away.

Irritated, she shuffled through her locker until she found the right book and then slammed the door shut with a little too much force. When she looked up Grayson was right there, standing almost as close as Aiken had been. Except it didn't make her uncomfortable. It actually made her feel at ease, something she didn't often feel anymore.

She peered up until she met those strange eyes. They seemed to be searching her own.

"You wanna get out of here? I know a place." His words were smoky, tinged with a chill.

This time, Cori nodded.

Chapter 11

THE BEST PART OF A GRAVEYARD

Grayson knew what he had to do. He now knew his life's purpose. Or at least the only purpose he really cared about. For a few precious seconds it had been so clear, like heaven had opened up and shined a light on him. Or something like that.

He'd made her laugh. Not *at* him — which would be a totally different thing — but *because* of him. He'd made her laugh like Aiken had, but better. Because not only had she laughed, she'd chosen him.

He felt like he'd inherited a slaughterhouse. Which to a zombie was gold.

He was certain the feeling wouldn't last. But still. He would ride the wave until it was gone. In fact, he was feeling so good that he hadn't even had to struggle with his temper when Aiken wedged his way in between him and Cori. His temper was still intact as the guy tried to convince her to go out when she so obviously didn't want to. And now…

Now they were walking past the student parking lot toward his favorite place. Even still, his good mood was bewildering. He was still a zombie — nothing to be happy about. Besides, as a rule, he didn't do happy.

Whatever.

As they passed the parking lot he decided they should walk instead of drive. It wasn't that far.

"Where are we going?" Cori asked.

"You'll see."

"We aren't going to walk, are we?" She sounded horrified.

"Yep."

"Ugh."

He glanced at her. She scrunched her face up as she dodged a puddle.

"What? Walking's good for you."

"Not when it's muddy." He watched as she tip-toed through some deeper water.

"Look who's a marshmallow now."

Cori jutted her chin. "Am not."

They went for a ways in silence, stepping over puddles on the sidewalk. He was fairly certain her shoes were soaked through to her socks.

When the ten-foot wrought iron fence of the cemetery came into view, Grayson sped up a little. He went around the south periphery and found the side entrance. He was already some ways past the gate when he realized he was alone. Turning, he found Cori standing stock still on the opposite side of the fence.

"What's wrong?"

"Uh, this isn't, uh, what I had in mind."

Of course not. She was human. Humans didn't like hanging out in cemeteries. That was a zombie thing. Why hadn't he thought of that?

He walked back to the gate. "You scared?" It was a taunt, but it was better than admitting this was a bad idea.

"No. It's just creepy. Why would you want to come here?"

"It's nice. I like it. Come on."

She didn't make a move, but those crystalline eyes were staring so intently at him. He held his hand out to her and then instantly wished he hadn't when she just stared at it. It hung there like an opportunity waiting to be missed. *Take it,* he thought. *Take my hand.* Suddenly, it felt like the most important thing in the world and he wasn't sure what he'd do if she didn't.

It seemed like an eternity that she stared at his outstretched hand, but still he held it there. Waiting, hoping. Like his life depended on whether or not she touched him.

Then she took a step toward the gate. With him on one side and her on the other, it felt like they occupied two different worlds. And in truth, they did. Would she cross over to his? Somehow he knew that if she did — if she took his hand now — things would change for the both of them. The question was would it be for the better or for worse?

But then, how much worse could things get?

With an exasperated sigh, she placed her fingers in his palm and stepped through the gate. For a moment, he just stared at her because some part of him couldn't believe she'd actually done it. Okay, yeah all she really did was enter a cemetery. So why did it feel like more?

Her hand was small in his. But instead of finding fault in that, he actually… *liked* it. In fact, now that he wasn't looking at her like she was his only hope of being human again, he liked everything about her. Yeah, he did. He liked her hair, how it was long and straight and her bangs fell to the side so her eyes weren't covered. He liked her short little fingernails and the fact that she didn't paint them. He liked that she could look at him and he instantly felt chastised, like it was a sin to behold her or something. Maybe it was. He liked the way her neck became flushed when she was irritated. And how her cheeks got all rosy when —

"Are you okay?" she whispered. "D-Do you need water again? I think I have some in my backpack."

He shook himself. He didn't feel dehydrated. No, his problem was something else entirely.

"No," he said. "I'm fine. Let's go."

He should have let go of her hand, but he couldn't make himself do it. So he pulled her down the path that led to some of his favorite plots.

Cori didn't say a word.

Not until he pulled up in front of an ancient looking mausoleum. Etched in the slate colored rock was the name, HAWTHORP. It had always been one of his favorites. Someone made sure there were roses there at all times. In the summer they were yellow and peach. In the fall they were usually pink, sometimes purple. In the winter, white. But in the spring — as it was now — they were always, always red.

But it wasn't the flowers that he liked. It was the stone itself. Angels, so beautifully carved, were posted at each corner. The one on the right had bright eyes and a joyful expression, her wings uplifted to the heavens, one palm resting on her heart. The angel on the left was the antithesis of the other. This angel was weeping, clearly distraught, mournful. Her wings were sagging and folded in, her hand pressed to her chest as if she were in pain.

The sight gave him some sense of calm, although it left him confused. He supposed it was meant to be representative of how a person might have conflicting feelings about death. On one hand you might mourn the loss of your loved one, but on the other you might rejoice that he is now in heaven. But then, Grayson didn't believe in heaven…

And his death hadn't been the end for him. No, his had culminated in something downright atrocious. Something wrong.

"Is this someone you know?" Cori asked, bringing him back.

He shook his head. "No. I don't know anyone here."

"Oh."

"I just like it. I think…I think I would want mine to be like this one."

He really did realize he was being creepy. He just couldn't help it. It was who he was, *how* he was. Usually he kept it to himself. Now here she was, bearing witness to it firsthand.

He looked over at her. She was fixed on the sad angel. A tremble fluttered through her—he felt it where their hands linked—and then she pressed her lips together. He'd seen her do that yesterday, just before she started crying.

"What is it?" he asked.

She swallowed hard. Stared at the ground. Squeezed her eyes shut.

"It's just that…my, uh…dad. He died a couple months ago and this is…well, it's hard."

Her dad. Grayson immediately felt sick. He'd brought her to a cemetery of all places. What a stupid thing to do. He wanted to kick something. Because he should've known about that. Aiken probably knew.

"I didn't know," he said finally.

She let out a little nervous laugh. "How would you?"

"You wanna go?" Dumb question. Of course she wanted to go. Who would want to hang out in a cemetery when they were mourning the death of their father? Better question: who would want to hang out in a cemetery at all?

Cori shrugged. "It's okay. I'm tougher than I look." He was beginning to realize that. "See, no tears." She blinked her lids a couple times to prove it. But why did he have the feeling that she would be crying herself to sleep when night fell?

"Well, that's good because you haven't even seen the best part yet."

She crinkled her nose, an expression Grayson was coming to like. "The best part? You do realize we're in a graveyard. The graves *are* the best part."

"Come on, shrimp. I'll show you." He started toward the river.

"What did you call me?"

"Shrimp." He popped the P.

She rushed to catch up with him. "Shrimp? Why would you call me that?"

"It's just a little nickname I came up with the first time I saw you."

"But…why?"

He smirked. "It's obvious isn't it? You're tiny."

She let out a sound of outrage. "I am *not* tiny."

"Um, yes you are."

"Just because you're a giant, does *not* mean I'm tiny."

He gave her a look. "You're tiny."

"Whatever. Giant."

His face cracked a little. Or rather, he must have grinned. "Just doesn't have the same ring as 'shrimp.'"

"I'll think of something," she muttered.

Just then they crossed through the tree line. He stopped suddenly, causing Cori to run into the back of him.

"Ooof. What—"

"Here we are. The river. Or part of it anyway." Really it was more like an oversized creek. The water was up today since it'd been raining and it rushed by in a dull, steady roar. It was hypnotizing, mesmerizing. It was like a Pied Piper's song, calling to him. As always, he wanted to jump in. Instead, he settled for removing his boots and soaking his feet. Instantly his cells responded, soaking up the cool, fresh liquid.

"What are you doing?"

"What does it look like?"

Cori came closer to the bank where he was walking through the current with his boots and socks in one hand and his jacket in the other.

"Try it," he said.

"Nuh uh." Her bangs brushed her face as she shook her head.

"What? Don't you like water?"

"Oh, sure," she muttered, a look of annoyance on her face. "I like swimming pools and showers and the stuff you drink. That kind of water."

Grayson ventured over to the rock ledge and sat down. The water was high enough that his feet were still immersed.

"You don't know what you're missing." He eyed her. "If you weren't here, I'd rip my clothes off and dive in."

She rolled her eyes and crossed her arms. "Yeah, right." But he thought he saw a faint blush.

"I'm serious."

"It's cold. You would freeze," she insisted.

Nope, not him. Zombies were impervious to the cold. In fact, the colder the better. There was a reason morgues had freezers.

He simply shrugged. No need to point out that detail, especially when she likely hadn't forgotten that mysterious bathroom incident. He was lucky she hadn't asked more questions about it. But humans tended to do that, ignore what they couldn't explain.

Cori tip-toed through the muddy grass until she'd reached the rock ledge and then carefully sat down cross-legged next to him. Her shoes stayed on, of course.

"So…you really like it here?"

He nodded, trying to read her. "You don't?"

She cocked her head, looking around. "It's just so…dreary."

He supposed she was right. The craggy moss-covered rocks and drooping foliage supplied a perfect setting for the incessant drizzle.

"I like dreary," he told her. Dreary meant moisture. Moisture meant life. For him especially, it meant life.

They were such opposites, the two of them. She was like a desert cactus — one with blooms, of course — craving the dry and arid, and he was like the moss on the rocks, always requiring moisture. Or maybe he was that slimy scum stuff that stuck to the bottom of the river bed. Either way, total opposites.

Why was she his *Save?*

"Well, on a normal day," she said, "I wouldn't like dreary too much. But I guess today it suits my mood so it's kind of nice. And you're right, this is definitely better than the graves."

They were quiet for a while, both of them just staring at the bubbling stream in front of them.

"Since you don't like the wet, I'm guessing you don't care too much for Asher."

She shrugged. "I don't know really. I lived in Indiana my whole life so…" Another shrug. "What's that on your neck?"

Grayson fingered the pocked mark that was several shades darker than his skin. Every zombie had one, a *skar*. Besides being bitten by a zombie who'd reached the Age of Death, there was another way to be turned. Though he had no memory of it, it had happened for Grayson that second way — several injections of zombie blood to the vein in his neck. The poison had left a nasty circular scar, the size of a nickel. He supposed he was lucky his wasn't a bite mark like Aiken's and Leiv's.

"Birthmark," he said. Not a lie exactly, though it was more correct to call it a death mark. It marked his birth as zombie.

Silence creeped between them.

He wasn't good at small talk. Apparently neither was she, so he decided to just say what was on his mind.

"Why did you help me, in the hall, when I needed water?"

Out of the corner of his eye he could see that she'd turned to look at him, but he remained staring at the stream. Safer that way.

"I helped you because you needed it."

Such a simple answer, yet it amazed him. He wasn't sure if he would've done the same thing if the situation arose. If it were Aiken in the hall mid-water-cramp, would he have helped him get to the bathroom?

"But I wasn't nice to you."

She snorted. "No. You weren't."

"And you still helped me."

"Yeah."

He rubbed his palms together, a nervous gesture he tried to avoid. "Because you're good."

She fidgeted next to him. "Oh, come on. Not that again. I told you, there's nothing wrong with—"

"No, I mean…" He met her gaze. "You're good. You're a good person."

Their eyes were locked, but she blinked several times and swallowed hard.

"I just…did what I thought was right. No big deal."

But it was a big deal. She didn't know how big a deal.

Grayson looked away, into the thick green of the trees that surrounded them. "I don't think you understand how bad…" He shook his head. "Never mind." *Just shut up.* He didn't talk to people like this, and why should she be any different?

"I think I know what's going on here."

He truly doubted that but he glanced at her anyway. Those sweet blue eyes were so compassionate in that moment that he found it difficult not to reach for her. But if he did, then what?

"You're sick, right? That's why you looked like that. And why you needed water."

She thought he was sick. This was getting dangerously close to complicated.

"Not exactly," he said.

"It's okay if you don't want to talk about it."

He *couldn't* talk about it. She could never *ever* know what he was. Which was exactly why he should've stayed far, far away from her. But now, here they were.

"I'd rather talk about something else."

"Okay. What would you like to talk about?" She reached for a small round rock and bounced it in her palm.

"Let's talk about you."

"Me? I'm really not that interesting," she insisted.

A few days ago he might've agreed, but not now.

"How come you didn't go out with Aiken?"

Cori blinked a few times before answering. "I don't know. I just didn't want to, I guess."

"Why?" he pushed.

She shrugged and kept bouncing that rock. "Sometimes I just don't want to be sociable. Yesterday was one of those times."

"What about tonight? Are you going to go with him?"

She narrowed those pale blue eyes. "Why do you want to know?"

He shrugged, trying to give off the vibe that it didn't really matter. "Just wondering." His tone was cavalier to help get the point across.

Cori chucked the pebble into the flow. "I don't know. Probably."

"But you don't want to," he readily reminded her.

She shrugged again but didn't answer.

"You don't have to, you know."

"Yeah, I know," she laughed humorlessly, still looking at the water. "I could stay home by myself like every other night, eat stale pizza for dinner, and go to bed at eight o'clock. Or…" She took a deep breath. "I could stop being a recluse, go out with my friends, and maybe, just maybe, stay up until eleven."

He didn't want her anywhere near Aiken. Peg and Rex were okay, but Aiken…he was dangerous. There must be something he could do to keep Cori away from the Reaper. Had to be. Because he may not know much about the girl sitting next to him, but one thing he did know: she was good — too good for a zombie.

Chapter 12

None of Your Business

Cori didn't really like the way the conversation was going. It was too focused on her and her loser-ness (Peg and Rex would've been proud of her for that one). Really, she needed to learn to paint herself in a better light—as her mom had always told her. But then, brutal honesty was more her style, and yeah, her life kinda sucked at the moment so why hide it.

She was about to attempt a subject change when Grayson leaped up from his sitting position. It startled her, but before she could ask him about it, he put his hand up to silence her. He cocked his head to one side as if listening. Cori tried too, but she didn't hear a thing. Not even the wind rustling the leaves of the trees. He snapped his head around, first in one direction, then the other, looking for some apparent threat. His nose went up in the air. It was almost animalistic. Then all at once, he seemed to relax, coming out of his aggressive stance, his shoulders loosening.

A question was on the tip of her tongue—along the lines of, "What the heck was that all about?"—but something stopped her. A beautiful, tall, dark-haired, must-be-a-supermodel something. The woman—girl?—bounded out from the trees and straight into

Grayson's arms. She was clad in hipster jeans and a shirt that showed her pierced belly button.

"Gray! Oh, thank god. I knew I'd find you here. Something terrible has happened. It's Leiv, he's—"

"Raina," his eyes darted to Cori and then back to her.

"—been taken in for questioning. They didn't say why. They just came and took him and, and…I don't know what to do." She was in tears, Cori noticed. Whatever was happening, the girl was completely distraught.

Grayson shook her a little. "Raina, this is Cori," he said in a strange way. Why was he talking like that, like her name meant something?

Then it hit her. This chick wasn't just someone, she was his girlfriend. This explained so much. Like the way he held her, protectively. Like the way he was consoling her—so gentle for someone whose go-to expression was brooding.

Suddenly, the girl—Raina—looked at her and it was clear that she was seeing Cori for the first time. She stepped away from Grayson but still gripped the sleeve of his shirt, the skin of her knuckles white.

"Oh! Uh, I…thought…uh…" She seemed confused.

Cori stood, since she felt like an ant looking up at two giants. Not that standing helped much. Was everyone in this town tall? And talk about awkward, she had to get out of there. Raina certainly wouldn't be happy finding her boyfriend in a secluded place with another girl. Cori was pretty sure stuff was fixing to go down.

"I'm just gonna go," Cori said, backing away. She resisted the urge to put both hands up in a placating gesture.

"No," Grayson barked. It made her jump because she'd forgotten he could talk like that. Geez, he'd been almost normal today.

Raina looked back and forth between Cori and Grayson. Cori wanted to assure her that she had nothing to be worried about. She and Grayson weren't even friends, much less anything more.

"Raina, go on home and wait for me there. We'll figure it all out when I get there. Okay?"

She was nodding. "Okay, yeah. But Gray…"

"Everything will be all right. I'm right behind you, promise." His tone was gentle once more and something about it made Cori's chest hurt. He loved this woman, Raina. You could hear it in his voice.

Raina nodded hesitantly and turned away. She glanced back once at Cori and then disappeared into the trees.

Cori waited until Grayson turned to her before trying her exit strategy again.

"So, uh, thanks for getting me out of class and everything but I think I'm just gonna—"

He was in front of her so fast she didn't even know how he'd gotten there. "You should stay away from Aiken."

Okay. "Why?"

"Because." His voice was hard steel.

She crossed her arms over her chest. He stepped closer until they were almost touching. Uncomfortably close.

"Because why? Because you don't like him? If that was a good enough reason to stay away from someone, I wouldn't be here with you right now."

His mouth was a grim line, his eyes lit from the inside. When he didn't say anything else, she stepped around him to leave.

"Where are you going?" he demanded.

She kept walking. "Home."

He didn't say anything else and she didn't really expect him to. When she got to the gate of the cemetery, she dared a glance back. Grayson was nowhere to be seen, so she stepped through and went toward home.

Along the way it started raining. It was a longer walk since she was coming from the cemetery instead of school so she was left with extra time to think. Even with him being bossy, she was glad she'd gone with him. She hadn't expected to enjoy the wet cemetery. And her suspicions about Grayson being sick were confirmed. She wondered if his girlfriend knew. He seemed like the type to hide it. Cori was curious what disease he had, but she wouldn't push him to talk about it.

As for his warning about Aiken, she thought it was baseless. Aiken was as nice as they came. And he was happy and easygoing and, well, basically perfect in every conceivable way. Which was exactly why she wasn't going out with him tonight—even if Peg and Rex were coming. She was the opposite of everything he was: not happy, not easygoing, and not perfect. Hanging out with him too much would only bring him down. At least with Grayson she was on an equal playing field.

But then, she wouldn't be hanging out with him too much either since she really didn't want his supermodel girlfriend for an enemy. And on that note, where did she go to school? Cori was pretty sure she didn't go to Westland. She would've remembered someone like her, all that dark hair and those dark eyes. She probably didn't even need makeup to achieve the smoky-eyed look. And her pale skin was the type that was flawless, even without a golden tan.

Cori was soaked through by the time she reached her empty house. To waste time and warm up, she showered and then threw on her old raggedy sweatpants and Purdue hoodie.

When she went downstairs, her cell phone was ringing. It was Asia. Instantly, tears pricked her eyes. She missed her friend so badly. And wow, she needed someone to talk to. But if she answered that phone…she knew she would waste all their time bawling like a baby. And plus, Asia had seemed so happy last time they'd talked. She didn't want to be the one to ruin that.

She set the phone on the counter and opened the fridge. The pizza was still there. She stared at it for a minute before deciding that she was on a pizza fast. No more, even if Mom brought it home every night until she graduated. She dug around in there: half-full jug of milk, week-old Chinese takeout, a couple cartons of yogurt, bread, butter, cheese. She opted for the yogurt.

While she was eating, her phone rang again. This time it was Peg.

"Hey."

"Hi, Peg," she answered in a bright voice that was as false as the flowers she'd seen at the graveyard. Except for those roses at the crypt. Those had been real.

"Aiken said you were coming tonight so I was checking to see what time you wanted to meet up."

Cori sighed. Okay, so maybe Aiken did have a fault: he was a wee bit pushy.

"Actually, I told him I wasn't sure."

"Oh. Well…Shut up, Rex! I'm trying to talk." Cori could hear him in the background spouting off movie times. "So, what's the verdict? You coming or not? Please say yes," Peg begged. "If you don't come I'll be stuck with two guys. They'll make me watch an action movie." Cori was a little surprised that Rex liked action movies. He seemed too intellectual to sit through two hours of guys with bad accents blowing each other to smithereens.

"I really can't tonight, Peg." Cori wished she could tell her yes, but she just didn't have it in her. Not tonight. She would get over things eventually. Soon the memories of her dad would fade and she'd forget why she was so sad without him. The thought made her feel infinitely worse. But not tonight. Tonight, she needed more of what had gotten her through it thus far: solitude.

"I'm sorry," she told her friend, and meant it.

"Oh well. It's all right." She sighed dramatically. "You doing okay, though? I didn't see you after school."

"Yeah. Yeah, I'm fine. I left early."

"How was lunch with Dracula?"

Cori had to smile. "It wasn't so bad. I mean, it was weird at first. But after a while he warmed up."

"Hmm. So, he's like mold, huh?" Peg mused.

"What?"

"After a while, he grows on you."

Cori laughed. Peg was good at making her do that. "Yeah, I guess you could say that."

"Well…Just a second, Cori. What? No, Rex, she's not coming. What? Oh, *come on*…Fine." Big sigh. "He says, for you and you alone he would have lowered himself so much as to watch a rom-com. But now you will be punished accordingly upon our next outing. Punishment includes, but is not limited to, a) watching an action movie, b) watching a sci-fi movie, or c) watching a documentary. His words exactly."

Cori grinned. "Tell him I apologize profusely and I shall accept my punishment with my head held high."

"Oh, don't encourage him, Cori," Peg grumped. "Anyway, guess I'll see you tomorrow."

"Bye."

When she hung up, she couldn't help feeling a little better. And when on a whim, she decided to check what food options were hiding in the freezer, things got even better.

Helllooo Ben and Jerry's.

As soon as Cori was safe inside her house, Grayson ran home. He didn't bother going back to the school for his car. He just ran until he was there. One of the pluses of being undead: you had terrific endurance and stamina. As long as you were hydrated. And lucky for him it was raining.

Raina was pacing the floor when he got there, a bottle of water in one hand and her cell phone in the other. "Oh, Gray! I'm so sorry. I didn't know you were even talking to her. You said—"

He quickly cut her off. "It's okay. Tell me what happened to Leiv." She hesitated, searching his face. But he couldn't think about Cori right then. "Raina, what happened?"

"Reapers. They came early this morning, three of them. Said Leiv had to go with them for questioning."

"Concerning what?"

"Suspicious activities. That was all they would say. I demanded an explanation but they refused. And Leiv went peacefully. He…he said he would be back soon. That's all. But then, it's been all day and I am just so worried."

Grayson looked at the clock. School would be out in ten minutes. He needed to talk to Aiken. "Raina, I need you to drive me to the school. I'll talk to the Reaper, find out what's going on. You come back here and wait for Leiv."

Her brow furrowed. "No! I won't sit here and do nothing."

"I'm just going to talk to him, not fight him." Hopefully. He'd already had his can kicked by the guy once.

She jutted her chin. "Still. What if—"

"You know the best thing to do is wait," he persuaded. "Leiv is smart, and we both know he isn't in any trouble. It's just a mistake. They'll clear it up."

He could see her thinking it over. And truth was, she'd probably have better luck fighting Aiken than Grayson would. But she was clearly shaken.

"Fine," she said in a voice reserved for those she wanted to intimidate. It didn't really work on him even though he let her think it did. "But you call me as soon as you find something out. Understand?"

"Of course," he said, then gritted his teeth. He hated being told what to do, but he let it go since she was so upset.

She dropped him off at school just as class was letting out. It didn't take long for Grayson to find Aiken in the parking lot. He was getting into the driver's seat of a sparkly new Ford F-150, cherry red with chrome wheels. Grayson wouldn't be caught dead — or undead — in something like that. Nope, he would stick to his black-as-midnight Corvette. Not to mention, it was a convertible.

Aiken spotted him and immediately his happy-boy persona shifted into hatred.

Grayson didn't waste time with pleasantries. "Why did you arrest my brother?"

"*I* didn't. My partner did. And that is none of your business," he answered hotly.

"It's totally my business. Where is he?"

"Again, NOYB. He'll be released when we're done with him."

Grayson's fingertips tingled with the urge to hit him. "He hasn't committed any crime. Why is he in custody?"

Aiken leaned back against his truck, his arms crossed, a grin on his face, the image of cool. "You just aren't getting it are you? See, when I say that it's none of your business, I mean — "

Grayson let out a growl. He didn't mean to exactly, but then let's face it, he'd been wanting to for a while. And yeah, it felt good.

Aiken's jaw ticked. "Did you just *growl* at me, civie?" he ground out, blatantly using the derogatory slang for "civilian."

"Tell me where my brother is," was Grayson's only answer.

Aiken stepped toward him in such a way that almost had Grayson falling back. "Your brother," he spat, "is nearing the Age of Death. He is dangerously close to decomposition — which as you know, is *my* business." He took another step, and this time Grayson was forced to back up. "He is being questioned to determine his state of mind. Tests are being done to confirm his age and to see if he is carrying the contagion. All this would be completely routine if not for the mysterious deaths occurring up north." He was glaring down at Grayson in a way that should have been impossible since they were roughly the same height. And just what was he implying? That Leiv could be responsible for those atrocities? For all they knew, humans were the offenders.

"Mysterious deaths. How does that have anything to do with my brother?"

"Since you must know, they occurred not too far from here. We don't know if the killer was zombie or human but if they're zombie—" his jaw clenched and unclenched "—we're looking at a possible *live eater.*"

A rogue. One who ate humans. He wanted to retch.

"We are trying to prove his innocence, Grayson. And you will *not* stand in the way."

Grayson knew in the zombie world it wasn't "innocent until proven guilty" but rather "guilty until proven innocent." Even though he hated it, he would have to accept it.

Yeah, but he didn't like being told what to do.

"And *you* won't tell me what I will or will not do. You might be a Reaper but you have no authority over me."

Aiken just smiled, sarcasm leaking from his pores. Why did it seem that he got more satisfaction out of the mental assault than a physical one? "Whatever you say, boss." Just then Aiken's phone rang. "Oh, lookie there, it's my partner. You might wanna stick around."

Grayson rolled his eyes while Aiken made a big show of hitting the call button.

"Hello? Uh huh. Of course, I have his progeny right here." Progeny? "Sure, the little guy is demanding to know the whereabouts of his *brother.* What shall I tell him? Okay. Uh huh. Sure. All right then, toodles." There was another big to-do while he punched the end button. "Your *brother* has been cleared and is en route to his home. Run along now, and you can meet him there."

"Fine." Grayson turned to leave, in a hurry to talk to Leiv.

"I know you were with her today. Where'd you go?" There was a disturbing edge to Aiken's voice.

Grayson couldn't help looking over his shoulder with a cruel smile. "That's NOYB."

Chapter 13

Jealousy Makes the Heart Grow Fonder

"It's really no big deal," Leiv was saying. "They just ran some tests, asked a ton of questions. Really, give it a rest, Raina."

Grayson stood, arms crossed, like a statue in the corner observing his brother and sister.

"So, they know you're not contagious then? They know you still have time?"

"Of course." He reached for her, wrapping her in a hug. Like that, she looked so small, her six-foot frame dwarfed next to his. "You worry too much. I told you, I don't have any symptoms. I'll be around for a few more years. Promise."

Grayson didn't know what to think of the arrest. Part of him wanted to believe what Aiken had said about it being routine. But the other part couldn't shake the feeling that something was off. Either way, Leiv didn't seem worried and that alone was most reassuring. Leiv was the oldest and the smartest. He was the most cunning of the three of them and if something was wrong, if he was close to deterioration, he would be the first to know.

And he wouldn't try to hide it like some zombies did. He wasn't like that. He was noble.

Leiv and Raina pulled apart and peered at Grayson.

"Raina told me you were with Cori today," his brother said carefully.

Grayson nodded once.

"Are things…going well?"

What was that supposed to mean? Like today was planned? It wasn't. Well, maybe lunch was but not the cemetery. And all of it was to keep her away from Aiken.

"It just sort of happened."

Leiv shot him a lopsided smile. "I know, dude. It's not your style to scheme." He went over to the sound system and cranked it on. "But you're talking to her now? That's good, right?"

Grayson didn't want to discuss it. Especially in front of Raina. There was too much hope in her eyes and it left him feeling uncomfortable.

"I guess." He shrugged one shoulder.

Leiv sauntered over to stand in front of him. "You know, Gray, it's okay for zombies to have human girlfriends."

Grayson jerked his head back and almost choked on his own saliva. After a couple coughs he was able to respond. "I don't want a girlfriend. And how in the hell is it *okay?*"

Leiv took a swig of water from the bottle Raina had brought him. "It's perfectly normal to fall for one of them. They are so…well, they're *alive*, for lack of a better word." He got a faraway look in his eyes. "I've done it. Raina has too. Really, I think it can't be helped."

Grayson almost didn't notice how his sister slipped from the room. Obviously this wasn't a conversation she wanted to take part in, and that was just fine with him. He glanced back at his brother—who was apparently lost in some memory of times past. He couldn't believe this.

"And just how did that work out for you, Leiv? When she found out what you were? Or did you never tell your 'human girlfriend' that you were one of the Dead Walking?"

Leiv's smile vanished. "I did tell her."

Anger itched at Grayson's being, brown flickering threateningly at his vision. Was he the only zombie alive that could see how wrong it was to act like they were normal? Even if the human never noticed the difference, they weren't normal, and no amount of pretending would ever make it so.

"And?" he pushed.

Leiv went back to the sound system and turned it off. "And everything worked itself out."

"So, you mean she thought you were a lunatic and ran away screaming. Realized you'd lied about what you are. Tell me, did you love her? Or was she just a plaything?" Like Cori was for Aiken. "And what happened when the Reapers found out? Because really, if you did love her, how could you ruin her life like that—"

"I loved her!" Leiv said, loud enough to shut Grayson up. Even his eyes changed, whites streaking yellow, irises a deep brown. Leiv never raised his voice, never got angry, never lost control. Within the second, he'd gained it back again.

"Brother," he said. "You have a lot to learn. There's so much that nobody can teach you. You have to learn it on your own, in time."

Grayson's chest heaved with the effort to catch his breath. To think of what might've happened to Leiv's human. The Reapers. They would have silenced her. Aiken had played dumb when he'd mentioned they didn't harm humans. But Grayson knew better. He *knew*.

But then, he wasn't any better than them was he? What he was considering doing with Cori…

Leiv's shoulders slumped as he came to stand in front of Grayson. His hand came to rest on Grayson's shoulder and it was all he could do not to growl and shrug it off. But he tried to remind himself, this was Leiv, his brother. The one who'd taken him in when he'd risen in a fog of lost memory, craving flesh, and filled with a despair so intense he'd cried for days.

"I know what you're thinking, but it wasn't like that. Look, there's a lot you still don't know about us zombies. But understand this: not all of us hate who we are."

"Yeah? Ever think maybe that's the problem?" With that, Grayson stormed from the house, desperate to get away. Because he did hate who he was. He truly did. And always had.

The question was did he hate himself enough to risk Cori's life?

He was terrified of the answer.

Cori was taking up the whole couch like only a true couch potato could: on her back, ice cream propped up on her belly, with her legs draped over one of the sides. She was halfway through a carton of chocolate chip cookie dough—having already polished off the Chunky Monkey—when there was a knock on the door. Reluctantly, she paused the TV and went to answer it.

Annnd hello headache. She must've gotten up too fast. She steadied herself for a moment before stumbling to the door. In Indy, she would have checked first before answering. But she was in Asher now and everything was harmless. Still though, instead of throwing it open wide, she just cracked it.

And then almost choked on a chocolate chip.

It was Grayson, a.k.a. The Last Person She Expected.

"Um, hi," she said, opening the door the rest of the way.

"Hey," was all he said.

She jammed the spoon into the half melted ice cream and tried to forget about the fact that she was in a pair of beat up sweats. "What are you doing here?" she asked.

He stuffed his hands in his pockets and stared at the ground. "I just uh, things got kind of crazy earlier. I wanted to make sure…" He drifted off. She waited but he didn't finish.

"So, is everything okay with whoever was in jail?" Wow this conversation was one for the record books. Awkward.

"Yeah," he said quickly, still staring at his feet. "It wasn't jail exactly."

"Oh. Okay. Well…good."

He finally glanced up. His expression was one she was beginning to get used to: cold and distant. "I see you didn't go with your friends tonight."

"Nah, I made new friends," she said, holding up the carton of ice cream. "Meet Ben and Jerry. They're real sweeties." The side of his mouth quirked a little and his shoulders eased a fraction. So she kept going. "Popcorn's hanging out in the microwave. I'm counting on the three of them and reruns of *Glee* to keep me up till at least eleven."

He nodded but didn't say anything else. She didn't know what to say either, but after a few uncomfortable moments she thought of something. "How did you know where I lived?"

He shuffled his feet. "Oh, uh, it's a small town."

"Not that small."

He glanced at her and then immediately away. "Yeah, you're right. I followed you earlier."

"Followed me?"

He nodded, unashamed.

That was so…creepy.

"I wanted to make sure you got home okay," he added gruffly.

That was so…sweet.

"Oh. Well, I'm, umm, good. So…" Why was he here? Should she ask him?

Before she could decide, he answered her question as if he'd plucked it from her mind. "I want to have lunch with you again," he barely mumbled. "Tomorrow."

"Okay, sure. We can sit with Peg—"

"No. I don't want that. Just you." His eyes went to hers, almost a challenge.

"Grayson, I really can't keep blowing off my friends. And besides, I'm pretty sure your girlfriend wouldn't like it if she found out you were—"

"My girlfriend?" he interrupted.

"Yeah, the girl from the cemetery. Wasn't her name Rain?"

Green eyes went wide for a moment, his surprise clear. "Raina is my sister," he said. "Not my girlfriend."

"Oh." Relief swamped Cori as she realized she was glad—very, very glad—that Raina was only his sister.

Grayson, however seemed troubled. "Why would you think she was my girlfriend?"

Because you were holding her and consoling her and I figured you'd only be like that with a girlfriend or a sister—and because I'm an idiot, sister never even crossed my mind.

"She just seemed like…your type," was what she said out loud.

"My type?" He was shaking his head and looking at her so strangely. "Not even close. I prefer a much different…type." When had he stepped closer? And why were his eyes suddenly so dark? Sultry, they were sultry. And hypnotic. Would she tumble into them maybe, if she kept looking?

"My mistake," she said, her voice sounding too breathless. After a second, she realized what was wrong: that tugging feeling was back, stronger this time. So intense that her head felt like a weighted balloon, airy but heavy.

"Are you okay?" Fine lines furrowed his perfect brow. That only happened when you were concerned. Was he concerned about her?

Suddenly, Cori felt as if the ground buckled under her, and she had to grip the doorjamb in order to stay upright. Like a lightning strike, his hand shot out to steady her, and as soon as he made contact with her arm…it all went away. The spinning heaviness just…gone.

She looked at him. "Yeah. I'm fine. Too much ice cream probably. This is my second carton."

Frowning, he took the container from her hands. "You should sit down."

She tried to protest. "No, really. I'm okay." But he was already herding her over to the porch swing. He made sure she was sitting and then backed away, as if dizziness was contagious.

Grayson peered into the container of ice cream like it was pureed liver instead of chocolate-chip-gooey-goodness. "You shouldn't eat this if it makes you sick."

Cori rolled her eyes and stuck her hand out, wiggling her fingers. "I'm not sick. Give it back."

He hesitated, regarding her with narrowed eyes, but finally surrendered the Ben and Jerry's. He stared as she took a few more bites.

"Want some?" she offered around a mouthful. After all, she didn't want to be rude.

His eyes seemed to grow heated again…and were they greener? What was up with him? Then, in a breath, his face closed up and he shook his head as if to clear it.

"About tomorrow," he said. "Lunch?"

Cori was glad she had a mouthful of ice cream to get through before answering because she had to think about it. She really wanted to help Grayson, wanted to break through his defenses and get to know the guy underneath. She loved that he was finally ready to say bye-bye to his loner days. But she really liked Peg and Rex and Aiken. And if she kept putting them off, they'd probably give up on her. The only fair thing to do was give them equal time.

"I have to sit with my friends tomorrow," she said eventually. "I can't keep telling them no."

"You mean, Aiken. You can't keep telling Aiken no," he said a little too calmly, like there was something hiding there under all that smoothness. The tone of his voice put her on edge.

"What does that mean?"

Grayson shrugged, a shrewd look on his face. "It means whatever you want it to mean."

"Aiken's my friend just like Peg and Rex and, well, you if you want to be."

He crossed his arms over his broad chest, making them look even bigger than they actually were and stared her straight in the eye as he said, "No. Thanks."

Cori's mouth hung open as his words bit her. Should've known the nice wouldn't last.

She stood up because she hated how he was standing over her. "Why are you doing that?"

"Doing what?" His voice was harsh. A cold winter when minutes ago he'd been tropic.

"Why are you being rude again? I thought we were past that." Her words were strong but inwardly she was trembling.

"I'm just being me." He smirked. "Sorry if you can't handle it."

Oh, he didn't know the depths of the things she could handle. He had no idea. The fact was, she was sick of having to "handle" everything. For once, couldn't things just be easy?

"I can handle it all right," she said, suddenly very tired. "I just wish I didn't have to." She walked past him to the door. "I'll see you tomorrow, Grayson. Maybe you'll be in a better mood then. Maybe you'll have lunch with us."

"Don't count on it," he spat.

She nodded, feeling heavy in the worst way. "Okay."

Cori went in, shutting the door behind her. Suddenly her pillow sounded like a great idea.

Grayson watched the door shut, all the time wondering why it felt like more than a couple sheets of wood had come between him and his *Save.* He wanted to hit something; he *needed* to hit something. But instead he went around the side of the house to look in the window like the creep he was.

In the kitchen, Cori chucked her ice cream in the trash. She stood there staring at it for a while as if she wanted to dig it back out. But she didn't. When she ran both hands down her face and stared up at the ceiling, he saw the wetness on her cheeks. She was crying again. Was it because of him? The thought left him feeling cold — in a bad way.

It hadn't been his intention for things to get ugly tonight. After talking to Leiv, he'd just wanted to see her again. Talking to her at lunch and then at the river had been the highlight of his day. But also, he'd wanted to see if she'd gone out with Aiken. He hated to think of what he would've done if she had. Mostly though, he'd wanted to see her. He was drawn to her — had been since the first day. He didn't like to admit what that might mean, but there it was nonetheless.

He'd never meant to make her sad. No, he wanted to make her happy, wanted to make her laugh, like at lunch.

Cori went over to the refrigerator and wrote something on the dry erase board that hung there: *G'night mom, Cori.* Then she left the room. Grayson ran around to peek in the living room window. She was there, clicking buttons on the TV remote. The screen went black. She switched off the lamp and started for the stairs.

Grayson looked at his phone: nine thirty. She was going to bed early again.

He watched until she disappeared up the steps.

He should do something. It wasn't right for her to be sad, especially because of him. He shouldn't have been so…so…*jealous.* He'd been jealous. Because she'd chosen her friends over him. Jealousy. It was an emotion he couldn't ever remember feeling.

This was wrong, all wrong. She wasn't going to cry tonight, damn it. Not because of him. And not because he couldn't handle his own crap. He would fix it.

Before he knew it, Grayson found himself in front of that door again, knocking.

Chapter 14

The Flip of a Coin

Cori had just closed her bedroom door when she heard the knocking for the second time. It had to be Grayson. Who else would it be? She didn't feel like talking to him any more, so she ignored it. Her bed, her refuge, was calling, and she was going to answer the call before the tears got the best of her again. If she could just fall asleep before her mind set to thinking about things…

She cut the light and climbed into bed, not bothering to change out of her slouchy sweats. The knocking started up again, louder this time, demanding, but she knew he'd go away eventually. And he did.

Cori pulled the covers up and willed herself to go to sleep.

But sleep didn't come. No, instead her mind assaulted her. Right then, she really wanted her dad. She wanted to tell him about Grayson and ask what she should do. Should she just give up on him? It wasn't what she wanted, but if he wouldn't let her in…if he was determined to be a callous jerk…

Her dad would have known what to do. She was so much like him, but he'd known so much more about life. And now he'd never be able to teach her.

The tears came again.

It was still early. She could call Peg, but they hardly knew each other and Cori didn't think it was fair to test their new friendship with all her troubles.

Actually, the truth was she didn't want to face anyone.

She was tired of being alone, and yet she couldn't stand being with anyone. It was a problem. There was one person she wanted to spend time with. But he was so hot and cold, it was next to impossible. And he'd said he didn't want to be friends. She wondered if he really meant it.

The tears fell harder, not the sobbing sort, but the kind of constant stream that came with long term agony. Yes, she was too used to this to sob anymore. Now, it was just quiet crying, even if it was in great volume.

At least she was alone and no one could see her crying like this. They would automatically think she was weak. And she wasn't. She'd just been through too much in too short a time. The junk built up inside all day and then it all came out at night like some type of cleansing. She'd be all better in the morning, ready to face another day.

But for now…there was crying.

Cori heard the front door open and knew her mom was home. Maybe if she'd stayed up a little longer, they could've talked. But then, Mom was in the same boat she was. Any attempt at talking was usually unbearably awkward for both of them.

So she pulled the covers tighter and waited for sleep to come. In the meantime her mind kept thinking of Grayson. *Why* was he so hard? She knew there was more to him than his cruelness—she'd seen it in the way he'd acted with his sister. She wished there was someone in her life to console her like that when she was distressed. She wanted that comforting voice telling her it would all be okay, even if deep down she knew it never would be.

More tears. More agony. More silence.

Until her door cracked open.

No. Mom couldn't see her like this.

She sat up, ready to sweep the tears away and spin a really good I'm-too-tired story. But then it turned out to be worse than she expected.

"What are you doing here?" Her voice was embarrassingly tear-soaked and trembling, which covered up her shock.

Grayson was standing in the doorway, eyes solemn, mouth grim. She couldn't believe he'd just walked into her house. Hadn't she locked the door? Probably not—she often forgot. Stupid!

She went to wipe the telltale wetness from her eyes.

"No, don't," he said, rushing forward. His tone was enough to halt her hand halfway to her face.

When he reached her, his fingers went around her wrist—they were so careful—and pulled her hand away from her face. He went to his knees by her bed. They made a loud *thunk* against the wood floor.

Cori was stunned, and she knew her eyes were probably huge.

"These are my tears—because of me," he whispered raggedly. "I'll be the one to make them go away." She couldn't believe the emotion spilling off of him when he'd been colder than ice only a bit ago.

Slowly and deliberately, he released her wrist and brought his hand up to her face. Ever so gently, his thumb swiped her tears away—tears that were still falling. A strange look came over him when he pulled his hand back. He just stared at the wetness, rubbing his thumb and fingers together in circles. Then he squeezed his eyes shut as though he were pained. When he opened them, he looked directly at her. Cori's stomach clenched. His eyes were so tender, so foreign.

"I'm sorry," he grit out through clenched teeth. "I'm so sorry." The tone was harsh, exactly opposite of his eyes, and she didn't fully understand it.

She blinked and another volley of tears cascaded down. Immediately, Grayson went for them. He was even more careful this time, his hand barely more than a whisper against her skin. And yet, it felt so significant to her, heavy almost, in its intensity.

Her eyes kept leaking. She couldn't seem to make them quit. And with each new rivulet came another brush of his fingers. "I'm afraid they won't stop," she mumbled, shakily, trying hard to sound normal.

"It's okay." His eyes locked on the place where his fingers touched her face. "I've got all night…if that's what it takes."

This made her let out a single nervous laugh. And more wretched tears.

"I mean it," he told her. "I'm staying until you're not sad." And more wiping.

Didn't he know that would take so much longer than one night?

Cori pressed her lips together which drew Grayson's attention to her mouth. "Really, there's no need for—"

"I was wrong, earlier, and I'm sorry. Cori…I'm sorry." She could never know how much. Words weren't enough to describe his remorse. Her tears were tearing him up inside. They smelled like the ocean, carried the same sorrow the ocean carried in with each new wave. And when he'd first touched them, his cells had sucked up the liquid just like they would water. But instead of refreshing him, it had seared him down to the soul. It burned, scalding hot. But he would take the pain.

He deserved it.

"It's okay, really. Like I was saying—"

"I was jealous," he blurted. He needed to tell her, to explain himself. "I was jealous because you chose your friends."

Her brow furrowed until there was a tiny crease between her eyes. "Why?" It came out a broken whisper.

This was the part he didn't want to tell her because it didn't make much sense. But he owed her the truth. "I wanted you all to myself." Her eyes went wide at that bit of information, her face flaring red—and still, she was crying. He caught the drops with his knuckles as they fell from her cheeks, his skin doing its job absorbing them and making them part of his being. Inside, he felt the burn of her grief anew.

"It can't be like that," she said quietly.

He knew that. Oh boy, did he know that. He wasn't even sure when he'd started wanting it to be like that, but he did. It was like that conversation with Leiv hadn't ever happened. As if he would start pretending, living a lie just to be with her.

Why couldn't he be normal? Right now, it felt more important than ever. Because if only he was a normal guy, then…

He nodded because he couldn't get his voice to work. Whatever he wanted didn't matter because she was telling him no. And why shouldn't she. He was awful and she knew it. He'd done nothing to disprove that fact. And most of all, they didn't make sense together. It was as he'd thought from the beginning: they were ill-matched. Except *she* wasn't the problem; *he* was.

Cori swallowed hard, her tears beginning to dry up. Her face was hot, but it was a sweet sensation against his palm. He couldn't pull his hand away even though it was no longer needed.

"Relationships don't work like that," she said carefully, almost like she was afraid to say the words. "If…if we are gonna be—" Her voice cut off, leaving him hanging like cat off a tree branch. The word "if" resounded over and over like a chant in his mind. What was she saying? Did she want to be closer to him, the way he wanted to be with her? Did she feel the draw, the pull, as strongly as he did?

Oh, how he wished she didn't. But oh, how he wished she did. Two sides of the same coin. If she flipped it, where would it land?

Grayson knew he should leave right then, before she finished. He should get up and walk out and never speak to her again. He was bad. An abomination. And she was sweet and sensitive and good. She was good, he knew it. He would *ruin* her if she let him. She was his *Save* after all, it was her destiny. Unless he could make himself stay away from her.

Looking into her soft blue eyes and hanging on her every last word as if it was his life breath, he didn't think he could. How could he?

Her mouth was parted just a little, warm breath escaping and taking the chill from his skin, their faces were so close. His thumb found her full bottom lip—it was effortless, his hand was already caressing her cheek—and went back and forth over the soft surface. He desperately wanted to taste her lips. Watching her eat ice cream had been downright unbearable. But he couldn't kiss her with his mouth. He wouldn't infect her or hurt her, and she wouldn't know he was different, but still. Her mouth was too perfect. It would be akin to an angel being kissed by a demon.

There had to be a way. Maybe if he was good too…he wouldn't ever be like her but maybe he could try to atone for what he was. Somehow.

I'll be better, he thought. *I can do better, try harder.* When she nodded, he realized he'd said it out loud. But he couldn't take it back. What had been meant as a silent promise was now a declaration. And really, that was okay because somehow he knew he would always try to be better for her. Maybe one day he would be able to leave her alone. The day would inevitably come when he would have to tell her what he was or leave her—but today was not that day.

Just then her eyes fluttered and a shy smile curved her lips. "Does this mean you changed your mind about being friends?"

"If you couldn't tell, I'm not very good at the friend thing. It's why I have such a friend deficit." He hadn't changed his mind at all—he had no interest in being her friend. He wanted more.

You don't deserve more.

But what did she want?

It doesn't matter; you don't deserve it.

His hand was still taking up her cheek, but she didn't seem to mind. The light from the night was coming in her window, and the reflection of it on her hair caught his attention. Of its own will, his hand gravitated to the strands that danced around her cheeks. He slipped his fingers through them and his breath actually caught. He had no clue they'd be so soft. Like threads of satin.

But did she want this?

"What are you thinking?" he managed to ask.

She blinked several times and swallowed hard. Instinctively, he knew she didn't want to tell him and that meant it was bad.

"I'm thinking that any minute now, I'm going to wake up back on the couch and realize all this was a dream."

He cocked his head to one side. That, he hadn't been expecting. Not at all. Would this really be a scenario that she might dream about? The fact that she would dream about him—and that it would be something other than a nightmare—was altogether baffling.

"And would that be a good dream or a bad dream?" he couldn't help asking. He had to know one way or another.

Cori ducked her eyes again, clearly uncomfortable. "A good one."

A good one. He almost smiled. Instead he twined his fingers in her soft, soft hair. "What would you say was the best part?"

Her eyes pierced his defiantly. "That, I will never tell you."

He did smile then. "Maybe one day," he mumbled, his attention still on her hair.

"Never."

He went back to her face, his hand dipping under her chin to tilt it up. He grew serious again. "Do you forgive me?"

She took a shuddering breath and nodded. "I just have one question though."

"What's that?" What would she ask? Would it be something he had an answer to?

"In the morning are you going to hate me again? Or are you going to be all marshmallowey, like now?"

Still serious, he said, "It's not possible for me to hate you, shrimp."

Chapter 15

AN OMINOUS WARNING

Lunchtime was, in a word, awkward.

All morning, Cori had been in a weird state of uncertainty, not sure what to think about everything that had happened the night before. It hadn't been a dream. That much she knew. But she wasn't naïve enough to think things would be smooth going. He'd opened up a little last night. He'd been vulnerable. That meant she was bound to endure some more of his crabbiness today. That'd be his emo-defense mechanism kicking in.

But that was okay.

Last night had done something to her, strengthened her. Or maybe it just distracted her from all the sucky things in her life. Whatever the case, she felt different. And it wasn't just because of the way he'd looked at her, the way he'd touched her, the way he'd made her think he was going to kiss her…Well, okay, maybe that was a lot of it. The thing was, she'd never had that kind of connection with anybody before—and in such a short period of time. She hadn't even broken the surface of knowing him, but they clicked. Deeper than that. They complimented each other. He was the rough side of the Velcro; she was the soft.

In first period, Grayson was already at his desk, doodling on his notebook. Nervously, Cori went and sat in front of him, as usual. He didn't acknowledge her at all. Clearly, she'd have to be the first to talk.

"Hi," was all she could get out. If only she was like Peg maybe a simple "hi" wouldn't be so tough.

"Hi." He kept his head down.

She waited, staring at his wild dark hair, but he didn't spare her even a glance. She tried not to let it bother her. After all, she'd been mentally prepping herself for this all morning. But still, it did. After another second, she faced forward. Best to leave him alone for now.

Aiken arrived and thankfully was enough of a distraction.

"Hey," he said, after he'd taken his seat next to her. "Missed you last night. Peg said you weren't feeling well." Did she? How sweet of her.

Cori shrugged, not wanting to lie. "I just needed some alone time."

"I understand. I get that way too." His smile was so friendly she instantly felt guilty for ditching him yesterday. "Listen," he said, turning serious. "I know you've had some bad times, with moving and everything." She knew when he said "everything" he meant losing her dad. "But if you ever need to talk or anything—about whatever—I'm here for you." He grinned again and she couldn't help noticing how it brightened the room. "I've been told I'm a great listener."

She grinned. "Thanks, Aiken. I'll keep that in mind."

As if he knew she didn't want to dwell on things, he was quick to change the subject. "Peg said she was going to talk to you about helping out with the EPO project."

"Epo?"

"I think it stands for Environmental Protection Organization. Peg is in charge of the student sector, I believe. From what I understand, this next month is a big deal. Every week there will be different projects, fundraisers, town-wide cleanups, and at the end there's a big party or something. Anyway, she said she was going to see if you wanted to help out. First meeting is tonight. Could look good on those college apps."

"She hasn't said anything yet. But I'm sure I could find the time to help her."

Another smile from him. "Great. I figured you'd be up for it."

Class dragged but finally the bell rang. Grayson rushed past her and out the door before she could even close her book. She glanced at Aiken. Sometimes, she realized, he could look so dangerous—a far cry from his normal good-natured ways—like the way he was glaring after Grayson right then.

She hurried to her next class. Once again, she sat near Grayson. This time, instead of trying to talk to him, she took her pencil and jotted something on his notebook since that's where his attention was.

Is everything all right?

He stared at the words for too long before he finally looked at her and nodded sharply. She couldn't tell what he was thinking; his expression was mostly neutral, closed off.

Not helpful at all.

She wanted to know what was going on behind those dark eyes. Once she might have thought that those eyes were hard and shallow and nothing more than a brick wall made especially for girls like her to knock their head against. But she knew better now. Last night she'd witnessed a whole different pair of eyes. Ones that were unexpectedly caring.

What was staring back at her now was definitely a brick wall.

She wrote something else—even knowing that the answer would likely make her feel worse. *Regrets?*

His shoulders slumped as if he carried the weight of a million worlds on his back. Holding her gaze, he nodded. The simple admission cut her deeper than she'd thought possible. But then, she'd asked for it, hadn't she.

Cori bit down on her lip, hoping to hide the expression that was threatening to surface. His mouth parted like he was going to say something—and that's when Aiken barreled through the door whistling Miley Cyrus's "Party In The USA." He plunked down next to Cori, seemingly oblivious to the fact that he'd interrupted something.

Cori quickly flipped open her own notebook and pretended she was urgently finishing some homework. Thankfully, he didn't try to talk to her. But he did keep whistling that obnoxious song until Mrs. Simon had to ask him to stop.

In her next class, she tried not to think about Grayson and failed pretty miserably. Hadn't he said he wanted to try? Maybe he'd changed his mind. Had regrets.

By lunchtime, she'd decided not to expect anything. It really wasn't fair for her to think someone like Grayson—who seemed to spend most of his time alone—could change his ways overnight. And besides, there was no need to rush things. Whatever had happened between them last night, there would be more of. She felt sure about that.

Still, she was shocked when Grayson walked right up to her table in the middle of lunch. She hadn't seen him in the cafeteria and assumed he'd skipped again.

"…but there's so much to do to prepare and I could really use all the help…I…can…and get…" Peg had been talking—rather animatedly—about the EPO project when her face, and apparently her mind, went blank. Cori noticed a similar expression on Rex's. Aiken just looked bemused. She turned to see what they were gawking at.

There he was, staring at her, his eyes alight once again. And just like the night before, her stomach flipped.

"Oh. Hi." She hated that she sounded so surprised. Why couldn't she just play it cool? Was that so much to ask? "You can sit here." She moved closer to Aiken to make room on the bench. But Aiken didn't budge and there wasn't enough room for Grayson to sit. "Aiken, can you scoot just a little?" she asked, her eyes still locked on Grayson.

Aiken did—like an inch. She tore her eyes away from Grayson to look at him. What was wrong with him? He was glaring at Grayson.

"Aiken," she said, annoyed. "We need a little room." He didn't move. Rex cleared his throat. But still, nothing.

"It's all good, Cori," Grayson said.

No. He wasn't leaving. She'd worked too hard to get him here. She snapped her head around to object—

But he wasn't going anywhere. Instead, he sat down in the tiny space, straddling the bench so he was facing her from the side. His long legs stretched out, one behind her and one in front. His right arm rested on the table and his left, on his leg—the same leg she could feel against her lower back.

Sitting like he was put them very close together, and Cori realized she might have liked it if not for all the sets of eyes that were currently pinned on her. It wasn't just Peg and Rex either. It seemed like everyone in the cafeteria was focused on them.

And that was how she came to be uncomfortably wedged between two muscled up hotties who couldn't seem to stop glaring. Why did she get the feeling that the only thing keeping these two from tearing each other to shreds was little ol' her?

"Uh…so, like I was saying, will you come to the meeting tonight?" Peg continued, as if she was speaking rote. She didn't give Cori a chance to answer. "Rex can pick you up if you want and bring you home. And I'll order pizza and stuff so you don't have to worry about dinner."

Cori speared some salad and shoved it in her mouth so she wouldn't have to answer yet. She was onboard with helping Peg with the EPO thing, but she didn't think her voice would be solid yet. Grayson sitting so close had thrown her, and she could swear he hadn't stopped staring at her since he'd arrived. Not to mention she was way closer than she ever anticipated being to Aiken. Oh, and Rex was running his tongue along his front teeth, which she'd noticed was common when he was annoyed.

When she'd finished chewing and the silence was becoming weird, she said, "Yeah, sure. I'll come. It sounds fun."

Rex smiled but it looked forced. "What time should I pick you up?"

"I'll pick her up," Aiken barked. Rex narrowed his eyes. Grayson stiffened next to her. Peg looked strangely uncomfortable. It was a weird look for her because she was the type who was never uncomfortable. The world changed to fit her, not the other way around.

Cori frowned at Aiken. What was wrong with him, talking to Rex like that?

Ignoring the hate beams he was throwing over her head to Grayson, she spoke up. "Meeting starts at six?"

Peg nodded.

"Five thirty, then," she said to Rex. "You know where I live, right?"

He gave her a sarcastic grin. "Of course, doll. You're the new girl. Everyone knows where you live."

Oh. News to her.

"I drive a red Passport, in case you weren't aware," he continued.

She nodded. "Red Passport. Got it."

To her left, Aiken snatched the bottled water he'd purchased. In one swift motion, he'd uncapped it and upended it, gulping almost frantically. She wasn't the only one at the table who stared at him strangely. She was sure, however, that she was the only one who noticed Aiken and Grayson had something in common besides their undeniable good looks. How had she not noticed it before? It wasn't a big thing but…it was the water. Just like Grayson, Aiken never ate anything at lunch. He just drank water.

When the bottle was empty, he crushed it and tossed it toward a nearby recycling bin.

Then there was nothing more to say. Not even Peg could come up with something to break the quiet. Rex was using his fork to make designs in his mashed potatoes. Aiken was tapping a frenetic rhythm on the table. Peg was twisting the cap on and off of her bottle of green tea. Cori had shoved her tray aside and was trying not to notice how she could feel Grayson's breath on her neck—he was that close.

The bell rang. And never before had anything sounded so good. It was like each of them breathed a sigh of relief.

When Cori had un-sandwiched herself from Grayson and Aiken, Peg grabbed her by the arm and pulled her away. She went with her because well, Peg was almost dragging her and because she desperately wanted to get out of the cafeteria. In the hall, Peg zeroed in on the bathroom. When they were inside and the door was shut, she looked under the doors of the stalls.

"All clear," she said, her bouncy red curls bobbing as she righted herself. Then her green eyes came at Cori like lasers. "What was *that* all about?" she asked.

Cori shuffled her feet. "What do you mean?"

"What do I mean? Are you serious? I'm talking about you spending lunch as the creamy center of a double stuff Oreo, that's what I mean." Peg was wearing jeans—green ones, the color of grass—and a navy blue and yellow striped shirt. But still, her eyes demanded the most attention.

"I told Grayson he could sit with us if he wanted. I don't know what was up with Aiken. He was being weird, huh?"

Peg rolled those eyes. "Yeah, weird. So, what's going on with you and Dracula?"

Cori fiddled with the hem of her shirt. "Nothing, really. We've just been talking."

Her friend crossed her arms and cocked one hip. The gesture screamed, "Yeah right."

"You gonna tell me or not?"

Cori pursed her lips while she considered it. Why shouldn't she tell her about last night? It wasn't like it was a secret. "He came to my house last night."

"And?"

Cori shrugged. "And we talked. That's it."

"That is *so* not it," Peg argued.

Cori went to the sink and busied herself with washing her hands. "He's not how he seems, you know, not once you get to know him. There's something about him."

Peg strolled over to stand next to Cori and met her eyes in the reflection of the mirror. "Something you like?"

Cori wanted to scowl, but instead the corners of her mouth turned up. It was like they had a mind of their own. "Yeah, something I like."

Peg huffed and checked her teeth in the mirror. "Well, if you insist on being masochistic I guess you have my support. I won't even say 'I told you so' if he ends up breaking your heart. I just have to know though." She glanced at Cori in the mirror and then looked away quickly, her voice too high. "Wouldn't you rather try your luck with someone like Aiken? He's obviously into you."

Cori frowned. She couldn't imagine him as anything other than a friend. She just didn't feel *that* way about him. And then there was the stunt he'd pulled at lunch. She shook her head. "No," she told Peg. "Aiken is just a friend. And speaking of, what was up with him?"

Peg blinked. "*That* was jealousy in action. That was basically two dogs attempting to mark their territory. Meaning you, of course."

"Ew. Gross visual."

Peg shrugged. "The truth is nasty sometimes."

"Well, I'm not interested in Aiken, so that's the end of that."

Peg nodded. The tension between her crimson eyebrows relaxed. "Okay then. Maybe tomorrow things will be less awkward."

Cori gave her a look.

"Hey, we can always hope." Peg grinned. "Come on, we're gonna be late."

In class, neither Grayson nor Aiken tried to talk to her. When school was over, she stopped by her locker to collect her homework. That eerie drawing feeling that was now becoming familiar swept over her like a wave, making her head swim. And then it faded away, replaced by an unmistakable presence. Grayson had come up behind her. She could tell by the way he smelled: woodsy like pine. She'd noticed it last night and again at lunch. It reminded her of the woods, the sweet smell of wet decaying leaves on the forest floor. She liked it. But even if it weren't for that, she would've known it was him. Instinct — or something — told her who it was.

She closed her locker and turned around. He was right there, nearly as close as he'd been at lunch, and staring down at her so intensely. She hoped she didn't have anything on her face. She resisted the urge to reach up and check.

He stepped even closer, his mouth inches from hers. Not a single part of him was touching her, but he might as well have had his hands all over her for the way she felt.

"Come with me," he said.

"W-Where?"

"Does it matter?"

She shook her head, which was probably stupid — it should matter. It just didn't. Grayson raised an eyebrow.

"I have the EPO meeting though. I promised Peg."

"You won't miss it," he promised. His jaw ticked. "Maybe I'll even come with you."

Was he serious?

"Okay."

Cori followed him out to the parking lot — apparently they were driving this time? When he stopped at the passenger side door of a shiny coal-black Corvette she had to work to cover up her surprise. For some reason, she'd expected him to drive an old clunker.

Grayson opened the door without a word and she got in. He stayed quiet while he drove. Cori did too. There was nothing to break up the silence except the radio, which was blaring Arcade Fire.

The car stopped sooner than she'd expected. Looking around, she realized they were at the cemetery again. She followed him through the gate and past the headstones to the thin line of trees and shrubs that separated the river from the graveyard.

While he did the whole wading in the water thing again, Cori watched his face. He seemed troubled. His dark eyebrows were drawn tightly over his eyes, causing his forehead to crinkle. His normally full lips were a grim slash set in his face. And his jaw was clenched so that it looked like it might crack under the pressure. After minutes of silence, he perched on the same rock they'd used the day before, his feet dangling over the edge. She followed, sitting next to him but not touching him.

"Why are we here?" she asked finally when he still hadn't said anything.

Grayson shrugged, staring into the white-capped water as it rushed by. "I wanted to be alone with you. This seemed like the best place."

"The cemetery?" she laughed, jokingly.

His brow furrowed more, his pale skin creasing deeper between his eyes. "The river," he corrected. He started to get up. "We can go now," he said roughly. But she caught him by the hand, stopping him.

"No, we just got here. It's fine."

Grayson settled back on the rock. But when she would have kept holding his hand, he pulled it away. Cori felt her face flare red. She had no idea how to act with him. Or what exactly they were. He'd had regrets about last night and nothing had really even happened, so she clenched her hands in her lap and took her turn staring into the water.

"This is the only place I ever go. Here and home," he muttered. "I don't know where else to take you."

"I like it here," she told him.

"Yeah, right." He smirked.

"I do. It's quiet and pretty and…"

"Wet and cold and muddy," he finished, picking up a stone and tossing it into the stream.

"Yeah, but…" He was here. And she would take being with him on the damp riverbank over being alone in her warm, dry house any day.

"But what?"

She glanced at him. He was still staring at the water like it was the only thing his eyes could see.

She sighed. "I'd rather be here than home."

He finally looked at her, his gaze searching. "Why? Don't you like your home?"

She traced the contours of the rock ledge while she thought about how to answer. What would be the least embarrassing thing to say but yet still the truth? She settled on a phrase her dad used to use. "A place is only as good as the people in it."

With him staring at her like he was—like he was trying to solve a puzzle—she got the undeniable urge to crawl under a boulder and stay there for a hundred years. But that was crazy, so she did the next best thing: looked away.

Suddenly, Grayson's fingers were curling under her chin, bringing her head back around. "Why do you always do that?"

"Do what?"

"Look away when I'm trying to figure out what you're thinking."

She shrugged, struggling not to look away again. Like he was one to talk. He was always avoiding her gaze.

"I'm confused about what's going on between us," she admitted.

Looking into her eyes, he shook his head. "There is nothing going on between us."

Oh. Cori felt her face turn cherry red. Had she misunderstood everything? But they were at least friends now, right?

Somehow she summoned the courage to say one more thing. "Well, I guess I'm trying to figure out what we are." She could barely make her voice work, her throat was so thick with embarrassment.

"We are nothing," he said with a cold dead voice that felt like a slap to her cheek.

"Oh."

Cori hugged her knees to her chest because she felt less exposed like that. *Nothing. Nothing. Nothing.* It reverberated through her mind. So they weren't friends and they definitely weren't more like she'd been hoping for. She rested her head on her knees.

"It's not such a great place now, is it?" Grayson whispered.

She remained silent.

"Do you want me to take you home?"

It was the tone of his voice that brought everything into focus: he sounded…hopeful. Did he *want* her to leave?

That's when the light bulb clicked on. They weren't *nothing*—she didn't think so and neither did he. He'd said he brought her here so they could be alone. That must mean *something.* So why did he sound like he was trying to get rid of her? There was one explanation and it also explained why she kept getting mixed signals from him.

Cori lifted her head to look at him with narrowed eyes. "Do you enjoy playing games with my feelings?"

His eyebrows raised in surprise. "No. I —"

"Why did you bring me here just to turn around and make me go?"

He didn't answer.

"That's what you're doing, right? Trying to upset me so I'll leave."

Grayson looked away, and Cori knew she was right.

"You know what I think?" she continued, uncurling her legs. "I think you're *afraid*." He didn't respond. Didn't even move a muscle. She got closer to him. "What are you afraid of, Grayson?" Was it because he was sick? Because he was terminal? Was he terminal? She didn't know for sure.

When he looked at her, his expression had changed. It wasn't aloof or cold or even angry. It was pained. Tortured.

"What? What makes you look at me like that?" she asked, almost to herself. Cori leaned even closer as if that would help answer her question. It didn't.

"You need to back up," he said, his voice strangled.

Her eyes roamed all around his face. She recalled last night when he'd been so tender with her, the way he'd looked. It had transformed him into something real — not the stony façade he so liked to wear. Now, gazing in his eyes, she could see it again. It was there just under the surface.

She didn't back up. She didn't shrink back at all. She inched closer.

His eyes widened, the brown-flecked green all she could see. His short breaths puffed between them. "If you come any closer I'm going to kiss you. I won't be able to help it," he said desperately.

The declaration shocked her, sent a jolt of anticipation straight through her. Even the rock beneath her felt warmer. And yet he sounded ominous, as if his words were meant as a warning.

What would it be like, she wondered, to be kissed by him? She was still reeling from the fact that he wanted to. She wanted the same thing. She'd wanted it last night. Maybe even from the first day. But then she realized he'd said "if." That meant she had to do something first. What was it? Oh yeah, move closer.

Just as she made the decision to lean in, his expression changed again. She could almost see his resistance crumbling as an ancient stone wall would, brick by brick, dissolving into dust.

"Never mind," he breathed and his mouth came down on hers, his hand reaching up to slip around her neck and pull her close. His lips weren't gentle. Neither were they careful. They were silken steel. And they demanded a response.

He probably meant to scare her—another attempt at pushing her away—but she liked that he wasn't timid. And she wasn't going to let him keep messing with her. Today, here and now—well, whenever they finished kissing—they were going to put a name to whatever they were.

Decision made, she wound her arms around his neck, leaning into him. A bold move for her. But then, he *was* kissing her.

Grayson's arm wrapped around her waist and hauled her even closer while his lips continued their assault. It was electric, the sensations she was enduring. And yet, she didn't think she would ever get enough. She'd kissed a few guys—barely meeting the definition of three or more—but none had ever left her feeling like this. None had held her so tightly or kissed her so firmly, almost possessively. Yes, he kissed her as though she was his to kiss. She sort of liked the idea. And wow, she might as well have been experiencing her first kiss all over again because those others could never hope to compare. She wondered if any future kisses would hold a match to the one she was locked in right now. Had he ruined her for any others?

When his mouth opened, hers did too, and the sweetness of his breath rushed in, causing receptors in her brain to misfire. There were bells and cannons and fireworks. Her heart pounded and her fingers felt numb. It was the best kind of disorientation.

She'd never been kissed like *this,* and she had no idea what to do. She might have gone limp for a second. But when his lips softened and became almost tentative, she pulled herself together.

She didn't want him to stop.

He was holding her gently now, his hand curved around her cheek as if she were delicate china. His tongue, so soft, lapped at hers. Was she in heaven? Because really, this feeling couldn't happen on earth. Right?

Right.

After a moment, Grayson pulled back. He was still close. She could feel his heavy breathing, but she couldn't open her eyes. Her mind was a fog, and it seemed like her physical body was miles away. Except he was holding her, so no, she wasn't floating. She forced her lids to open and met his brilliant mossy eyes—eyes that appeared to question. What were they asking? At that moment he seemed almost vulnerable.

She said the first thing that came to her mind. "Am I dead?"

His forehead crinkled. "No," he said, sounding defensive.

"Oh." Cori tried to clear her head. "Because that was heavenly."

In an instant, his brow unfurled and his eyes widened in surprise. "I shouldn't have done that," he muttered even as he planted more kisses on her cheek and jaw.

"Why?" she mumbled distractedly. He rested his forehead to hers, breathing ragged. She didn't have to wonder if he'd felt the same way about their first kiss—it was there in his actions.

Grayson didn't answer her question though; he just said quietly, "I lost control."

Cori took a deep breath and noticed how badly she shook on the exhale. "I wish you'd lose control more often."

Chapter 16

Secrets and Regrets

Grayson tried to calm down. He called to mind every trick Leiv had ever taught him…and then he would feel Cori against him and the thing that thumped behind his chest—he wasn't sure it could really be called a heart anymore, not since his rising—would pump faster, trying to distribute the water his body needed. He just couldn't believe he was holding her, that he'd kissed her.

He was so very ashamed.

But then she'd said things like "heavenly" and "more often" and he found it hard to contain the joy that snaked through him.

He wanted to do it all again. Her lips had been just as sweet as he'd imagined—no, sweeter. And soft. She was soft as the clouds looked. He wanted to remember it forever. And he would. Zombies had near perfect memory from their rising—even if everything before was a picture riddled with holes—so he'd retain it all. Her softness, her breath, her tongue. The way her eyelids drooped. Her hands in his hair.

His heart pumped wildly, requiring more water. He placed one palm against the rock where moisture had pooled. It would have to do for now.

He hadn't known he could feel so torn over a simple kiss. Oh, but there was nothing simple about it. He'd kissed *Cori*. And that was different. Not simple at all. He'd kissed his *Save*, the one who was supposed to die for him.

The thought sent a powerful kick to his gut. He knew in that instant that he would never allow it to happen. She was too good to ruin. She was meant to live and thrive. Really, he'd known from the beginning he would never go through with it. Maybe that's why he'd hated her at first.

He forced himself to release her. She still looked dazed, and there was a long stretch of silence between them while they both stared at the water that rushed by.

Cori broke it. "Look, I know you're worried because of your… sickness. But whatever you have, it isn't contagious, is it?"

Contagious? No, not yet. He was years from the Age of Deterioration. He shook his head.

"I know you said you didn't want to talk about it, but maybe we should. Just get it over with."

"It's not something I can talk about, Cori."

"It's bad?"

He nodded. He wanted to get mad and storm off and leave her stranded. That would show her for bringing it up. But he couldn't find a reason to be angry. She was observant. Who could blame her for asking questions?

"Is it…fatal?" she asked, her voice unsure.

Aaannnd that was one he absolutely couldn't answer. Because he was already dead.

"Why are you asking so many questions?" His voice was sharper than he'd intended.

"Because, I'm tired of being the one who's confused about where we stand," she snapped right back. When she got all sassy like that it made him want to smile.

"I thought I just cleared that up for you."

"No." She shook her head. "That was you, kissing my socks off. How am I supposed to know if you'll have regrets later and start pushing me away again?"

He gazed into her searching eyes. "I'll always have regrets." A hurt look came across her face, and he hated seeing it. But he was telling the truth. He *would* always regret getting involved with her.

Even still, he had to work to keep from reaching for her.

"Always?" she asked in a small voice.

He nodded and she looked away.

"So, I guess that means you don't want to…I guess we aren't…" She drifted off and put her face in her hands.

Grayson scowled. "What?"

"This is so embarrassing."

"Why are you embarrassed?" Now he was confused. And quickly running out of patience.

"I keep thinking there's more going on here and you consistently tell me there's not. I just don't understand. I mean, why…why did you kiss me like that?"

"Because I wanted to. I've wanted to for a while. So I did." Simple answer.

She looked up at him. Her expression was almost annoyed. "You wanted to. Even though you knew you'd regret it. That makes no sense."

"I don't regret kissing you, Cori."

She threw her hands up in frustration. "Would you please just tell me what is going on here? I need to know where we are. I can't stand the wondering." Her eyes were fiery with aggravation, but they were also pleading. He understood her need for reassurance. He wanted it too, but he couldn't ask her for such a thing. For him, there would never be any reassurance.

But for her there could be.

Grayson took her hand because it was safer than taking her mouth again. And besides, if he did that he might lose his nerve.

"I think about you all the time," he told her. "When I'm not with you, I'm wondering what you're doing, who you're with, if you're smiling or crying, what you're eating." He smiled a little and let the tips of his fingers brush over her bottom lip. It was hard to tell her these things—even harder to believe he was actually feeling them—but it was easier when she was blushing like she was. "I like being close to you. I want…" He wanted so many things. Suddenly, being human again only topped them because it meant he would be free to be with Cori. "I want the same thing you want. I think. I mean, I think that's what you want."

She tilted her head to the side, almost like she found it hard to make eye contact, as though if she looked at him sideways it would be easier. "Then why did you say you had regrets?" she whispered. She seemed so vulnerable, so unsure.

Of course, it took him that long to realize she didn't understand the reason behind those regrets and he probably just seemed fickle.

Grayson pulled her close again — he couldn't help himself. "Because." His voice was riddled with gravel. "No matter what happens, in the end you'll be the one who gets hurt. So yes, I'll always regret being with you." He swept some of that silky hair back from her face so he could see it better. "But that doesn't mean I don't want to be with you."

Her eyes were big. He could see the darker blue ring around her pupils.

"You want to be with me?" she repeated in an almost inaudible whisper.

More than anything, he wanted to say. But he had to watch himself, had to be careful with her, so he just nodded.

"Me too," she said.

With her words, he was torn in two because the part of him that knew it was wrong was battling ferociously with the part of him that wanted it so badly. In the end, he couldn't deny that the idea of them together made him happy, and happy was something Grayson hadn't been in a long, long time. He craved being happy again, so that was the part of him that won the battle — the part that wanted happiness.

"Are you sure?"

She bit down on her lip and nodded. He felt sorry for that lip. After all, there were better things she could be doing with it. With that thought in mind, Grayson bent his head to hers and kissed her again, not bothering to be ashamed this time. He would deal with shame later. For now he would be happy. Not an ounce of shame entered his head when Cori wrapped her arms around his neck, drawing closer. Nope, not even a little.

The kiss was just as powerful as the first but he didn't let it go as far. He pulled back just enough to see her eyes. They helped ground him. Those eyes…Yes, they were like a lighthouse in a storm. And he felt like he'd been in a tempest since the day of his rising, only now, since having met her, finding his way. Was this the basis of the connection between a zombie and his *Save?*

After a minute she said, "Are you going to ignore me tomorrow?"

He rested his forehead against hers, his arms still holding her firmly in place, and breathed her in. "No, why?"

She half shrugged. "I don't know, you're pretty moody. I'd just like to know beforehand if you think you'll change your mind."

Moody? Him? "Yeah, well you're pretty short," he grumbled.

"But that has no bearing on how I feel about you."

He pulled back once more to stare into her eyes, but she refused to look at him. So he made her. "I told you how I feel about you," he said seriously. "It won't change."

After a second she nodded. "We'll see."

He ignored that and took her hand to help her up. "As for me being moody…well, I guess you'll just have to put up with it."

"Yeah, and I guess you'll just have to put up with me being short."

"Yeah, I guess so."

A red Passport.

Cori was in it, buckled into the passenger seat as it whipped haphazardly around a corner and then barely made it through a yellow light just as it turned red. Rex turned out to be a truly crazy driver.

But Cori really wasn't paying all that much attention. She was thinking about everything that had happened earlier while she'd been at the river with Grayson. Mostly she was thinking about the things he'd told her, trying to figure out the mysteries he refused to reveal.

No matter what happens, in the end you'll be the one who gets hurt.

Of all the things Grayson had said, that statement left her feeling cold. Deathly cold. He'd sounded so certain that she would end up brokenhearted. His voice, the way he'd shivered as he spoke, had left no room for doubt. When she pieced it together with the fact that he avoided her question about the fatality of his illness, she could only come to one conclusion, one that made her eyes prickle with fresh tears: Grayson was dying. Whatever disease he was suffering from, it was killing him.

It wasn't fair, how people had to die when they hadn't had a chance to fully live. Her dad hadn't been done living and he'd been thirty-eight. Grayson's situation was even worse than that. Seventeen was too young to have to leave this world—even if the next one was better.

Rex took another corner so fast Cori thought the Passport might have gone up on two wheels. She grasped at her seatbelt with one hand and the dashboard with the other.

"Oh, I'm terribly sorry, Cori. I forget you aren't used to my driving."

"Uh, that's okay," she uttered as he ramped a set of railroad tracks.

"I live out of town," Rex explained, as if that was a good enough excuse. When she raised both eyebrows and pursed her lips he put some more effort into the justification. "In order to get to my house you must travel halfway up a mountain via a supremely winding and bumpy dirt road." He shrugged one shoulder. "I guess you could say I attack the road when I drive."

Cori watched his profile so she wouldn't have to look out the windshield. He seemed relaxed, though he had been curiously quiet for the drive. She thought maybe it was because Grayson had been there when he'd come to pick her up for the EPO meeting.

She studied her friend. Rex was tall like Grayson and Aiken, but he didn't have their muscle mass. Not to say he was muscle-less. His was just the lean sort, his height making him seem lanky. He dressed nicely too. She would label his style "Geek Chic": casual black pants, tight-fitting plaid button-up (sleeves rolled up, of course), red Converse sneakers, and those dark wire-rimmed glasses.

"So, Cori, I hope you don't mind my asking but…are you and Drac—uh, Grayson together?"

The question surprised her, even as she'd expected it. Too bad she hadn't really thought about how to answer it.

"Yes. I mean, no. Uh, I think so. Yes."

Rex jerked the wheel left as he pulled into the parking lot of Asher's only park. As far as parks went, the setting was gorgeous. Hiking trails wound in and out of tall pines laden with green shrubbery. A play area took up the main part of the grounds, but there were so many trees surrounding it, it almost seemed as if the colorful structure actually belonged in the woodsy scene. Even the picnic tables that dotted the area felt natural.

Rex parked the vehicle and turned off the engine before giving her a wry smile.

"Glad you're clear on that." He pulled the keys out, sighed dramatically, and rested his forearms on the steering wheel. "As long as you're happy, that's really all that matters, I suppose. Are you, Cori?"

She thought about it before she answered. Some of the things Grayson had told her at the river thrilled her. To know he thought about her when they were apart—just like she thought about him—was a relief.

And then there was the kissing. That made her happy for sure. She supposed she was mostly happy.

She nodded at Rex. "But listen, please don't say anything because I don't know if he…" She realized how stupid she sounded and stopped.

But Rex gave her a friendly smile. "Don't worry, doll. I'm not a gossiper. Well, unless you count Peg. I tell her just about everything. I have to, you know. It's a rule or something."

"Thanks, Rex."

They both got out and started walking toward the giant gazebo that marked the center of the park. It wasn't your average gazebo. Cori could plainly see its white and blue spindled roof from the parking lot even though they were quite a way away. As they got closer, she could see students gathered inside. Peg was easily spotted thanks to her red and white polka-dot head scarf. Aiken was there too, standing close to Peg, arms crossed, leaning against a whitewashed side rail. Other students—she knew some of their names—were huddled in groups, their chatter leaching out into the rest of the park.

Rex cleared his throat in an awkward way and then whispered, "Dracula's here."

Cori's head whipped all around, but she couldn't see Grayson anywhere. "Where?" she whispered. "And quit calling him that!"

"Over there by the trees." Rex conspicuously nodded in the right direction.

Peering through the thick green foliage, she spotted Grayson leaning against a tall pine tree, all casual. His leather jacket made him seem dangerous, but when their eyes met, she couldn't feel afraid. His expression was stony, but even from that far away, she could see his eyes soften. In response, her heart sped.

"Go on ahead," she told Rex. "Tell Peg I'll be there in a minute." He nodded and continued toward the gazebo, loping forward with his hands jammed in his pockets.

As Cori walked over to meet Grayson, she hugged her thin sweater tighter to her body and shivered. It was still too cold here in Asher.

The term "spring" meant absolutely nothing in this part of the country. It was less of an intro into summer and more of a continuation of winter. She wished she'd remembered her jacket.

When she finally made it to Grayson, she suddenly felt unsure. What if he'd changed his mind about her? When she'd left, he told her he was going home and he would see her tomorrow. What if he was here to tell her never mind about all that stuff at the river?

Nervously, she stepped forward.

It only took a second for her to realize there was no need to worry. As soon as she was close enough, Grayson reached out and yanked her close, burying his face in her hair. He let out a long sigh, and she was bombarded by his fresh woodsy scent. Cori shivered, this time not because of the cold.

"Hey," she murmured against his chest close to where her hand rested. She could easily feel his muscles through his thin gray T-shirt. "I thought you were going home."

"Do you want me to?" he whispered.

Her fingers curled around his shirt of their own accord. "No. I was just curious as to why you were here."

"You know why," he said, his hand moving around to her back to hold her better. "I wanted to see you again. Stupid, huh? I started for home but ended up here instead."

"Not stupid," she insisted.

He pulled away to shrug off his jacket. "Here, put this on."

"Why?"

"Because you're cold."

She shook her head. "But what about you?"

"I won't need it," he said dismissively. He held the leather out to her and she gladly took it, anticipating the residual warmth from his body. Except, the jacket was cold. Now that she thought of it, the few times they'd been close Grayson hadn't exactly been warm. Not cold, really. Just not quite average as far as body temp should go. She knew it was because of his illness.

Cori started to take the jacket back off.

"What are you doing?"

"You've got to be freezing," she said, touching his bare arm and confirming that he wasn't very warm. "You need this more than I do." She at least had a sweater, after all.

Grayson raised a perfectly arched eyebrow. "Trust me, that is *not* the case." He went about slipping the jacket back into place and zipping it up. When he was done he cradled her cheek with one hand and kissed her lightly on the lips. "I'm not cold at all," he said. "Now, you're going to be late."

Cori glanced at the gazebo full of students and nodded. "Come with me."

"I don't think that's such a great idea."

Frowning, she said, "Why not?"

Grayson touched the tip of her nose with his forefinger in a playful gesture. Playful Grayson. That was new. "Well, if I remember correctly, lunch didn't go so well, did it?" Ah, so he'd noticed that. Huh.

"So what?"

"I wouldn't want to make your friends mad." He said it sarcastically, but the edge in his voice made Cori think he meant it.

"Come on." She grabbed his hand and pulled him toward the gazebo. Surprisingly, he didn't put up much of a resistance as she wound her way back through the trees to the walkway.

"We don't have to do this, you know," he said as she dragged him along.

"Do what?"

"This. I can just wait for you over there." He jerked one thumb over his shoulder, indicating the group of trees they'd just come from.

Cori shook her head and kept walking. Things were a bit tricky now, but she knew her friends would get used to him. Eventually.

As they climbed the white steps of the gazebo, Cori noticed most of the other students had quieted down and were waiting for Peg to start. Peg was over in a corner with Rex. From the looks of things, they were arguing. Or at least something was wrong because they were whispering harshly back and forth. Aiken was still leaned up against the railing, but now his head was tilted up to the domed ceiling and his eyes were closed.

Still holding on to Grayson's hand, Cori ignored the strange looks coming from the other students and headed toward her friends. When they neared, Aiken's head snapped up and he gaped at them. His eyes went to their linked hands before landing spitefully on Grayson. Cori snuck a peek at Grayson. His face was once more a stone, but his eyes were leveled on Aiken and it seemed like there was a challenge in them. But then maybe she was imagining it.

At that moment Peg stepped up to the front holding a clipboard. "Okay, everybody, let's get this party started." Immediately she had their attention. That was the kind of person she was, though; she commanded attention and people gave it willingly, gladly. Cori admired that about her—especially since her own personality demanded as much attention as a flea on the sidewalk. It was highly likely that Peg was the yin to Cori's yang. They were opposites that complemented each other. She'd always thought of Asia that way, but now she wasn't sure if that description fit. Cori realized Peg filled that role now, maybe even better than Asia had. The thought made her happy even as it made her sad. She should call Asia soon. It wasn't right to just ignore all her voice mails and Facebook messages. Soon. Soon she'd get in touch with her.

"As you all know," Peg continued with a grin, but the smile was tight, "next month is April and that means that I need all of you beautiful EPO members to help me out. There's so much for us to do, but first I'd like to focus on the city-wide cleanup." She consulted her clipboard. "I've cordoned off Asher into sections. I'd like you all to commit to overseeing the cleanup of one of these areas for the duration of the month. Groups of two or three for each section would be ideal. So who would like to volunteer to take care of section one—this would include the park and its bordering neighborhoods?" Peg held up a giant map with a big area highlighted red. At the top it was labeled "Section 1."

A few hands shot up, and she smiled more easily. "Great!" she exclaimed, rolling up the map and tossing it to one of them. Then she proceeded to jot something down on her clipboard. "All right, now for section two…"

Cori listened patiently as sections two through eleven were claimed. She had to admit, she hardly knew where any of the sections were. Until Peg reached the last one.

"Okay, that leaves section twelve," Peg said with a weary sounding sigh. "Any takers?"

No one volunteered.

"Come on, guys. It's not that bad. I did it last year. Anybody?" Peg sounded nearly desperate.

Cori hadn't volunteered yet—mostly because she was clueless about the layout of the town she now called home. Aiken and Rex had already taken section five—the school and its surrounding neighborhoods—so they couldn't speak up.

"W-Where is it?" Cori asked and then cleared her throat because she hadn't meant to sound so timid.

Peg glanced at her. "Oh, sorry, Cori. I forget you weren't here for this last year." She gave her a bright smile, so Cori grinned back. "Section twelve includes the river and its surrounding neighborhoods." She hesitated. "And also, Stonehenge."

"Stonehenge?"

"Oh, um, that's what we call the cemetery."

The cemetery. Now she could understand why no one wanted to claim section twelve. Cori knew that part of town. Plus the graveyard didn't bother her, really. And the river…well, she really was starting to like the river.

"We'll take it," she blurted.

Rex raised an eyebrow. Aiken's gaze narrowed even further.

Peg looked at her, perplexed. "We?"

"Me. And Grayson."

"Oh. Yeah." Peg was nodding *way* too much. "Sure, sure. Great idea. Okay. Thanks, you two." She jotted some more on her clipboard. "All right, next order of business. As most of you know, our VP, Maria, who also runs our Facebook page, recently moved to California and we need someone to take over for the rest of the year."

While Peg started fielding questions, Cori couldn't help feeling like a bug under a microscope. It was Aiken. His gaze wasn't necessarily angry but it was intense. His eyes would trek from Grayson to Cori to the joining of their hands, like it was a lock he was trying to pick it apart, before landing back on Peg. It took several rounds of this before Cori realized the way Aiken's expression changed when his attention landed back on Peg. It was laser beam focus, furrowed eyebrows, working out a puzzle and then…solution found.

Rinse, repeat.

Except, the puzzle of Cori and Grayson holding hands didn't seem to correlate to Peg, so his expression didn't make sense. With every pass of his eyes, Aiken inched closer to Peg, seeming to get taller and even more dangerous. Grayson stiffened, back going straight as a plank, his hand squeezing Cori's tighter. Unlike Aiken, he *did* look angry. His glare could melt the polar ice caps and send them all into the next ice age.

Cori squirmed when Aiken's gaze shot back over to them. Jaw tight, hands clenching…and then another shuffle toward Peg. She must feel his breath on her neck by now. But this time his eyes stayed focused on Grayson. If it was a staring contest — or more appropriately, a glaring contest — it would be hard to determine a winner.

As Peg was wrapping up the meeting, Cori realized she'd probably contributed to Grayson's mood. What was she thinking, volunteering him for the cleanup? She hadn't asked. What if he didn't want to do it? She supposed she could handle it on her own if it came to that — or beg Peg or Rex to help her.

As students began filing out of the meeting, she peeked at him, embarrassed.

Grayson stared straight ahead, his jaw clenched in that way she thought of as normal for him. His eyes were dark, even browner than normal.

"Let's go," he said, ushering her away.

She should say something, give him an out. "Listen," she started, trying to sound casual, "sorry about volunteering you like that. I'm just gonna go tell Peg that I'm doing section twelve by myself—"

He jerked his stare down to her, his brows forming black slashes above his eyes. "What?"

Cori tried for an easygoing laugh, but it came out a nervous giggle. "I shouldn't have done that. Sorry. I'll go fix it. Nothing to get angry about." She turned quickly away.

Only to find herself being swung back around to face him.

"I'm not angry about that." He glanced at something over her shoulder — or maybe glared was a more accurate term. "It's that damn Reaper."

"What? Who?" Reaper?

Grayson focused on her again. "Don't worry about it." He grabbed her hand. "Let's go."

She let him pull her down the steps before she asked again. "What's wrong?"

"Nothing," he said, walking quickly toward the parking lot.

But he'd said…

"Wait, Grayson, hang on." He wasn't listening so she dug her heels in. "Wait!"

"What?"

She stared at him. Once again, he was stone-faced. "Is everything all right?"

He forced a small and an obviously fake laugh. "Yeah. Or it will be once we're out of here." Before she could ask what he meant, he brushed his fingers gently across her cheek sending a warmth flooding through her veins…question forgotten.

"Come on, shrimp. Let's go."

But wait, she had to make sure. "You don't mind that you're stuck helping me clean the cemetery?"

Grayson rolled his eyes. "Of course not. It's my hangout, remember? This is just a really great excuse for us to be there together."

"Oh. Well, then. Okay."

Less urgently now, they went toward the parking lot where Grayson's Corvette was parked.

Chapter 17

Looming, in a Good Way

The rest of March passed by in a blur.

Cori spent a lot of her time at the cemetery or the river with Grayson. They picked up trash sometimes. Other times they just sat and talked. Often they didn't talk at all—either because they didn't need to or because their mouths were busy doing other things.

Cori liked going there now. It felt like she belonged there, but not in a creepy, foreshadowing-of-death kind of way. She especially liked it because it meant getting to know Grayson a little bit better. Thanks to their graveyard rendezvous, she knew he adored indie music; he found horror movies to be hilarious and not in the least bit frightening; he loved the rain—or water, period; his favorite food was beef—he failed to specify further, just beef. She'd learned he was adopted by a couple but he didn't refer to them as mom and dad.

"They're more like my siblings. They were too young to be parents."

Too bad. She'd much rather think of Raina as his mother figure than accept that she was his non-blood related sister.

"So why'd they adopt?"

He shrugged, reaching to wipe a dew drop from a nearby leaf. "I was in a bad place. I'd just lost my family. I was…sick. Experiencing symptoms I didn't know how to deal with."

"What happened to your family?"

"I don't know. I can't remember."

"Anything?"

He shook his head.

"But you could find out. Don't you wonder?"

"I guess. Sometimes."

"We could look online. Where are they from?"

He shook his head. "No, Cori. I'd rather not know."

"But—"

"No. I have a new family now, and I can't be dragging anybody else into this…life."

She understood what he was saying.

He'd laid his jacket on the ground for her to sit on so she wouldn't get wet. She fingered the zipper just for something to do.

"It's bad enough I brought you into it."

She tried not to let his words hurt her. She knew deep down that their time was limited, even if she chose to ignore it most of the time. He'd never been clear about what disease he suffered—but she was certain they didn't have forever.

And she knew about his regrets. She didn't want to be his biggest regret. She wanted to be his greatest decision. Or even his good choice.

"Don't do that," she whispered. "Don't regret me."

His gaze caught hers, and she could see it all. The war between whatever he thought was right and wrong. The pain of whatever he kept from her, of time missing from the back of his life. But most of all, remorse. Not a single ounce of hope or joy.

It wasn't right. She might end up being his biggest regret, but she'd at least be the regret that made him happy.

She dropped the zipper and scooted closer to the edge of the rock ledge where he'd perched. Like a magnet to metal, he inched closer to her as well until they were face to face, chest to chest. Her fingers gently traced the shadows above his cheeks. They matched the shadows in his eyes. Except the ones in his eyes had names. Guilt and fear were mixed with deep longing.

"I don't like what I see here," she whispered.

His eyes flared brown. He licked his lips. "You don't?"

Slowly, she shook her head. "So every time you look at me like that, like we're bad or wrong, I'm going to do something to remind you it isn't true. To remind you what we have is good. That you're not making a mistake. That *you* are good. That you shouldn't look at me like I'm part of that Y in the road and you took the wrong way."

He took a sharp breath. She let her lips come so close to his but never fully touching. Her hands trailed to his chest and planted there.

"I'm going to do this." She took a deep breath…

And shoved as hard as she could. He tumbled from the rock ledge and into the water with a splash and a curse.

She jumped to her feet, laughter pealing even though she'd covered her mouth with her hands.

The water was swift but not deep, so Grayson was already climbing out, shock still firmly on his face. Which made her laugh harder. A hold-your-belly kind of laugh.

His mouth twitched, one side struggling not to grin. "You think you're funny?"

She nodded. Yes. Definitely. More giggles escaped.

He took a step toward her, his eyes narrowing. "Maybe I'll throw you in since it's so funny."

She gasped. "You wouldn't!"

He tilted his head to one side. "You better run."

Oh crap. "Grayson, no."

He lunged for her, but she squealed and ran. She didn't watch where she was going as she raced down the path that led back to the main part of the cemetery with him hot on her heels. He'd catch her any minute, but her only goal was to be far enough away from the water.

"I'm going to catch you, shrimp." His voice wasn't very far behind. "And when I do, you're going in the river."

She giggled, ran faster. The tree line just ahead was thinning. Almost there. But when she broke through into the clearing, it was at the very back of the cemetery where no graves had been dug yet. She'd taken the wrong path and there was nowhere to go. There was Grayson mere steps behind her and the wrought iron fence in front of her. She ran for it even knowing she was trapped. But at least the river was still a good trek through the trees.

She slammed against it, exhilaration erupting in the form of laughter. Gripping the bars, she peeked over her shoulder just in time to see him rush up behind her.

He held the bars, caging her in. "Gotcha," he breathed against the back of her neck. His breath tickled, forcing another giggle from her.

She turned in his arms and he swooped down to kiss her, his mouth first rough and playful, then growing soft, sweet. She shivered when he pressed his wet clothes against her in retaliation, but it was worth it because when he pulled back to stare at her, his eyes had changed. They danced. It was slow and tentative, like they were just getting used to the feeling, like they didn't want to step too far away from the wall of misery they leaned upon, but still. Mission accomplished.

Her grin widened. He traced it with a finger. "I like what I see here," he said, mimicking her earlier words. "I want it to stay like that. I don't want to be the reason it goes away."

This was what made Grayson special. He cared more about whether he was hurting the people he was closest to than about himself dying. The problem was he thought the solution was avoiding meaningful relationships. It was the reason he'd avoided her. The reason he didn't want to find his family.

He was wrong.

But she'd done enough for today. Enough trying to prove him wrong. At least they'd had fun.

And besides, if she pushed too much it might just make him pull away again.

Even though the truth of it was that he was good and special, Grayson hated himself. Cori could see it in his movements, in the way he hesitated sometimes when he touched her, as if he would contaminate her. She could hear it in the way his words were clipped any time she complimented him or spoke fondly of their time together. It was as if he thought he was dirty. A leper, who should be warning, "Unclean!"

She couldn't understand it, why he would feel like this. But until he opened up, she'd have to do her best to make him see otherwise. Or throw him in the river again.

Grayson and Cori spent their lunchtimes together. Just as she'd assumed, her friends had gotten used to him. Well, it wasn't so much that they'd gotten used to him, they'd just learned to ignore him, and really, he seemed fine with that. In fact, he made it easy for them since he didn't talk during lunch.

At all.

At first Cori had been nervous about it. There had been awkward attempts by Peg to engage him in conversation and once in while she would randomly try it again, but basically things just seemed to go smoother if they all talked *around* him instead of *at* him. Since there was no talking *with* him.

That's not to say he didn't communicate. He did. Plenty.

He communicated his barely-hanging-on-by-a-thread tolerance for Aiken by glaring at appropriate times. Like when Aiken had offered to drive Cori to an EPO meeting or when he sat next to her on the bench. Eventually, Aiken had started pulling a chair up to sit at the end of the long table.

And of course, Grayson communicated with Cori. Sometimes that meant excessive PDA, but she didn't mind.

Sometimes when he'd fidget and look around as if he was about to get up and run away, his eyes would settle on her. He'd take her hand and hold it—and she would let him. There were times when he would squeeze her fingers and it seemed like he was asking some kind of question: *Is this okay? Am I all right? Are you all right?* She would always smile and squeeze his fingers back. Still, he looked so uncertain at times.

On the occasion that she would ask him a question, he would look directly in her eyes and in a low voice, answer as simply as possible. This, also, she was okay with.

Sometimes, without realizing it, she would lean into him or her hand would land on his leg, his arm. He always responded as if no one else was around, wrapping his arms around her. Little things like that made her feel special even if it got her some weird looks.

It was a complex sort of relationship, but it was working. And Cori was glad because for the first time since her father's death, she felt…okay. Better than okay. She wanted to cling to this feeling—and Grayson—for as long as it would last.

April was half over before Peg started talking about the dance.

After they'd finished lunch Cori noticed her nervously pecking at the table with her canary yellow nails. "So, the Earth Dance is the twenty-eighth. It's a Saturday. All of you are going, right?" she asked without looking up from the wood-grained veneer.

"Earth Dance?" Cori questioned. What dance was Peg talking about? Why was she just now hearing about it when it was only three weeks away?

Peg shrugged a shoulder. "It's a big fundraiser to benefit EPO. I thought I told you about it?"

No, she most definitely had not told her about it. Cori would have remembered.

"Anyway," Peg continued. "You have to come. It's the biggest dance of the year, even bigger than prom, and it's held outside, so it's totally awesome. We hire a DJ and go all out for the lights and stuff. Say you'll be there."

Cori shook her head. Dancing was not her thing. Not anymore. "I can't. I don't have a dress or anything."

Peg stared up at her, almost stricken, before recovering. "That's okay. We can go shopping for one. It'll be fun."

Cori crinkled her nose. "Really, Peg, I don't think—"

Peg squeezed her eyes closed. "No! Don't do this to me. I'll have to go with Rex again. Alone."

Rex hmmphed. "What makes you think I'm going?"

Peg turned her gaze to him aghast. "You *have* to! I can't go *alone, alone.*"

Cori peeked at Aiken. He was picking at the label on his water bottle. "Aiken, what about you? Are you going?" Cori asked him.

Something flickered in his eyes before he flashed her a wicked grin. "Why? Are you asking for a reason? You need a date?"

Grayson stiffened beside her, but Cori just replied by giving Aiken a sarcastic smile. "No, Aiken. I was just wondering what Peg's other options are, that's all."

The mockery left his face and his eyes bolted away to peer out the window. Strange reaction.

Rex cleared his throat. "Look, Peg, I'm not one to dabble in rumors…" Peg rolled her eyes. "But there is one I've heard lately that warrants a second look."

"Oh, really," she said, unconvinced. "And what might that be?"

Rex jerked his head to the left indicating another table. "Rumor has it Caleb Thorten has, shall we say, the 'hots' for you. I believe he wishes to ask you to this dance you're so concerned about."

The words were barely out when Aiken's water bottle came down hard on the table top, making everyone except Grayson jump. "Sorry," he gritted out and then pretended to be interested in his fingernails.

After a moment, attention returned to Rex.

"That's just not true, Rex," Peg was saying. "I mean, he dated Brittany Messer last year." She shook her head. "He's not interested in me."

"I wouldn't be so sure," Rex mused. "I mean, he *has* been staring at you for the last twenty-five minutes."

"What?" Peg ducked her head.

"I swear," Rex said, crossing his heart for emphasis. "See for yourself."

Peg shifted a bit to peek over Cori's shoulder and then immediately ducked her head again, putting her hand to her forehead in a nervous gesture. "Oh. Wow," she said.

"Told you," Rex muttered.

Cori glanced over her shoulder and grinned. "Which one, the blue shirt?"

Peg nodded.

"He's cute, Peg. You like him?"

A smile played at her lips. "I don't know. I hardly know him. I mean, yeah, he's cute. Do you think—"

The sharp crackle of plastic being crushed in a strong fist interrupted her. Aiken had done it. Cori could swear she'd never seen him like this: his jaw was clenched as tight as a vice, his lips were pressed together so they were a nearly-white line, his forehead had enough creases to make him look like one of those wrinkled up dogs, and his eyes were nearly invisible because of his brows. He very nearly looked like someone else. A far cry from the happy-go-lucky Aiken they were used to. Come to think of it, he hadn't been himself lately. He'd been…edgy.

Clearly shocked, no one said anything. They just stared. Until some kind of twilight zone took over.

Abruptly, Grayson held out his water to Aiken. "Here man, you need a drink?"

At first Cori thought he was joking. But Grayson didn't really joke—especially not with Aiken.

A kind gesture?

Sweet of him. Strange of him.

Even stranger, Aiken snatched the bottle from Grayson's hands and downed it in one huge gulp before crushing that one too and tossing it aside. Still, he seemed different. In fact, Cori thought he looked ill. And were his eyes turning sickly?

"Aiken, are you all right? Do you need to see the nurse or something?" she asked him.

He squeezed his eyes shut but didn't answer.

Grayson answered for him. "He's okay. He just needs some space. Why don't you go get a drink, dude." Grayson was obviously trying to be light, but Cori heard the rigidness in his voice.

Aiken shoved his chair back from the table and took off toward the exit. They all stared after him. Cori noticed he was walking funny, sort of hunched over and stiff. And slow. It seemed familiar to her. Where had she seen that before?

Grayson cleared his throat. "He's fine," he said. And he wasn't just talking to her this time; he was addressing the three of them.

When Cori looked at her friends, she was surprised to see Peg staring open-mouthed at Grayson and Rex glaring at him.

"Well, whatdaya know. He speaks," Rex said in a hard voice that Cori wasn't familiar with.

"Of course I speak," Grayson laughed.

At that point, Cori had to turn and stare at him too. Something wasn't right here. He was acting funny.

"Hmm," Rex continued. "Could have fooled me. I thought you were just here to glare at Aiken and loom possessively over our girl, Cori."

Grayson's jaw ticked and he ran his tongue across his front teeth. "I do not loom."

"You most certainly do," countered Rex. "In fact, I believe you gave the term its definition."

"Rex!" Cori said, completely surprised at his scathing tone.

"I do apologize, doll. I simply can't believe you put up with him."

Cori glanced at Peg who was dumbstruck. She wanted to tell Rex exactly why she put up with Grayson, why she put up with each and every one of them. How dare he judge something he knew nothing about? She wanted to tell him that things weren't as they seemed with her and Grayson and that it was none of his business. But she couldn't say all that with Grayson sitting right next to her.

"It's the same reason I put up with all of you," she finally said. "Because I *like* him."

With that she got up from the table too, aiming for the exit. She assumed Grayson would follow her and he did. But he didn't say anything until they were standing by her locker.

"Are you okay?"

She leaned against the cold metal and let its chill sink into her anger-heated skin. "Yeah, fine."

He was silent for a bit. "If you want, I can stop eating lunch with you. Just say the word and it's done."

She peered at him. There wasn't much emotion in his features, but she could tell he wanted her to be happy. "No, I don't want that. I like how things are." She truly did. She had no idea what had caused Rex's outburst. But whatever it was, it wasn't her problem. And it wasn't Grayson's.

He nodded once. "Okay."

Cori reached for his hand and coiled their fingers together. His expression didn't change much, but she was learning to decipher the minute things, like the lines around his mouth easing or the ever so slight lift of his brow.

"You never answered Peg about the dance," he said in a flat, unassuming tone.

Cori frowned. "Yes, I did."

"No, you didn't."

"Uh, well, I meant to. Answer's no."

Grayson came closer, looming, she realized. Looming in a good way. Cori decided she rather liked looming if he was the one doing it.

"If I asked you would you say no?" His question caught her off guard and even though she hated the idea of going to a dance, the fact that he would ask her sent a warmth through her body.

"I don't know," she said, because she really didn't know the answer. "Ask me and find out."

He took some of her hair between his fingers, so gentle. He stared at it, seeming perplexed. He'd done this several times in the past, and it always made her self-conscious. Was there something wrong with it?

When he looked into her eyes again, her heart started a rhythm that wasn't a simple pitter-patter.

"Cori, will you let me take you to the Earth Dance? It would make me incredibly…happy."

The way he said it struck a chord in her chest. Where she might have said no before, she now found herself wanting to say yes. Not because anything had changed with regard to her wanting to go, but because she realized that this might be the only chance they would ever have to go to a dance together.

Cori stared hard into his eyes. What did she see there? What was he thinking right then? Was he thinking what she was thinking, that this was a one-chance thing? That next year at this time they might not have the same opportunity?

It seemed like he was holding his breath, waiting for her answer. He really wanted this, she realized. And that was all she needed to know.

"Yes," she whispered. "But I'm warning you, I don't dance."

"I'm not worried," he said, breathing easily again. "One thing—" he twirled that strand of hair around his finger "—will you wear your hair down?"

"But I wear it down almost every day."

"Yeah, I know. I like it that way."

"Oh. Okay."

The bell rang then and students started rushing into the halls.

"I won't be in class today," Grayson mentioned as an afterthought.

"Why not?"

"I've got something I need to take care of. Will you meet me at the river after school?"

"Sure, I guess."

Grayson leaned down and kissed her quickly on the cheek before heading for the exit.

As Cori went to class her thoughts returned to Aiken. Was he all right? Something about the incident was bugging her, but she couldn't put her finger on what exactly it was. He wasn't there when she got to class, which wasn't too surprising. He'd looked awful at lunch—two shades away from death…

That's when it hit her, what was so familiar about the incident. It was eerily similar to how Grayson had looked when she'd found him in the hallway her second day of school. Grayson had been so much worse, but the symptoms were the same: sunken eyes, dried up, powder-like skin, stiffness. And Grayson had offered Aiken his water. There was only one reason for that: he knew Aiken needed it.

And how did he know?

Cori felt chills travel up her spine as she realized the answer. He knew because they shared the same strange illness.

Chapter 18

Call Me Jiminy Cricket

Grayson was on a mission: find the Reaper immediately. He didn't know how much of the puzzle Cori had pieced together. She wasn't stupid, not at all. If Aiken's dehydration had gone any farther, she would've recognized it as the same thing that had happened to him the day she helped him to the bathroom. He could only hope he'd distracted her enough to give him some time to find Aiken and make him leave town.

Not that he didn't want to go to the dance with her—he did. Yeah, he really did…she would be so beautiful in a blue dress…But he wasn't above shamelessly using the dance as a distraction either.

Grayson checked the bathrooms first. No sign of the Reaper. He knew Aiken wouldn't have gone to class. He'd need some time to recuperate.

He found him in the parking lot, standing in the open door of his truck, chugging water as if there was a forecasted drought. He seemed to be recovering, though.

Miraculously, Grayson held his anger in check. It wouldn't help for both of them to be dehydrated. "You look better," he said and smirked. "Which really isn't saying much."

Aiken regarded him with wary eyes. "Go away, civie."

"Actually, that's what I'm here to talk to you about." He stared hard to get his next point across. "Except you're the one who needs to go away. Leave Asher."

The Reaper straightened, a deadly glint in his eye, and faced Grayson full on. "Not happening."

Unfortunately the leash on Grayson's anger wouldn't hold indefinitely. "Look, I don't know what your problem is and I don't care. All I care about is the fact that you almost lost it in there. I don't want Cori to know what I am. And you can't afford for anyone to know about you either."

The Reaper smiled, but it wasn't the playful mocking thing that it usually was. This one was the smile of someone determined to have their way. It was the sort of grin a crazy man might enlist. "I'll leave when I go to my grave—permanently, that is—and not a second sooner."

So he was throwing down the gauntlet, was he? But why, Grayson wondered. Inwardly, he shrugged and stepped up to the challenge. "That can be arranged."

Aiken laughed. "You wouldn't risk trying to kill me. I *think* you're smarter than that."

Grayson felt his skin turn to fire and his vision flip to beige. "I would risk anything, *anything* to keep Cori from learning about us."

The Reaper pursed his lips. "Would you now?" he mused, a bit more relaxed. "And exactly why is that?"

For a minute Grayson thought the guy was actually wondering. But of course he already knew the answer…he was a Reaper.

"You know why," he spat. "I would never let a zombie touch her. Ever. I will make sure she is safe from harm if it's the last thing I do."

Instead of clearing the question mark from Aiken's face, Grayson's words actually seemed to make it bigger. Aiken shook his head as if to clear it.

"Wait a minute, you want to keep her *safe?* You mean from other zombies, not yourself, right?"

Grayson was growing increasingly frustrated with the Reaper. Oh, he knew why Aiken was here. It was clear he'd been watching Cori from the beginning, waiting to see what Grayson would do, what he would reveal to her. But he would tell her nothing, wouldn't give the Reaper a reason to eliminate her. "From *all* zombies. Including myself. Especially myself."

Aiken's eyes squinted as if he were trying to see through some kind of substantial fog. "From all zombies? Including yourself?" he repeated in a strange voice. "You mean…you don't plan on…killing her?"

At the mere thought Grayson felt nuclear, like a ball of fire was seated in his insides, threatening to explode and bring all to ruin. His eyes went wide and the vein in his neck popped out as if to say, "Look, buddy, you messed with the wrong jugular."

Kill Cori?

It hadn't been that long since he'd stood in the hallway looking at her for the first time. Even then he'd known that killing a being like her would be a sin one could never be forgiven of. Angel or not, she was a soul—a precious human soul—just as Grayson had once been, and he would never take that away from her. His murder was something he couldn't fix. He'd accepted that now. But he'd make sure she didn't come to the same ruin he had. He couldn't imagine a better way to spend his death.

Kill her?

No. But he *would* kill. The person—or zombie—who ever dared to lay a hand on her would pay with their blood. He would see to it—

"Grayson." A raspy, choked voice brought him back to the land of the living—or semi-living, as was the case. He was horrified to see that he'd lunged at Aiken and now had him by the throat, fingers digging deep into his windpipe. "Let. Go."

He did, stepping back and struggling to catch his uneven breath. Aiken rubbed at the skin of his throat. "A simple 'no' would have sufficed. Geez, civie."

Aiken reached into his truck and pulled out a bottle of water, tossing it to Grayson. "It seems we have a lot to talk about," he said easily. Too easily.

Grayson caught the water but he didn't open it. He was a little confused. Why weren't they fighting right now? Hadn't he just tried to strangle a Reaper? A Reaper that hated him.

"What…what do you mean?" he barely got out. His chest was so tight from the emotion that had wracked him at the thought of Cori's death.

"I mean…" Aiken climbed into his truck and slammed the door. "It's about time you and I get some things straightened out between us. But not here. Somewhere safe."

A chill ran across Grayson's overheated skin. Of course the Reaper wouldn't kill him in public. No wonder they weren't fighting. He wanted to get him alone somewhere first. Grayson locked his jaw. Well, that was just fine. He would fight him, especially if it meant a chance at killing him. Because he wanted the guy away from his Cori. At any cost.

"Meet me at Stonehenge in half an hour."

Grayson had barely enough time to stop by his house before meeting Aiken, and he was exceedingly glad no one was home when he got there. He had some stuff to take care of—just in case things went bad for him at the cemetery.

Not wasting any time, he ran to his room and started writing a letter. A letter to Leiv. He stuck to the important points—no need to get mushy—and when he was finished he pried the monstrous ring off his middle finger. Leiv had given it to him shortly after his rising. It was truly a hideous piece of jewelry—gunmetal gray, gnarled and twisted carvings that made no recognizable shape, just a mass of weirdness, and in the dead center sat the tiniest ruby you'd ever seen. The sad little jewel might have measured out to be an eighth of a carat. Maybe. His brother had promised him, in that casual yet mysterious way he had about him, that one day he would come to love the ring.

That day had never come.

But it was his single possession, the one thing that he could claim ownership to. And he wanted Cori to have it if anything happened to him. He paused, wishing he could give her something better. But the ring was all he had, so that's what she would get.

Grayson sighed, still not resigned to the fact that Aiken might kill him. The letter and the ring were unnecessary. But…just in case. The ring would have to say all the things he'd never have a chance to.

He set the letter on his pillow and placed the ring on top. Then he went downstairs to collect water and weapons. He picked his favorite dagger from the case in the living room—it had an ivory handle. Grayson liked it because it fit his hand perfectly, almost as if it had been fashioned for him. Whenever he trained with Leiv and Raina, it was always the first weapon he chose. He buckled it into a holster around his forearm. Next, he fitted a thick leather collar around his neck. It had steel studs embedded in it. Its purpose was to help prevent beheading—the only *real* way for a zombie to die.

As he hurried out the door, he stopped to look at his reflection in the mirror. He looked deadly. If Cori saw him like this…but she wouldn't. It was still hours before school let out.

When Grayson got to the cemetery, Aiken was already there. He was leaned casually against the door of his truck, arms crossed. The instant Grayson stepped from his car, the Reaper rolled his eyes.

"Oh, you've got to be kidding me. A *steel?* You're wearing a *steel?* Oh, and a dagger too."

He came out of his casual lounging posture. "I'm not here to fight, civie. I said we needed to *talk*. Talk, not fight. You do know the difference, right?"

Grayson approached him warily, not ready to believe him and not really wanting to. If they didn't fight he'd lose his chance to kill Aiken and get him away from Cori. "I know the difference." He regarded the Reaper. He didn't have any weapons on him—well, unless you considered his stupid earrings to be weapons. "What do you want to talk about?"

Aiken raised an eyebrow. "For starters, we could talk about why you showed up here with weapons."

Grayson simply shrugged.

"Okay, listen." Aiken sighed. "I think there's been a misunderstanding. I don't want to fight you, Grayson. I don't want to kill you either, so you can take off the *steel.*"

"I think I'll keep it on for a while."

The Reaper shrugged. "Suit yourself."

"What do you want, then?" Grayson asked.

Aiken came to stand in front of him. He seemed almost apprehensive. "I need to be sure first."

"Sure about what?"

"Cori is truly your *Save*, right?"

"Yes. So what?"

"You were told by an Oracle? Face to face?" he prodded.

Grayson frowned at the question. "Yes, of course."

"How will I know it's her?" he'd stupidly asked Hannah.

"The same way everyone knows: you will know her by the pull, it will draw the two of you together." She stopped, closed her eyes for a moment, and then opened them again. They were completely gray, with a hint of… excitement? "There is something about her eyes that will appeal to you."

So, yes. As Grayson nodded at the Reaper, he was absolutely sure Cori was his.

Aiken looked at him strangely, like he was from another dimension or something. "Lemme get this straight: she is your true *Save* and…you have no desire to…use her?"

Grayson glared at the guy. Hadn't they already covered this?

Aiken held up both hands in an appeasing gesture. "I find that a teeny bit hard to believe, especially seeing how close the two of you have become. I'm just trying to understand you."

Bile rose in Grayson's throat with every word out of the Reaper's mouth. The trees that surrounded them turned a morose antique as he tried to harness his temper.

"I could *never* hurt Cori. I love her," he growled.

As soon as he said it, he knew he meant it and had to look away. He couldn't believe he'd said it in front of the Reaper, couldn't believe he'd said it out loud. Grayson swore right then and there, he would never repeat it. Doing so would bring a whole new set of complications to his and Cori's already too complicated relationship. And besides, he didn't want her to know.

Steeling himself, he looked at Aiken. He was surprised to see the hardness gone from the Reaper's face. In fact, he almost seemed shaken.

"Okay, then," he said, his voice wavering. "I guess that settles it."

"Settles what?" Grayson still didn't know why they were talking.

Aiken ignored him and went over to his truck, resting his elbows on the side of the bed. He stared into the emptiness while Grayson paced behind him.

"Do you know what a *Reaper* does?" he finally asked.

Grayson knew. "Yeah, I know. You kill the zombies who've reached the Age of Death."

Aiken glanced at him, eyebrows raised. "There's a bit more to it than that."

"Oh, right. I forgot. You do whatever it takes to prevent humans from finding out about us," he said with venom. "Including, but not limited to, *killing* innocent humans." This was why Grayson hated Reapers.

"No," Aiken countered, his voice harsh. "We do whatever it takes to *protect* humans. That is what we do, even at the expense of our own kind. Otherwise we'd just let the contagious ones run rampant."

Grayson scoffed, crossing his arms over his chest. He knew what happened to a human who got too close to a zombie. It had happened to him…when he'd become friends with Raina. For all he knew a Reaper had done the deed, made him into a monster just to keep him quiet. "So you protect them by killing them? I'm willing to bet they would take their chances—"

"We don't kill them," Aiken barked. "Not under any circumstances, ever."

He could call it what he wanted, but in Grayson's eyes taking a human's life and giving them a zombie one in exchange was no even trade. It was murder.

"Turning humans into zombies is the same as killing them," he said simply.

"Is it?" the Reaper countered. "Aren't you still alive? Though in a…different way?"

Grayson scoffed, disgusted. "Yeah, whatever helps you sleep at night."

Aiken's face turned curiously sad. "You've got it all wrong. We don't turn humans into zombies. At least not the way you're thinking. Not against their will."

What? He was lying. Who would choose this? Grayson sure as hell hadn't and someone turned him.

"You're wrong. I didn't go willingly."

"You sure about that? Do you remember?"

Grayson fell silent. There were bits from before but nothing that amounted to a full memory.

"That's what I thought. Look, what I'm saying is Reapers don't hurt humans. We cherish them. We used to be them, Grayson, each and every one of us. Before we mutated, we were human. Even the Oracles, though they've mostly forgotten that fact. Too long since they've felt human." He shook his head and stared at the ground as he continued. "We *choose* this, to be guardians. We take an oath '…to *protect* those from which we were born…'"

The resolute tone to his voice sent a chill up Grayson's spine.

"Zombies are powerful creatures, more powerful than humans in most ways. We have a duty to see that they're never harmed by our kind, to keep the fragile balance between the two species." He let out a long sigh. "So, yes, okay. We kill zombies who are a potential danger to the human population. And, although you seem to despise that fact, most are grateful for our services. Let me ask you, when you reach the Age of Deterioration, don't you want someone to stop you from infecting humans? Or are you the type who wishes to pass this curse on to someone else?"

Grayson was a ball of shock—on the inside. On the outside, however he was like a stone.

Could the Reaper be telling the truth? And if he was then how could Grayson explain his own existence? He'd been led to believe that this was simply what happened to humans who got too close to zombies. *The secret must be kept…* The phrase had been uttered repeatedly for the first five years of his undead life.

But the conviction in Aiken's voice was clear. When he spoke of loving humans, well, that was sort of how Grayson felt. Except maybe it wasn't love, really. It just seemed to him that they were special, not to be messed with. They should never be forced into a life of death, as convoluted as that sounded.

Aiken called their zombie nature a curse. Grayson thought he was the only one in the world who viewed it that way, the only zombie unhappy with his life. The Oracle had implied as much. Could this Reaper possibly have the same feelings?

If so, that meant he wasn't a danger to Cori. In fact, it meant he could help.

"I would want you to kill me," Grayson finally answered. "Without a doubt."

Unbelievably, the Reaper smiled, though it didn't completely reach his eyes. "I thought you'd say that. Too bad I won't get to." He smirked. "I'll be long gone by then."

A joke. The Reaper was trying to be cute while Grayson was still making sense out of this new information. Aiken was telling the truth, Grayson could sense it. But he trusted Leiv and Raina above all. He'd talk to them about this as soon as he got home.

"Have you told Cori yet?"

Grayson frowned. "Told her what?"

Aiken rolled his eyes. "That you love her, that you're dead…any of the above?"

"No. And I'm not going to."

"Hmm. Probably smart for now."

Grayson met his curious expression with a glare. "What do you mean, for now? I plan on never telling her."

"I don't think that's such a great idea, civie."

Grayson didn't really care what he thought. And what made him think he could go digging around in Grayson's love life anyway? He'd put a stop to it.

"So, you got a thing for Peg?" Grayson asked before the Reaper could dig any deeper.

All humor drained from Aiken's face like water draining from a bathtub. "No," was all he said.

Grayson cocked an eyebrow. "Oh, really? Then what was that at lunch?"

"Drop it," Aiken demanded.

Grayson grinned evilly. "Now, why would I do that when it is so obviously bugging you?"

Aiken turned his back on Grayson, pressing his palms into the side of the truck. When he spoke, it was a low hard sound.

"She's mine. My *Save*."

Grayson's sarcastic smile melted away as cold ice encased him. All that talk about loving humans…and here was the Reaper coming face to face with his own *Save*. If Aiken truly felt like Grayson did, that being a zombie was a curse…

He didn't want to ask the obvious question, couldn't actually. He was too afraid of the answer. Peg was Cori's friend. If Aiken killed her…

"Well, go ahead," Aiken snapped. "Say something."

Grayson shook his head, his face grim. "I've got nothing to say."

The Reaper rounded on him. "Don't you want to know if I'll use her? Don't you want to know how a Reaper gets around his oath to protect humans?"

Grayson said nothing.

"A Reaper's *Save* is the only thing not bound by the oath. It isn't illegal for a Reaper to use his *Save*." Aiken said this hastily, as if to clear his conscience, to alleviate his guilt.

Grayson knew the look in his eyes, knew it so well.

"You want to, don't you?"

Shame blanketed Aiken's face making it almost unrecognizable. "Yes," he breathed. "I do." His eyes were almost pleading, begging for absolution. But Grayson had none to give.

He clenched his jaw as he finally gritted the words. "Will you? Will you kill her?"

Aiken hung his head, but instead of answering the question, he blew Grayson's mind again.

"From my rising I knew I was an abomination, something twisted and perverted, not meant to be." He spoke in a somber tone that reminded Grayson of himself. "I spent many miserable years hating my life…until I became a Reaper. Suddenly, this life-after-death thing had a point, a purpose. When I was approached by the Oracles concerning my *Save*, I told them to screw off." He grinned wryly. "They were extremely offended, of course. But after much groveling, I convinced them I had no desire to ever meet my human. It wasn't true at all. Truth was, I knew—as all zombies do—what happens to them when it's all said and done. And I just couldn't…"

He shook his head, a disgusted look on his face.

"I didn't want to take the chance of ever meeting her. I didn't want to take the chance that I'd be too weak to resist her. That I might use her and regret it every hour of every day." He turned and kicked the side of his pretty red truck leaving a dent in the shape of his size-twelves. "I had no idea I'd meet her anyway. Had no clue that the *pull* would be so damn strong."

Grayson clenched his fists as the Reaper grew quiet, his eyes staring at the gravel beneath their feet. While he'd been so anxious to meet his *Save*, Aiken had purposely avoided his. Aiken had been determined not to kill her. Grayson had needed to fall in love with his in order to have that same determination. It occurred to him then that the Reaper was probably the one person in the world who hated what he was more than Grayson did.

"I think you're the only person who can help me," Aiken said suddenly.

Grayson looked at him, skeptical. "How could I help you?"

"You understand how I feel, how badly I don't want to hurt her, because you feel that way about Cori."

Aiken's eyes grew wide, the wheels turning in his mind.

"You just have to make sure I don't cross any lines. Yeah, you can help me, civie."

Grayson stared at him, doubtful. "What? You want me to be your conscience or something?"

"Yeah, kinda. Just…when I start to forget why it's a bad idea, you can remind me. Convince me. Or, well, even kill me if you have to."

The statement stunned Grayson. He stared at the Reaper unable to believe what he was hearing.

"And what if I become weak?" Grayson knew that would never happen, but he tried it on for size anyway.

Aiken shook his head with certainty. "You won't. I saw the look on your face when I questioned you. And yeah, you do remember choking me, right? You'd die before you hurt Cori, wouldn't you?"

Grayson nodded immediately. "Yeah, I would."

"That's what I thought. So, will you help me?"

He thought about it. Here was the chance to save a human from death. And she was a friend of Cori's. But even if she wasn't, Grayson knew it wouldn't change his answer.

"Yes. I'll help you." He sighed dramatically. "Just call me Jiminy Cricket."

Chapter 19

WHAT'S WORSE THAN DYING

Cori found Peg at her locker, fumbling with the lock. Her friend didn't have her normal effervescent expression on her face. Instead she seemed glum.

"Oh, hey, Cori," Peg said. "Listen, Rex feels just awful about how he acted at lunch. He said he was going to call you tonight and talk to you."

Cori waved her off. "It's already forgotten." It wasn't a lie. She had other things on her mind now. "Peg, I was wondering if you could give me Aiken's phone number."

Peg peered at her through stray red curls with curiosity. "Sure. I uh…I've been trying to call him since lunch but he's not answering." Peg got her phone out and started moving her thumb around on the screen. "I mean, I was a little worried after lunch. He seemed sick or something. And I didn't see him in the halls. He wasn't in class was he?"

Cori looked at her friend. She was nervous, flustered, and talking without taking a breath. Her shiny yellow nails seemed to shake as she tried to navigate her phone.

"Peg?"

"…I don't even know what happened, really. I mean, we were talking about the dance one minute and then suddenly he was just mad…"

"Peg."

"…Or at least he seemed mad. Did he seem mad to you? He's usually so easy-going. I don't think I've ever seen him like that…"

"Peg!"

She looked at Cori. "Yeah?"

"Are you okay?"

Peg smiled half-heartedly. "Oh, yeah. Sure. I'm fine. Here it is. I found it. Are you ready?"

"Peg, what's going on?"

She laughed, but it sounded forced. "Nothing. I'm just a bit frazzled today. I've been busy getting everything ready for the dance. Can I ask why you want Aiken's number?"

"I needed to ask him something."

Peg nodded. "Oh."

What was that in her voice? It sounded like defeat.

"Am I missing something here?" Cori asked, totally puzzled.

Peg's shoulders sank and her hands went up to cover her face. When she spoke, it was through her fingers. "No, Cori. You're not missing anything. I'm just having an off day. I've been hella busy and I've got a headache that doesn't have a clue it's supposed to go away with aspirin." Her hands came down and she let out a slow measured breath. "Besides the number, is there anything I can help you with?" She smiled and Cori was relieved to see it was more natural than forced. But she wondered if there was something else bothering her friend. Knowing that Peg was trying to be strong, Cori decided it would be a good idea to give her something else to think about besides whatever problem was plaguing her.

"Well, here's the thing. Remember how I told you there was something wrong with Grayson, that he was sick or something?" Peg nodded. "Well, I was right. But he won't talk about it at all. I've never pushed him on it because…well, because I didn't want to upset him and he's such a private person, you know."

Peg shut her locker and they started toward the parking lot.

"What little information I've gotten from him hasn't been good. I know that he's not contagious but…whatever he has, it's…it's…"

Cori's throat closed up. "I'm afraid he's dying," she managed to squeak. Saying it brought on a wave of emotion she hadn't fully expected, and she fought the urge to curl up in a ball and sob.

Cori stopped walking.

Peg was saying something. She forced herself to listen.

"Are you sure? I mean did he tell you that? He doesn't really look like he's that sick, much less dying. Cori?" Peg's eyes were worried, sympathetic.

How could Cori tell her that she'd seen him looking already dead? How could she explain that he'd consumed a little water and was suddenly back to normal? She couldn't. Part of her wondered if it had happened at all. If it weren't for Aiken's little episode at lunch…

"I'm sure, Peg."

"Then you should talk to him about it. Definitely."

Cori shook her head. "He won't. I've tried."

"Well, try harder. Because—" she took Cori's hand and squeezed it "—I can see how much you care about him, and losing him so soon after losing your father would be devastating. At least if you talk about it there's no mystery. You'll know exactly what you're in for."

That was the scary part. Cori didn't want to think about losing Grayson. She wanted to ignore it completely. Or at least part of her did. Sometimes when she was alone and contemplating it, she could almost convince herself she was jumping to crazy conclusions. Grayson couldn't die. Like Peg said, he seemed so vital. He wasn't weak. She'd only seen him weak once. But what if she kept ignoring it, kept pretending he was fine, and suddenly one day he was gone? Like her dad. With no warning. The thought terrified her.

Peg was right. She had to know.

Cori looked at her friend. "That's kind of why I wanted to talk to Aiken."

Peg's lightly freckled forehead scrunched in confusion. "Aiken? Why Aiken?"

This was where she had to be careful. "Well, I think the two of them have some history. I was hoping he might be able to shed some light on things. Anything he could tell me might help."

Peg nodded. "Yeah, that makes sense. Just…" A worried look flitted across her friend's face. "Be careful okay, Cori?"

Cori nodded, understanding that Peg was concerned.

"And listen, if you need anything—even if it's just to talk—I'm here for you. Okay?"

"Thanks Peg."

On her way to meet Grayson at the cemetery, Cori dialed Aiken's number. Three times. He never answered. Along the way, a red Passport screeched to a halt next to the sidewalk she was on.

Rex leaned out the driver's side window. "Do you need a ride?"

Cori went over to the SUV. "No, I'm almost there."

Rex managed to look sheepish. "Cori, I feel I must apologize for my behavior at lunch today. I was terribly rude. There was no excuse for it and I am immensely sorry."

"I'm not sure I'm the one you should apologize to."

"Yes, Peg informed me of that already. I will…" He seemed to swallow something distasteful. "Apologize to Grayson as well. And I will try to be more tolerant in the future. Can you forgive me?"

Cori wondered if she should inform him that the future was short for Grayson.

"All is forgiven, Rex."

He seemed relieved. "Good. All right, good."

By the time Cori stepped through the gates of Stonehenge, she'd tried Aiken's phone two more times and had left a message. As she meandered through the gray-tinged gravestones on her way to the river, she passed by the Hawthorp crypt that Grayson liked so much. Red roses of varying shades were clustered around the entrance. A sudden feeling of anguish had Cori stopping directly in front of it.

She gazed at the two angels that flanked the cement structure. The more she stared, the more she realized that she despised the one that was rejoicing. How utterly insensitive for her to be rejoicing while those left behind mourned their loss. How could she be happy that a life was taken so early? Cori understood the other angel so much better. Losing a loved one meant you *should* mourn. Forget being happy that they'd made it to heaven when their absence from earth was such a tragedy. Cori wasn't ashamed to admit that she would much rather her dad be here with her on earth than watching her from the clouds.

Would she feel like that when she lost Grayson too?

She already knew the answer.

Cori forced her feet to walk the remaining distance to the outcropping of trees that bordered the river. As soon as she'd stepped through the thick foliage, she spotted Grayson perched on their rock, his forearms resting on his knees. His boots were nearby, so she knew he'd been walking in the water.

Immediately he got up and came to her, embracing her so her feet weren't touching the ground. He was strong. Solid. How could he be so strong if he was dying? It didn't make sense.

"Where have you been, shrimp?" he whispered into her hair.

Cori shivered as she clung to him. Maybe she was wrong. Maybe he was fine.

Grayson set her back on her feet and tried to pull away but she was holding on too tight.

"What's wrong? Did something happen?"

Cori shook her head; she couldn't speak yet.

"Cori? Talk to me. What's wrong?"

She spoke into his chest, so quietly she hoped he wouldn't hear. "I'm scared."

Grayson went stock still. The hand that had been rubbing her back reassuringly rested frozen on her shoulder.

"Scared? Of what?" His voice was hard. He tilted her head up until their eyes met. "I would never let anything hurt you."

Funny for him to say it like that. Didn't he remember telling her if they got involved she would inevitably get hurt?

"What if…what if you can't help it?"

That little crease formed between his black eyebrows. "What are you talking about?"

"Remember when you told me about regrets? You said…" She stopped talking because he'd suddenly let her go and stepped away.

Grayson stared down at her with a harsh expression she didn't quite understand. "I remember what I said."

Cori swallowed back the lump in her throat. She didn't like how he was acting. "I think…I think we should talk about it, Grayson."

"Talk about what?" He turned and went back over to the riverbank.

Cori followed him. "I think we should talk about whatever's going on with you —" she took a deep breath "—and with Aiken."

His back went rigid. "We don't like each other. That's all. We'll work it out eventually."

"That's not what I'm talking about," she said to his back.

"Where did you go after school?"

"I didn't go anywhere. I had to talk to Peg and then I walked here. Don't change the subject, Grayson. You know what I want to talk about."

He picked up a pebble and chucked it into the river. "Yeah, well I *don't* want to talk about it. So…"

She stepped closer to him, wet leaves sliding under her shoes. "Listen, I need to know what's going on with you," she told him quietly. Maybe if he understood. "It hasn't been that long since… since I lost my dad. I just need to know what to expect." Her throat closed up on the last word.

Grayson hung his head, still not looking at her. It was forever before he answered.

"Expect the worst, Cori. With me, just expect the worst."

When Cori got home, she tried for two hours to get a hold of Aiken without success.

Around six o'clock her mom walked through the door. Cori was so stunned that she dropped the bag of chips she'd been holding.

"Oh, hey, honey." Her mom spoke around two stuffed paper shopping bags. "I'm making dinner tonight, so don't spoil your supper." She stepped delicately around the chips that Cori was plucking off the floor.

"Dinner? Really?" Cori didn't mean to sound so surprised.

"Yes, really. Pasta sound okay?"

Cori nodded numbly. It sounded great.

She watched as her mother went into the kitchen. Then looked at the clock again. Yep, it really was six fifteen.

She followed her into the kitchen. For a while she just stared, not sure what to say. "Need help?" she finally asked.

Mom was busy filling a pasta pot with water. "Sure. Why don't you spread some butter on that loaf of bread? Cut it length-wise first."

The kitchen was mostly silent as the two of them went about their tasks. The clock on the wall ticked away the minutes and Cori heard every one of them as they inched by. She desperately wanted to break the silence but had no idea what to say. And she'd never been great at conversation anyway. Her mom was the outgoing one.

"So how's school going? Do you like Westland Heights?"

Cori nodded as she started chopping lettuce for a salad. "Yeah, it's nice enough."

"Made any friends?"

"A few."

Her mom stopped stirring the alfredo sauce and looked up in blatant surprise. "Really?" Cori nodded and tried not to take offense at her mother's astonished tone.

"Well, tell me about them."

She didn't really want to, but she supposed this was how you had a conversation and she definitely preferred it over the awkward silence. "I met Peg on my first day. She's the outgoing type. She invited me to sit with her at lunch and that's how I met Rex. He's Peg's best friend. He's the brainy one of the bunch…" Cori stopped because her mother was staring at her, slack-jawed.

After a second she seemed to catch herself. "Go on, honey."

Should she tell her about Grayson and Aiken? Might as well.

"Then there is Aiken. He was a new student too so we had something in common."

Mom stopped stirring again. "Is his last name McGrath?"

Cori nodded and went to work on the tomatoes.

"I know his mom, Cota. She's an OB nurse at the hospital. Nice lady. I was shocked when she told me she had a son your age; she looks so young. But she's part Cherokee I think. Remember your great-great aunt on your daddy's side, Launa, she was half Cherokee and that woman was simply ageless…"

Cori looked down at the salad greens to cover her shock. Mom never wanted to talk about Daddy—even if it was just to refer to his great-great aunt Launa.

Mom let out a shaky sigh. "Anyway, finish telling me about your friends."

"There's just one more. Grayson." Cori tried to keep her voice neutral but her mom caught the slight inflection and looked up from the bubbling sauce.

"Grayson, huh?" She turned down the burner a notch. "And what is it about this Grayson that makes my only daughter's voice get all wispy?"

What could Cori tell her mother about Grayson? She didn't want to talk about him being sick.

"First of all, my voice is *not* wispy." Her mother raised one eyebrow and Cori ignored it. "Well…he's kind of like me. He likes to keep to himself. He lives with his older brother and sister. I'm not sure what happened to his parents; he doesn't like to talk about it."

Mom's brows furrowed, adding crinkles to her forehead that were not normally there. "What's his last name? Maybe I know them too?"

Cori doubted it, but she knew her mom was trying to investigate without seeming nosy so she played along. "Patch is their last name, Leiv and Raina."

Mom put down the spoon she'd been using and looked at Cori. "Leiv Patch?" Cori nodded. "I know him. He's an EMT."

That was all she said. But from her tone, Cori guessed she might not be fond of him.

"Oh. Well, I've never actually met him or anything. I don't know much about him. Is…he a nice guy?"

Cori's mother returned to stirring the bubbling pot, nodding slowly. "Sure. Nice enough."

Oookay. Time to change the subject.

"Well, Grayson is too. I like him. We have a lot in common, you know, and we get along."

Mom didn't respond so Cori busied herself with mixing up the salad dressing.

Sometime later she said, "You're never alone with him are you? Cori?"

Cori was stunned by the direct question and couldn't come up with an evasive answer quickly enough. "Uh…sometimes," she said stupidly.

Mom's mouth formed a grim line.

"Do you think that's smart thinking?" It was the question she always asked Cori when she wanted her to rethink something she'd done.

"Mom, there's nothing for you to worry about. We're always in public." Mostly. "Besides, you and I have already had all the 'talks.' I'm not going to do anything stupid."

Neither of them said anything more.

When dinner was finished, they ate in silence at the bar—apparently the table was off limits ever since Cori's dad had passed. The few times she and her mom ate together it was never at the table.

As they were clearing the dishes, Cori tried to jumpstart the conversation again.

"Dinner was good, Mom. Thanks."

Her mom smiled sadly. "You're welcome, Cori." That was all she said as she put away dinner and started the dishwasher. Mom had reached her limit.

"Do you want dessert? I think there's still some Ben and Jerry's in the freezer," Cori offered as a last ditch effort.

"Not tonight, honey. I'm exhausted. Think I'll go to bed early."

"Okay."

Cori looked on as her mother plodded up the stairs with sunken shoulders.

Later, when Cori was alone in her bedroom, she dialed Aiken's number one last time. She was fully prepared to leave yet another message, but he answered on the fourth ring.

"Hello?" His voice was brusque.

"Hi. It's Cori."

"Oh, hi, Cori." He sounded distracted.

"I've been, uh, trying to call you. Didn't you get any of my messages?"

"Ah…no. I haven't checked my voice mail."

"Oh."

There was a weird silence while Cori tried to figure out how to ask him what she wanted to know.

"Did you need something, Cori? Or did you finally come to your senses and decide you needed a date for the dance?" he said in a teasing tone.

Cori rolled her eyes even though he couldn't see it. "No, I have one, thank you. Actually, I needed to talk to you about something else."

"Okay. What's up?" There was a slam—a door?—and then all background noise was cut off.

"Well, it's about what happened at lunch."

"Oh, that. It was nothing. I just needed some—"

"Water," she said at the same time he did. "Yeah, I know."

Aiken was silent.

"Listen, I need you to tell me what's going on with you and Grayson," she pleaded.

"Uh, I'm not really sure what you're talking about…"

"You're sick right? That's why you need to stay hydrated and why you can't eat. I'm guessing that's how you knew Grayson too. From the first day, I sensed the two of you already knew each other somehow, I just didn't put it together until today."

"Cori—"

"I know it's not cancer, but just tell me what's going on with you and don't lie about it, Aiken."

There was a long minute of silence.

"It's not exactly what you think, Cori."

"Well, clue me in then."

"I can't," he said shortly.

"Okay, then tell me this, whatever is wrong with you is the same thing that's wrong with Grayson, right?"

There was a hesitation but Aiken answered with a "Yes."

"And whatever it is, it's bad right?"

"Yes."

The next question stuck in Cori's throat. "How long does he have?"

"Uh…I don't really know."

"Aiken…"

"Look, you need to talk to Grayson about this, Cori," he insisted. "I really can't tell you much."

"I've tried, believe me. He won't talk about it."

"Well, maybe that's for the best."

Cori sighed heavily. Part of her agreed. But a bigger part of her *needed* to know. "At least tell me what the illness is, Aiken. Please. I'm going crazy here."

There was a long stony silence. Cori was desperate.

"I know he's dying," she croaked. "I just want to know why—" She cleared her throat, trying to make her voice sound better. It didn't help. "I need to know how much longer I have with him. It can't happen like it did with my dad. I just can't handle that again."

Cori heard Aiken sigh over the phone, and she felt like she'd said too much.

"If I could tell you everything, I would. I think you deserve to know," he said gently. "But it's not up to me. It's Grayson's call."

They were both silent. Cori tried to stop tears from forming in her eyes but it was useless.

"Tell me something," Aiken said in a totally serious, totally humorless tone of voice. It sounded odd on him. "Do you love him? I mean, really love him? You know, that no-matter-what sort of love?"

Cori thought about it and knew she did. And she knew it was the exact kind of love Aiken was talking about because, face it, Grayson wasn't easy to love. But then there were also things about him that you just couldn't help but love. They hadn't known each other long but she felt like he'd unlocked something inside of her, something she'd been trying to find the key to for ages. And in the meantime, she'd learned things about him that he probably didn't even know himself—like that he was good, genuinely good.

"Yes," she said, barely a whisper because tears were falling all around her. "I love him."

There was a long pause. "Then there's one thing you should know. This…thing, that Grayson and I are dealing with, it's so much worse than simply dying." The words sent chills up Cori's spine. "Dying would be paradise."

<h1 style="text-align:center">Chapter 20</h1>

Zombies Can't Keep Secrets

Grayson found Raina in her room. Not her bedroom, but her computer room, which to her was loads more important than where she slept. She was hunched over a pink bejeweled keyboard, her eyes focusing between two different twenty-seven-inch monitors. The glass top desk also contained a speaker system that could rival Leiv's, an iPad, an open laptop that was too big to really fit on anyone's lap, and, yeah, a goblet full of ice chips — she hydrated like the stars.

The room was ridiculous. Only Raina would have a setup like this and then hang a crystal chandelier above it.

"Oh. Hey, Gray," she said, not looking away from her computer.

"Hey. You got a minute?"

"Sure. Hang on." She clacked at her keyboard, a low growl forming. "They want these graphics more lifelike, but it's impossible. If they were any closer to life they'd be a freaking video." She grabbed a handful of ice and tossed it in her mouth. Not much like the stars after all. "I mean, if they want a video they should call a videographer. Almost done…there." She leaned back in her faux fur-lined chair and cracked her knuckles. "What's up?"

Grayson sat on the white leather couch.

"I talked to the Reaper today."

She looked at him blankly. "You talk to him every day."

He rolled his eyes. "Yes, but today he told me some things I didn't know. Like, he claims Reapers don't kill humans."

Raina cocked her head to one side. "I suppose it depends on your definition of kill, Gray."

Both his brother and sister knew his opinion on turning.

"Right. But they don't turn them either. He said they only turn ones who want to be turned. He said everything they do is to protect humans. So that leaves me wondering, you know, about me. About what happened to me."

Her expression tightened. She never liked to talk about this. Grayson knew she felt somewhat responsible for his death because their friendship had been the catalyst.

"I thought you didn't want to know about your past."

He nodded. "True. But…I don't know. I'd like to know who made me this way." The name of his murderer. Who killed him, who turned him. One thing Aiken said haunted him. Did he agree to be turned? He wanted to throw up just considering it.

No way. He couldn't have.

Raina shook her head, her fingers tapping at the arm of her chair as if they missed the keyboard. "We just don't know, Gray. It could've been anybody. We suspected Reapers of course, because of the law. When you found out I wasn't human…" She shrugged.

A door slammed downstairs.

"Yo, Raina," Leiv called.

"Up here."

"Have you seen Gray?" he asked as he climbed the stairs.

"Looking at him."

Leiv appeared in the doorway. "Oh, good. You're both here. We need to talk."

Raina eyed him. "Not until you drink. Geez, Leiv. You look at least fifty."

She reached under her desk for the built in mini-cooler and retrieved several stainless steel water bottles.

Leiv smiled. "Awesome. Because I'm actually closer to one hundred. Fifty's a compliment, baby."

She rolled her eyes and tossed him the water. He downed the first one in a couple gulps.

"Seriously, Leiv. You're either balding or you're using too much gel," Grayson chimed in.

Leiv's smile vanished until he'd examined his reflection in the chrome cover of Raina's laptop. "Dude. Show an old man some respect, will ya."

Grayson shook his head. Old man. Raina was exaggerating. Leiv didn't look a day over thirty. He just needed to hydrate more often.

"Something happened at work today," he began. "Got a call to help out in Haute."

Haute was the closest town to the north and it was a level tinier than Asher. They had only two ambulances, so anything involving more bodies garnered a call out. But what did this have to do with him and Raina?

"Five bodies," he said, gravely. "Don't know why they bothered calling the ambulance. They were mutilated beyond recognition. It was a rogue."

"No," Raina gasped.

Leiv nodded. "I wasn't sure at first but, yeah. There was brown blood at the scene and all over the victims. A lot of it. So much, they thought they'd been drowned in the lake."

"Why would there be…?" Brown blood. Grayson couldn't even finish the question. Too many emotions warred inside him. Rising to the top like cream, was fear. Fear for Cori. This was too close.

"It was like…like they were trying to turn them or something. Mud everywhere. I've never seen anything like it."

Raina looked as horrified as Grayson felt.

Mysterious deaths up north. This must've been what Aiken was talking about.

"Something's going on and I don't know what it is but we need to be very careful. Haute doesn't have a registered tribe. If someone's eating human flesh, Reapers are going to come looking for me. Again."

But that wasn't even their biggest problem. *Who* was doing this? And why? And most of all, was Cori safe?

Grayson was suddenly glad three Reapers had made Asher their temporary home.

"So, you're going to the dance now?" Peg asked Cori.

It was lunchtime. They were all in their normal seats. But today didn't feel normal.

Grayson watched every minute detail of Cori's face as she answered. "Yep."

Everything felt so off kilter today. He knew it had something to do with their little chat at the river yesterday. For example, she hadn't let go of his hand since they sat down — not even to eat her cheeseburger. And she'd been unusually quiet as well.

"Did you talk to Caleb? Are you going with him?" Cori asked.

Peg shook her head, staring at the fake wood grain on the table. "Nope. Going with Rex again," she droned.

Rex rolled his eyes. "Don't make it sound so dreadful, Peg," he scolded. "There are plenty of girls who would love to go with me… and yet, I asked you."

Peg yanked her red curls into a high ponytail before answering. "Yeah, because I begged you," she muttered.

"Hey, I got an idea," Aiken broke in. "Why don't we all go as a group?"

Grayson glared at him. He hated that idea. He wanted to go with Cori. *Only* Cori.

Peg and Rex both raised their eyebrows and then nodded. Funny how the same expression looked so different on each of their faces. "What do you think, Cori?" Rex asked.

Cori looked at Grayson.

He wanted to say no. No way. He wanted to spend that night with just her. Yes, he was a mush, but he wanted to show up at her door with flowers and see her for the first time in a fancy dress and pull her close as they danced to a slow song. And when the dance was over he wanted to spend the rest of the night with her somewhere, anywhere, just the two of them. Maybe they could watch the sun come up and then he would take her home and kiss her good night and watch her walk back into her house.

It would be a perfect night. Just one before it was all over, before the clock that was counting down to the end — the end of them — hit zero. Because whether he wanted to admit it or not, their time was quickly coming to that inevitable end. It was racing there actually, like a runner on steroids. The sick thing was he never wanted it to end. All those things he'd said to Leiv about loving humans, none of it mattered one bit now. He wanted her forever. And if he'd learned anything yesterday, it was that he couldn't keep the zombie thing a secret forever.

That meant he couldn't keep Cori forever.

It meant their time was running out.

Suddenly, his chest locked up. She was still looking at him, asking a question. He needed to answer but he couldn't even breathe. Then he felt her thumb rubbing soothingly against his palm. A second later her slender fingers squeezed his and somehow his breath returned.

"Whatever you want is fine with me," he told her.

Cori cocked her head to the side. "Are you sure?"

Grayson nodded because he didn't trust his voice to speak again.

Cori turned back to her friends. "Sure, I guess we can do that."

Rex and Peg's bickering over dance details took up the rest of lunch. Cori didn't participate in the conversation, and neither did Grayson. He was too busy looking at her, trying desperately to figure out what she was thinking, why she was so quiet.

When the bell rang, Aiken gave him a strange look and motioned toward the hall.

Grayson leaned close to Cori and whispered, "I'll see you in class." When she nodded, he kissed her cheek and went out into the hall where Aiken had already gone.

Both of them slipped into the nearest men's room.

"Great idea, Reaper," Grayson growled before Aiken could even provide an explanation.

"Look, sorry if it cramps your style but I need the safety of numbers…" Aiken took a deep breath. "And I need you close by. You know, to watch me."

Grayson rolled his eyes and crossed his arms. "What, you think you're going to kill Peg at the dance? You have more self-control than you think. I never agreed to babysit you, Aiken."

"Yes, you did," he said simply. "And no, I don't think I'll kill her. Ever, if I get my wish. But that doesn't mean I feel like taking chances."

"It's done now anyway," Grayson said with disgust. "You got your way."

"Whatever," Aiken muttered. "That's not what I wanted to talk to you about."

Grayson raised one eyebrow at the Reaper's pensive face. "Yeah? Have anything to do with the zombie who's eating humans?"

Aiken's features hardened. "No, actually. But mind telling me how you know about that?"

"Leiv. He got called up to Haute. Said there was muddy blood everywhere like they'd tried to turn them after they ate them."

"Or before," Aiken muttered, a sick look on his face.

"Zombies eating zombies? What kind of sick—"

"NOYB, civie." He wasn't being smart though. More like a warning. "NOYB."

Grayson shivered and didn't even try to hide it.

"I think you should tell Cori what you are."

"No way."

"She'll be safer if she knows there are monsters out there."

"There are just as many human monsters. Besides, I can keep her safe."

"You need to tell her."

"Are you telling Peg?"

"No."

"No. You're not. You're going to do your job and make them safe and that settles it."

"Of course. But your situation is different. She came to me, asking questions."

Grayson ground his teeth together. Both at the idea that Cori had reached out to Aiken and because he had no idea how much the Reaper had told her.

"It doesn't matter," he gritted out. "I'm not telling her that zombies exist and that she's been kissing one for the last two and a half months."

Aiken pursed his lips and eyed Grayson in an annoying way. "Tell her."

Grayson just looked at the guy. The Reaper didn't understand. If he did, he wouldn't be insisting that Grayson reveal his darkest secret to the only girl he'd ever loved.

"I can't," he said, his voice a hard edge.

"She's worried, Grayson. She thinks you're dying."

"I know!" he shouted out of frustration.

Aiken stared at him, no trace of sarcasm or humor in his eyes. The laughing, taunting Reaper was nowhere to be found. There was only a fellow zombie now. "The longer you wait, the worse she'll be hurt."

He knew that. Grayson knew that.

But there was no way he could look into her sweet blue eyes and tell her what he was. He would rather die and rise all over again. Fifty times. A hundred times.

He was a coward. He knew it as he said his next words. "I *cannot* do it."

"Fine. Then I will."

"No." The word that was meant as a command escaped Grayson's mouth as a breath instead.

"She deserves to know, Grayson. If you don't tell her by tomorrow, I will."

Grayson couldn't tell her. Couldn't stand the thought of her knowing at all. But he especially couldn't imagine actually saying it.

I'm not human. I'm dead. I'm a riser. I'm a zombie.

There must be something he could do to stop Aiken.

Grayson felt like his world was crumbling, as if his feet stood upon a foundation of collapsing stones. He realized that his dream of dancing with Cori and watching the sunrise would be nothing more than that—a dream. He felt his limbs go numb as he realized that after tomorrow, his arms would never hold her again, his lips would never kiss her again, his fingers…they would never slip in and out of her hair again. But worse than all that, he wouldn't be able to make her smile any more or dry her tears or watch her laugh at Rex during lunch.

"Y-You can't do that," he tried. "Leiv said Reapers can't interfere with a *Save*." His voice was a broken mess.

"In this case, I can." Aiken didn't say it in a cruel way. He was just stating a fact. "My job is to keep zombies from hurting humans. You are hurting her by not telling her what you are. Think about it, Grayson. Her dad—"

"You asked for my help and in return you want to…to ruin me?" Grayson was grasping at things, something to sway him.

The Reaper shook his head. "No. I'm not trying to ruin you. I'm trying to *help* you."

It was over. The end was coming quickly and hard and brutally.

Grayson was breathing hard. His chest ached. His eyes burned. The bell rang and he noticed that even his ears hurt.

Half in a daze, half in terror he went from the bathroom as fast as he could.

Grayson was late to class, but Cori wasn't thinking about that. *Worse than simply dying…*

Aiken's words and the chilling way they'd sounded over the phone last night snaked through her mind for the thousandth time.

What did they mean?

Dying would be paradise…

Cori didn't know a lot about terminal illnesses, but she'd always assumed that the suffering was so great that when the end came, it was a welcomed thing. She supposed that was what Aiken had meant. But something about it struck her wrong. The feeling that she was missing something nagged at her.

Grayson arrived, looking ill. He'd been fine at lunch. Did he need water again?

Cori bit her lip. Hard.

Something was wrong.

She reached out and touched her fingertips to his cold hand and he flinched. Flinched? What was wrong with him?

While she continued staring at their hands — hers trying to make a connection and his lying lame against the desk — Aiken walked in. He too looked wrong. Not himself. She glanced at him questioningly and got a shrug in return.

The classroom was relatively quiet and she shouldn't have tried, but she felt like she would be sick if she didn't figure out what was wrong. So she said, "Grayson?"

He still didn't look at her. She felt like she did that day after he'd been up to her bedroom, when he'd made her cry and then apologized so sweetly. She felt like she'd been slapped.

Cori swallowed hard. "Please," she barely whispered. She didn't even know if her voice had made a sound or if her lips had just moved.

Grayson finally looked at her, though. His eyes were so green they almost matched the grass outside. His mouth was a wide flat line. But he squeezed her fingers once, quickly, and then pretended to pay attention to whatever the teacher was saying.

After class the two of them walked silently through the hall until they'd reached Cori's locker. As she fumbled with the combination she decided to try again.

"Are you okay?"

He nodded, looking at the ground. Still, he said nothing as they went on to their next class.

For the rest of the day, Cori worried. She tried to catch Aiken in the halls to ask him about it, but he was elusive. When the last bell finally rang she went looking for Grayson. He wasn't at his locker or hers. Cori waited until most of the students had cleared out and it was obvious that he wasn't coming before she ventured outside.

She found him waiting just outside the main doors. He was leaned against the brick wall, his hands looped in his pockets, but he looked anything but casual. He straightened when she came near.

Cori approached him warily, like you might approach a wounded animal, afraid he would bolt away or something.

"I thought you'd left," she said quietly.

Grayson shook his head, his eyebrows forming a deep V above his nose. When he stepped toward her and grabbed her hand, Cori released the breath she'd been holding.

"Do you have plans tonight?" he asked. He was staring at the hand he held, running the pad of his thumb across her nails.

"It's Friday," she said softly. "You know I don't."

He met her eyes for a moment, and her heart stuttered. The intensity there was alarming, and it sent a wave of panic through her. Somehow things had changed drastically since lunch—and not for the better.

"Can you…will you…spend tonight with me?"

The request was strange, and she was sure the look on her face reflected her thoughts.

"I mean, uh, you've never been to my house and I thought tonight we could, you know, go there instead of the river. If you want to, that is."

"Yeah, sure. As long as I'm home by curfew it should be fine."

He looked at their hands again. "Could you…stay later than curfew? Could you stay until the sun comes up?"

Cori squinted up at him. "What exactly are you asking?" Her heart was pounding. A silly girl might have assumed his request meant he wanted to "spend the night" with her, in the biblical sense. But she wasn't a silly girl and she had the sinking feeling that this meant something else — something bad.

Before he answered, he brought her hand up to his lips and kissed it carefully.

"I just want to spend time with you," he said, trying too hard to sound normal. "Nothing more. I promise."

Immediately Cori's mind raced, trying to figure out a good cover story — if her mom even decided to wonder where she was.

"Okay," she told him. "What time do you want to meet?"

His hand went up to her hair. "Right now sounds good."

Cori smiled a little. "I have to go home first."

"I'll come get you in an hour?"

Cori nodded. "An hour."

Chapter 21

Racing toward the End

Tonight might as well be the last night of Grayson's life.

At least it was the last night of his life that he would consider actually living. Every day and night after this one would simply be existing. Because he had to. For his family's sake.

Before, when he was human, he didn't know when the end was coming so he didn't celebrate his last night. But tonight he would make the best of things. He would make memories to hoard away for when he could no longer recall being happy. Since he was a zombie, perhaps the ones he made tonight with Cori would last him until the Age of Deterioration.

Leiv and Raina would both be gone tonight—Leiv was pulling a double shift, something he'd been doing a lot lately, and Raina was traveling to Portland for an overnight shopping trip (electronics, not clothes, she'd specified)—so Grayson and Cori would have the house to themselves.

On his way to pick her up, he stopped to get flowers because that's what he would've done on the night of the dance. He chose tulips even when the saleslady tried to get him to go with roses. Roses reminded him of the Hawthorp grave. Tulips reminded him of Cori. Simple and not simple all at the same time.

At her house, Grayson knocked on the front door. No peeping in windows this time…

Memory #1: The way she looked when she answered the door. She'd changed into a dark purple shirt that made her eyes look like ice. A dark curtain of hair framed her face, and Grayson swore he'd never seen a more beautiful sight.

He didn't say anything, didn't know if he could. He just handed her the tulips. Cori's polar eyes got really wide then.

"What are these for?" she murmured through a smile.

Grayson shrugged. "Just because."

"They're pretty. Thank you."

He could tell the flowers made her happy, and he couldn't help the little ribbon of pride that went through him.

"No one's ever gotten me flowers before. Well, no one except my daddy."

"I'm glad I was the first," he said.

Grayson waited, feeling slightly awkward, while she went and put the flowers in water.

When they were both buckled into his car, he said, "Are you hungry?"

Cori nodded. "Maybe a little."

Good. He wanted to take her to Erma's. He'd never eaten there since they didn't serve raw meat, but it was the kind of place where every table felt secluded. Grayson wanted to try to guess what she would order off the menu, and then watch her reaction as she sampled the meal. Would she order ice cream for dessert? He knew how much she liked it.

They'd never gone on a dinner date before. This would be their first. And most certainly their last.

She ended up ordering lasagna and Caesar salad. He'd guessed spaghetti and meatballs. For dessert, she had cheesecake.

Memory #2: The way she looked when she tasted that cheesecake. On the first bite, her eyelashes fluttered closed over those expressive eyes and for a moment, Grayson was annoyed that he wouldn't be able to read her. But then she made a little noise of intense satisfaction and all annoyance was instantly erased.

"Wanna bite?" she asked when she realized he was staring at her lips.

Grayson shook his head. But then he leaned forward and kissed the flavor from her lips like he'd wanted to do when he'd watched her eat that banana. When he pulled back, Cori was staring at him.

"Tastes good," he said.

Her cheeks blushed ten shades of red.

"How come you never eat?"

"I do. Just not…I have…a special diet."

A crease formed between her eyebrows. "Like what?"

He downed some ice water before answering. This was a horrible topic. "Just…you know, things that are easy to…digest."

Cori stopped chewing, her eyes falling to her plate.

Luckily, the waiter came with the check.

Next stop was his house. He gave her a short tour of the place he called home before showing her his room. For the first time in his memory, he was a little nervous. What would she think of his room? It was kind of dark. He liked blue and black and gray so that's what his room was done in. There was a large TV hanging on the wall and dark wooden bookshelves with books and DVDs loaded into them and a desk with his computer on it. He'd put away all his weapons earlier, so there was nothing like that lying around.

Grayson held the door open for Cori as she stepped in and looked around.

"You know, you didn't tell me you lived in a mansion."

He looked at her quizzically.

"I'm pretty sure your bedroom is the size of my living room," she explained.

"Oh." He shrugged.

"Whose money funded this castle anyway?"

He gave her a sideways grin. "It's hardly a castle, but mostly Raina's. She's a computer genius. She helped develop that video game, Grave Raider. Ever heard of it?"

"I've heard of the movie."

He grinned. "It was a video game first."

She raised an eyebrow. "Really? Wow. So, Raina the gamer. She's so, you know, glamorous. I never would've expected that."

Cori went and sat down on his bed. He sat next to her.

"Well, what are we going to do until the sun comes up?" she asked.

He thought about it. Really, they could count sheep and stare at the carpet for all he cared. As long as he could be near her while they were doing it.

"We can watch a movie if you want," he suggested.

Cori nodded. "Whatcha got?"

Grayson went over to one of the bookshelves. He didn't have any movies she would be interested in, so he ran downstairs to check the den. He brought up an armful of miscellaneous videos and Cori chose one.

The two of them settled back against his headboard, Cori nestled in the crook of his arm. He wished…he wished…

Grayson cut the thought off before it got started. It didn't matter what he wished. He had to remember what this night was really about. It wasn't a casual movie night, just one of many. No, it was a night to say goodbye, both to what they had and to what would never be. Wishful thinking was not allowed.

Grayson didn't watch a single second of the movie. He only watched her.

Memory #3: Her facial expressions. He wanted them burned into the backs of his eyelids. How she looked when she was happy. How she looked when she was excited. Even how she looked when she was sad. He wanted to remember how she always pressed her lips together when she was thinking.

Suddenly, the same sense of loss that had overcome him in the bathroom with Aiken threatened to overtake him again. He pulled her closer, his arms already aching at the idea that by this time tomorrow, she would be forever out of his reach.

When the movie concluded she turned her face up to him. They were so close he could feel her short little breaths hitting his cheek.

"You want to watch another one?" he asked. He wouldn't mind watching her face for another hour and a half. He still had a lot to memorize: the curve of her cheek, the ridge of her eyebrow, the wisp of her lashes, the few freckles that dotted her nose…

Cori shook her head. "I'd rather talk."

"What would you like to talk about?" he asked while he kissed her by her ear.

Memory #4: The way she smelled. Her fresh rain scent. He breathed it in, willing it to burn into his lungs in a permanent way.

"I want to talk about serious things," she said, looking into his eyes.

"Like what?" But he knew what, and it made him feel cold all over, the kind of cold that almost burned.

Cori reached for his hand, linking her fingers with his. "I want you to tell me about your illness."

He stared at her for a long time. He was suddenly aware they wouldn't make it to see the sunrise he'd hoped for.

"I already told you, I can't."

"Grayson, I want to understand what's going on with you." She gave his hand a squeeze. "Tell me," she urged.

"You don't need to understand," he barked. "It's none of your business."

Cori yanked her hand away and stood up. "How can you say that to me?" She said the words so very quietly, but Grayson knew there was a fire behind them.

"Because. It's true. You don't need to be thinking about my problems."

Her eyes grew narrow and her chin lifted stubbornly. "Do you ever think about mine?" she asked. "Do you concern yourself with my mom never being home or how I'm handling my father's death?"

Grayson's brow furrowed and he sat up to get closer to her. "Of course I do. You know that."

"But you expect me to ignore yours? What kind of relationship is that?"

"The kind that works," he snapped. She was quiet for a minute, and he wished he hadn't said it.

"I can't figure out why you don't trust me with this," she said almost to herself.

Damn it. He didn't want to fight tonight. He didn't want her standing so far away from him; he wanted her to be in his arms. So he tried to make it happen, but she pulled away.

"Cori…"

"No, Grayson. We need to talk about this." Her voice was shaky but her expression was firm.

No matter though, there was nothing to talk about.

Grayson crossed his arms and stared at the bathroom door.

"Listen to me," she urged. "I need you to talk to me about things. I want to be there for you. I…I…Grayson, please let me in. Let me help you."

He kept his eyes locked on the door, his arms remained crossed, doing exactly the opposite of letting her in.

After several moments passed she said, "Are you just going to ignore me? Grayson?"

Finally he looked at her. "I don't want to talk about it and I'm asking you to forget it."

Tears glistened in her eyes, but they didn't fall. "You want me to forget that you have a disease that makes you deathly ill if you don't drink enough water?" she whispered. "You want me to forget that at any given time you could…could…" Her voice cracked.

"Yes," he said immediately. "That's what I want."

Memory #5: The way her face looks when she's hurt. He didn't want to remember it, but he knew he would. And he would always know that he'd made it look that way.

"I can't do that," Cori said in a surprisingly strong voice. "You're asking for the impossible. I can't not care, Grayson."

There was nothing more to say. They both stared at the floor as he tried to brace himself for what was coming next.

There was plenty he wanted to say. Like, "You're everything I've been waiting for" and "I want this night to last longer" and "I can't believe I love you so much." But none of it would ever be said. Grayson just couldn't fathom forming those kinds of words. Ever. And it wouldn't be fair to her anyway because after tomorrow none of what he said would matter.

So he ended up saying, "Do you want me to take you home?"

She looked at him and slowly shook her head. "I can walk."

Memory #6: "Bye, Grayson."

Memory #7: The way it felt to watch her walk out the door. Like a lung being ripped out.

Memory #8: The way it felt knowing that this was how they were ending. And here, he'd planned for a kiss under the rising sun.

Cori made it down the stairs and out the front door before the volley of tears started falling. She didn't bother to brush them away. She just walked as fast as she could toward home. It was dark outside, but the quaint little streetlamps that were a signature in Asher lighted her way.

She couldn't believe how the night had ended. How could Grayson be so…so…stubborn? Why did he insist on doing this alone? Why couldn't he let her be there for him?

It was obvious he was getting worse. Soon he would be gone just like her daddy.

Her chest was tight, the compulsion to return to him hard to resist. It was the same feeling she'd had on her first day at Westland. The same way she'd felt when she helped Grayson get to the bathroom.

She ignored it.

Cori was about two blocks from home when her phone rang. She didn't check the ID before she answered.

"Yeah?" Her voice was thick with tears but she couldn't care.

"Cori? Is that you?" It was Aiken.

"Yeah, it's me."

He was silent for a moment before he said, "Are you okay?"

She wondered if she should lie and say yes just to get him off the phone. "What did you need, Aiken?" she said instead.

"Well, uh, I just got a call…from Grayson."

This surprised her enough to make her stop walking. "Since when did you two become buddies?"

"Doesn't really matter," he said. "He called because he wanted me to talk to you."

Cori started walking again. "Well, save it because I've already had enough for tonight."

She didn't want to hear any more about how she should just forget that her boyfriend was sick.

Aiken sighed over the phone. "He didn't tell you."

"Oh, he told me a lot of things. Like I should ignore the fact that he's dying and that I don't need to concern myself with his problems. He doesn't trust me."

There was some more silence and then an irritated huff. "I will tell you."

Cori stopped walking for the second time. "What?"

"I'll tell you everything, Cori," he promised.

"You will?"

"Yes. But not tonight. Tomorrow."

Cori knew she'd never be able to sleep. "Why not tonight?"

She passed two lampposts before Aiken answered her question. "Because I want you to be absolutely sure. You need to realize that what I tell you will change everything. For you, for Grayson. You have to decide if knowing is that important to you."

Aiken's tone was so serious Cori felt a worrisome chill slide up her spine. "What do you mean, exactly?"

"I mean you have a choice. You can let this go and keep things the way they are. You two seem happy. It would be smart to just let Grayson deal with his…sickness. Or I can tell you the truth and I promise, things will be different."

"Different good or different bad?" Cori asked. Her fingers felt numb for how tightly she held the phone.

"I guess that's up to you, really."

Well if it was up to her, it would be different good. "Okay, then I want to know the truth." Decision made.

"Sleep on it, Cori. Decide tomorrow."

"Fine," she agreed, frustrated. But only because she knew he wouldn't give in.

As Cori started toward her house again, she couldn't help feeling like tomorrow was doomsday.

After he called Aiken, Grayson walked to Cori's house. Just to make sure she'd made it home all right. When he got there, the light was on in the kitchen, so he peeked through the window. Apparently he would be peep-tomming it tonight after all.

Cori was leaning against the counter, a carton of ice cream in one hand, a spoon in the other. Her eyes were red-rimmed. Angrily, she jammed the spoon into the carton and came out with a gooey lump of ice cream. Grayson continued to watch as she dumped the ice cream back into the container and slammed it down on the counter.

He wanted to go to her, wanted to say something to make things better, but it was too late. It was over now. They were no longer racing toward the end—they were there. It was only a matter of hours before she found out his horrible truth. Now he just hoped that when she looked back over their time together, she didn't despise what they'd had.

Please don't let her regret our time together. Who he was pleading with, he wasn't sure. It didn't matter.

Grayson took one last look at his *Save* and, with despair that squeezed his chest like a vice, pushed away from the window.

Chapter 22

Monsters Are Really Real

Cori slept horribly that night. Dreams of Grayson watching a sunrise haunted her. He was so alone. She wanted to be there for him, with him. She could feel the bitter despair as the rays went from muted to brilliant. And every time she tried to go to him, the rays reached out and burned her. They wouldn't let her near.

When she'd woken, she couldn't get back to sleep. She even heard her mom leaving for work before dawn. Her nerves were too raw for sleep, and she didn't want to revisit her nightmare.

To busy herself until Aiken called, she decided to make pancakes. She cooked several stacks of them even though there was nobody but her around to eat them.

By noon he still hadn't called and she couldn't wait a second longer. She'd already chewed all her nails off—and she wasn't even a nail biter.

She dialed his number.

"Oh, hey, Cori," he answered casually, as if she wasn't waiting on pins and needles for him to explain Grayson's mysteries to her.

She got right to the point. "I made my decision," she said. "I want the truth."

"Okay," he said slowly, seriously. "I'll be there in half an hour."

As she hung up she wondered briefly if she'd made the right choice. For so long she'd worried about pushing Grayson to talk because she feared it would complicate things. But after last night she realized that no matter what, this illness was going to come between them. Somehow, some way. The best thing to do was to face it head on. Right?

Once she knew everything, she would go to him and make him see that they were in this together. No matter what. No matter if he was dying. No matter if she would lose him eventually.

She loved him.

Cori was sure he didn't love her back. Not yet. But that was okay. She assumed it was hard to fall in love with someone when you knew you were going to die. Probably even harder to let someone love *you*, she realized.

Aiken showed up twenty minutes later.

"I think you should sit down, Cori," he said when she brought him into the living room.

She was anxious and nervous and really didn't want to be sitting but she did it anyway. Anything to speed things along.

Aiken didn't sit, though. He stood off from her, against the wall.

"What I'm about to tell you…You're going to find it pretty unbelievable. It might even scare you. But rest assured, you're not in any danger and you never have been." His voice was flat, neutral.

Cori's brow furrowed but she didn't interrupt.

"You know how you think Grayson's sick?" She nodded. "Well, that's not exactly the case. Grayson and I…we're different. Different from you or Peg or Rex. We can't eat food like you can, and well, you know about the water. There are other limitations as well. However, in many ways we are like you: we think like you, have feelings like you, we breathe like you—" Aiken paused, waiting for her to say something. So she did.

"What do you mean different?"

"We are…not exactly human. We used to be, though," he added quickly.

Cori's jaw dropped, her mouth hanging open like a baby bird waiting for its next meal.

"That is not funny, Aiken," she hissed, her expression scathing. "Did you and Grayson make this up to get me to stop asking questions?"

Aiken raised an eyebrow as if he hadn't considered that tack. "No, Cori. It's the truth. And you're right. It isn't funny at all."

Cori jumped off the couch, fists clenched. "You really expect me to believe that you aren't *human*? What are you then? A vampire? A werewolf? Wait, lemme guess…a leprechaun?"

"We're risers."

Riser. She'd never heard of that. For a moment she felt dumb about her outburst.

"What does that mean?"

"Okay, don't freak out. A more common name for what we are would be…zombie."

Riser. Zombie. Riser, like rising from the dead.

"It's not as bad as you think." Still he stood there with that calm demeanor. As if he wasn't claiming to be a walking Mary Shelley tale or something.

Cori crossed her arms over her chest. Un-freaking-believable. Here she thought she'd be getting answers today. Real ones.

"I don't expect you to believe it without proof," he offered.

"And you can do that? Prove to me that you are a zombie? Shouldn't your skin be falling off or…or shouldn't you be trying to eat my brains or something?"

"Our skin doesn't fall off until we reach the Age of Deterioration, and we don't eat brains. Well, most of us don't." As an afterthought he added, "And yes, I can prove that I am not human."

Cori just stared at him. Even if he could prove it, she wouldn't be able to believe it. It was ridiculous. Zombies didn't exist.

"Would you like me to show you?" Aiken asked after she'd been glaring at him for too long.

Cori shook her head. "No. I want you to leave."

"Look, I told you this would change things. I tried to make you see that some things you're better off not knowing. But you said you wanted the truth. Well, here it is," he insisted.

"You're *crazy*. You can't expect me to believe what you're saying. I won't fall for this…this…whatever it is."

He stared at her for two seconds. Then he pulled out a serious looking dagger. The shiny black handle glinted in the light.

Cori threw her hands up. "Whoa, whoa—"

Her protests were interrupted when he sliced the blade down the inside of his forearm. Instantly, his skin split open and brownish colored flesh peeked out. Another millisecond later the wound was bleeding. But it wasn't blood. It was…it was…dirty water? Or that's the only description Cori could come up with.

"Aiken!" Cori exclaimed, panicked. "What did you do? Oh God, Aiken!"

"Look at it, Cori." He seemed to not be in any pain, his expression solid. "Look at my blood. It isn't like yours. It isn't human."

Cori was too alarmed to care. "Aiken, we have to get you to a hospital. Now! Oh my God, you're gonna need stitches. Lots of them."

Calm as ever, Aiken walked to the kitchen, dripping brown blood on the tile. Cori followed him, pleading.

"Where are you going? We have to go now, Aiken. Aiken?"

He went to the sink and grabbed a glass. "Cori, calm down and watch."

She was still stuttering out protests as he filled the glass from the tap and downed it. Then another. And another. She was about to attempt to physically drag him out of the house when she noticed the wound was getting smaller, the skin weaving back together as if by magic. Two more glasses and the cut was completely sealed, only leaving a thin gray-brown line. Another glass of water and even that was gone.

"W-Wha—" She'd lost the ability to form intelligent words.

Aiken dried his arm off and looked at her. "Water. It is our life force, for lack of a better word. It heals us, sustains us…we have to have it to survive."

Cori knew her eyes were as big as bowling balls as she looked back and forth from his arm to his face. Only then did it really hit her that his blood had been *brown*. Brown.

She stepped backward, away from him.

He noticed. "Cori, you have nothing to be afraid of."

Yeah, right, she thought. And then realized she'd said it out loud.

"We don't hurt humans."

She took another step back.

"Grayson?" was all she could manage.

Aiken's slow nod confirmed it. "He's like me. Did you hear what I said, Cori? We don't hurt humans."

"Who do you hurt then?"

His brow furrowed, deep ridges. "Nobody. Unless we're provoked. Or there's a threat. We're not evil."

Cori took another step back and hit the doorjamb. "You're telling me you're a good monster?"

She thought his eyes might have flickered with hurt, but then it was gone. "I guess so. Yeah. I mean, it's complicated."

He was still standing by the sink. He hadn't moved an inch. Probably afraid of spooking her.

"You…you shouldn't have told me," she mumbled.

Aiken rolled his eyes and for the first time since he'd arrived, he seemed like himself…like the Aiken she knew. "I gave you a choice, remember. Come on, Cori. If I wanted to hurt you don't you think I could've done it by now?"

It was true. He was massive when compared to her—and he had a knife.

"I just—I can't. I need to think for a minute."

He held up both hands. "Fine. Take a minute. Take five." He propped his hip against the counter and crossed his arms over his chest. Casual. How could he be casual in a moment like this?

Cori's mind was a load of jumbled up thoughts. She couldn't believe what he was telling her, that zombies existed. But then, how could she deny it after watching his arm heal? The thought that Grayson was some sort of mythical monster was…disturbing? No, that wasn't an accurate enough description.

Oh God, was this for real? Her *boyfriend* was a *zombie?* But Aiken had said they weren't dangerous. No, he'd said they didn't hurt humans. She was pretty sure they were in fact very dangerous.

But when she thought of how gentle Grayson was with her the night he'd dried her tears…

How could he be a monster? It didn't make sense.

Just then, a horrifying thought hit her.

"Am I…? Will I turn into one?"

Aiken looked amused, which annoyed her. "We aren't contagious. The contagious ones are…obvious. Think rotting, shuffling, and drooling. And trust me, you'd know it if you were gonna turn into one."

Cori let out a relieved breath. "How do you turn into one?"

"No one is sure how the first riser came to be but as long as there have been humans, there have been zombies. These days, most of us are turned by another zombie."

"D-Do I want to know how?" Her heart was racing, her breath coming fast.

"It involves our blood."

Cori's eye darted to the sink. "A large amount of blood being placed directly into a human's veins," Aiken added. "They have to die first, and then rise before they can become one of us. Or you could get bitten of course, by a rotter, one that's contagious."

"And when—*how*—does one become contagious?"

"It happens when we get old. Our bodies start to decompose at an accelerated rate and the contagion in our blood becomes more potent. It infects our saliva, our cuticles…and it can be spread to others. We call it the Age of Deterioration or Age of Death because we can't last long in that state."

Cori shivered involuntarily.

"So Grayson isn't dying?"

"Not *dying*. No." The implication was clear. He wasn't dying because he was already dead. Or undead.

Cori recalled all the time she'd spent with Grayson. Not once had she felt like she was in danger. Never had she wanted to escape him; she'd only ever wanted to be with him more. What did that say for her? That she was drawn to monsters? That two of her closest friends—one of whom she was in love with—were zombies?

Aiken shifted, crossing one ankle over the other. "Remember when I asked you if you loved him?"

Cori nodded, feeling that her eyes were wide but seemingly not capable of doing anything about it.

"You said you did."

Cori nodded again.

He gave her a sharp look. "Do you still? Can you love him, knowing how flawed he is?"

Flawed. Cori thought about it. She'd already known he was flawed. Though this was significantly different. She loved Grayson because she'd gotten to know who he was, the kind of person he was under his tough outer shell. He was still that person, wasn't he? He might be a—she swallowed hard—zombie, but that didn't mean he was a monster. He was good. Cori knew she hadn't been wrong about that. But…

"I don't know," she whispered, a tremble running through her.

Aiken nodded. "Then that's what you need to figure out. Grayson is not going to hurt you. You can be sure of it."

"I am," she said, realizing it was true.

Aiken came to stand in front of her. "I need you to keep our secret, Cori. Peg and Rex can't know about us. Can you do that?"

"Why can't they know? They're our friends."

He shook his head gravely. "People can't know, Cori. It's very important. Not everyone is as open-minded as you are. Besides, there are laws we must follow and I for one cannot break them under any circumstances. So. Will you keep this a secret?"

"Laws? Zombie laws?"

He nodded.

"And who upholds these laws? Are there zombie cops?"

Another nod. "You're looking at one. We're called Reapers."

God. Reapers? "As in, 'take your soul' reapers? Black robe and scythe?"

He smirked. "Nah. Not my style. You're thinking of my grandpa."

Cori's eyes bugged.

"I'm joking," he said.

She clenched her jaw. "Not funny, Aiken."

"Reaper is just a title. It comes from our oath of office. Everything sown must eventually be reaped, blah, blah, blah. We're not in the business of yanking anyone's soul."

This was so much. Too much.

"So can you keep a secret or not?"

"Will I be eliminated if I don't?"

Aiken rolled his eyes again and actually laughed. "Yeah, we might eat your brains."

Cori tried to smile because just like with Grayson, she knew Aiken wouldn't hurt her. He was good too.

"I won't tell."

Chapter 23

WHEN WRONG FEELS SO RIGHT

Grayson was still awake when Leiv came home from work early that morning. He'd gone ahead and watched the sunrise—because he was into self-torture, apparently. Truth was he just couldn't sleep. Every time he closed his eyes he saw Cori's face and his chest would start hurting so bad he couldn't breathe. Then he'd have to get up and drink water. He'd drunk enough to fill a nice-sized lake by the time the first rays of light snaked in his window, so he figured he might as well watch the stupid ball of fire come up.

He'd just settled back into bed when a knock sounded on his bedroom door.

"Hey, bro." Leiv poked his head in. He looked tired. Real tired. Of course he had just worked a double. "I thought I heard you moving around up here. Everything all right?"

Grayson tucked his hands behind his head and stared at the ceiling as he nodded.

"Why do I not believe you?"

Because you know me too well. "Because you're getting nosy in your old age." Grayson tried to joke but his voice was void of humor.

To Grayson's disappointment, Leiv came in and shut the door behind him. "What's going on with you, buddy?"

"Nothing to worry about."

"Yeah, right. I know that look. Like a kid who lost a puppy or something."

No, it was worse than a puppy.

Grayson just shrugged.

"Does it have something to do with Cori?" his brother pushed.

He winced. Didn't mean to, but just the sound of her name…

"Okay, so something happened with Cori. You guys get in a fight?"

Grayson didn't want to talk about it. "Yeah, that's it. No big deal," he lied too easily.

Leiv stared at him for a long time while Grayson tried to ignore him away. "Bro, you've fallen," he said strangely.

Grayson glanced at him, annoyed. "What are you talking about?"

"In love. You've fallen in love."

Surely he wasn't that obvious.

"Whatever," he said, hoping his brother would just drop it.

Surprisingly, he did. Leiv stood and started for the door. "Good. This is good," he murmured.

Grayson stared after him, confused.

When he got to the door, he turned back. "Gray, you know I'm here for you right? If you need me. For anything."

But he wouldn't always be. Soon it would just be Grayson and Raina. That sadness layered itself on top of what he was already feeling about Cori. Leiv was his rock. Whatever the question, Leiv always had an answer. And not just any answer. *The* answer. The solution. Except this time, it was different. Leiv couldn't help him with this.

Grayson nodded. "Yeah, sure. I know."

One side of his mouth quirked. "Good."

Just as Leiv was about to go, Grayson noticed he was walking funny.

"Leiv, why are you limping?"

"Oh, that. I just hurt my foot at work. I haven't had any water yet. I'm fine."

"Okay." Grayson let it go.

After his brother left, he was once again consumed with thoughts of Cori. He wondered when Aiken would drop the Z bomb on her.

Last night he'd told the Reaper to go ahead and tell her—he'd said his goodbyes. Aiken had said to have faith, that things would be okay. Grayson didn't know what faith was, so it was an impossible request.

Somewhere in the middle of hating himself and wondering if she would hate him too, Grayson fell asleep.

The house was a stifling prison. Or at least it felt that way to Cori. She'd been stuck in it all day trying to figure out what to do about Grayson.

Fantasy and reality had *Freaky Friday*-ed it and switched roles. What should be true wasn't. And what shouldn't be, was.

Fantasy: Cori was in a complicated yet happy relationship with a guy who made her heart race and gave her butterflies like no tomorrow.

Reality: zombies existed, and Grayson was one of them.

Plus side, plus side…At least she wouldn't have to worry about him dying until he was old. Yes. That was a good thing.

Hours passed as Cori tried to sort out the messy knot of emotions that came with that knowledge. There were so many questions left unanswered. Like, what happens when a human falls in love with a zombie? And how long do they live? Or…are they really dead? And can the two of them be together still?

That was when she realized she still wanted that—to be with him. Even though he was different. To her, he was still Grayson.

Cori paced the living room floor. Glared at the TV.

She wished she'd heard the truth from him, though. Why hadn't he trusted her? This was the question she struggled with the most. Maybe he was ashamed? If Grayson resented the fact that he'd been turned into something not human, that would explain a lot.

It was late afternoon when Cori gathered the courage to call him. He didn't answer, and when his phone clicked over to voice mail, she couldn't leave a message. Some things couldn't be said on a voice mail.

Seven more times she tried to call him. And seven times there was no answer.

At dusk, she decided to go to his house. By this time she was getting desperate to speak with him. They had so much to talk about.

But when she got there, all the lights were off and no one answered the door.

There was one more place to look. And if this strange sensation she was feeling drawing her there was any indication, that's where she would find Grayson.

Cori went quickly in the direction of the cemetery.

The water felt good. It was icy and it helped. He felt so hot, feverish.

Grayson hadn't ever heard of a zombie getting sick, but there was a first time for everything. He'd been this way since waking two hours ago.

He ducked his head back under the water and hoped that the frigid liquid would help dispel thoughts of Cori.

Where was she? What was she doing? Was she as miserable as he was? He hoped not.

It wasn't working. Grayson came back up for air.

There was a slight breeze and he was glad for it. It added to the chill of the water. Maybe he would stay out here all night. It would be better than going home where he could still smell her.

A rustle of leaves caught his attention. Who would be out here at night? Grayson kept himself still as possible while the noise grew louder, the steps got closer.

And then Cori was there, standing on the bank of the river.

When he realized she was real and not a figment of his imagination, a lump jammed in his throat and he couldn't swallow. She looked at him and then at his clothes that were piled on the rock. He couldn't read her face and she said nothing. After a second she turned her back to him.

Somehow, he managed to climb out and pull on his jeans. He didn't bother with his shirt.

"He told you."

She turned around and nodded, still not saying a word.

So, it was done. She knew.

Grayson was frozen in place. He couldn't move, couldn't breathe. Cori's eyes danced around before landing back on him.

"I just…I don't understand." Her head was shaking back and forth. "I mean, he showed me about the water. But everything else, he said I had to talk to you about it. How…how is this possible? How…? What…?"

She wanted explanations. How could he tell her? How could he tell her any of it? If he told her, then it would be real. And he couldn't stand that. He couldn't bear the thought of her knowing the truth, knowing everything about him. That they were so different. That she was life and he was death. He could imagine the look on her face when she discovered that he could only eat raw animal flesh. Or when she found out his blood wasn't red like hers, but brown like watery mud.

His mouth opened and shut like a fish so many times but nothing would come out. His chest burned like it was wrapped in barbed wire.

"It's okay," she whispered. "You don't have to talk about it right now."

He forced himself to look into her eyes. They were the same, full of life and love and so caring. They were his lifeline; she was everything to him. Everything. How would he ever get through this?

She stepped toward him. "It doesn't really matter anyway. I love you."

Grayson felt his face contort into something awful. His ears burned. His throat closed up. He backed away from her, his head shaking back and forth. "Y-You can't," he croaked in a hard voice.

She cocked her head, her eyes never leaving his. "I do."

"No, Cori. You can't love me. Save it for someone good and real."

She moved closer to him and he kept backing up until a tree trunk stopped him from going any further. The rough bark of it scraped against his bare back as he tried to move further away.

"You are both of those things, Grayson." She stopped right in front of him and reached for his hand. He yanked it away. She furrowed her brows. "I love you," she said firmly.

"No," he managed.

She snatched his hand and brought it to her face. "Yes." She placed his palm against her cheek — the same way he usually touched her face. Her skin was soft — the same way it always was.

He wished so badly that he could rewind life a few days, a few weeks. If only they could go back to the time he'd first kissed her lips, first touched her skin. If only he could keep on pretending that he was normal. Why had he condemned his family for pretending? He wanted to pretend right now, but he couldn't.

Cori knew what he was. And there was no going back.

She closed the distance between them so that she was pressed against him, chest to chest, touching his dead skin. "I don't care what you are, Grayson. I love you and that's just the way it is."

He hated that she felt like that, wished she didn't. With all his being, he wished it. It didn't matter that he felt like he couldn't live without her. It didn't matter that the very thought of losing her took him to dark places.

"I'll ruin you." His voice broke and he hated himself a little more for it.

She turned her face and kissed his palm. "No, you won't."

Her eyes…they were so pure in that moment, so full of hope and love. They were full of love. She loved him. *How* could she love him?

Her arms went around his waist.

With that gesture, he felt everything inside him crumble. Everything that made him *him* just broke apart and came back together in a different way. He didn't want to go on without her. He wasn't sure just what kind of person it made him, but he couldn't hold back any more. Whether it was wrong or right, he *wanted* her.

"Cori…" He tried to remember all reasons why he should push her away. In truth, he'd never expected to need to push her away. He thought he would lose her when she learned what he was.

"I need you," she whispered, shakily. "And I think…I think you need me too."

She had no idea how badly he did. The need was raw and powerful and enough to consume him. But even more, he *wanted* her love. He wanted the peace that her eyes brought and the comfort of having her near. He wanted to be worthy of her; he wanted to be human for her. But that would never happen because what good was living without her? What good was living if *she* wasn't living?

Whether he was worthy of it or not, he wanted her love.

And she was offering it.

He couldn't hold back another second. His lips crashed into hers with force and still, he couldn't stop. Shamelessly, he lifted her off the ground and switched places with her so that she was the one against the tree. Her hands went to his shoulders, clinging close. He kissed her like heaven was falling on them, threatening to end their existence. Her mouth was sweet and her scent swamped him and he nearly came undone when her little tongue licked against his lips. He couldn't get close enough to her, couldn't get enough of her mouth. And her body, it was tiny against his but it was so very perfect.

With effort, he forced himself to slow down. He wanted to savor this, needed to.

He pulled back, out of breath. "I need you to know that I would never hurt you. I could never —" His voice broke again, coming out in a ragged wordless noise.

"I know that." She was panting too, eyes glistening. "Of course I know that."

He buried his face in her neck, inhaling her scent. He wanted it in his lungs, traveling through the oxygen in his muddy blood, in the cells of his mutated body.

"You shouldn't love me," he breathed. "You just shouldn't."

Cori held on to him tighter, her whole body shaking against his. "It doesn't matter. I have to. My heart says so."

Grayson kissed her sweetly then, relishing the feel of her lips and the closeness of her body. Tilting her head to the side, he kissed her neck and the freckles on her shoulder where her tank top left off. Her hands found his hair and snaked through.

A shaky sigh escaped her. "I thought I would lose you," she murmured. "I thought you would die and leave me."

He kept kissing her because he couldn't look at her while he said it, even if it was the truth. "I *am* dead, Cori."

She pulled away to look in his eyes. "You're not dead. You breathe. You move. You think." She put a hand over his heart, the heat of it burning like a brand. "You feel."

"It's not the same," he said, brokenly. How he hated this.

"When you kiss me, I feel like a live wire. What do you feel?"

He just stared at her.

"What do you feel like when we kiss?"

"I feel…I feel…awakened…" *Alive*, he realized.

Her cheeks flushed red. "See, it's the same. Yes, we are different. Very different. But you are no less alive."

He couldn't believe what was in front of him, what he held in his arms. He'd been so wrong about her in the beginning. She was stronger than he could ever have imagined.

"I don't know if I believe that or not," he murmured in her ear. "But you make me feel like I am. Alive."

Cori's hands skated along his bare chest. "You're not even wet," she observed.

"It's my skin. It absorbs the water."

"That's amazing." Her voice was laced with awe and he hated hearing it.

Grayson shook his head. "Don't say that."

"Why?"

"It's not amazing. It's freakish. Just another thing that makes me different from you."

She wound her arms around his neck. "Different isn't so bad."

Yes, it was. It was bad. Even if she couldn't see that.

His conscience nagged at him. He should put a stop to this. Somehow, he should find the strength to push her away.

"Cori…" What could he say to make things right? He'd known from the start that this was messed up, that it could only get worse.

So why did it feel so damn good? To be holding her like this, without secrets. To see the acceptance in her eyes. How could something feel so right and so wrong at the exact same time?

"Cori—" he tried again. But her head was shaking and she'd put a finger to his lips to stop him.

"Don't," she said. "I won't let you do it any more."

"What?"

"Push me out." Her face was stern but her bottom lip trembled. She was scared. But not of him. Of *losing* him, he realized with a pang. "Tell me you won't do it any more," she demanded.

Grayson brushed his knuckles across her cheek.

"Grayson, tell me that we're together now." Her voice was rough. "And that means we face things together. Tell me."

He squeezed his eyes shut, leaning his forehead against hers. He couldn't fight this. Who was he kidding? He was the weak one all along. Zombie be damned, miniature humans could be fierce.

"We're together now, Cori." His arms gripped her tighter. "And you know what that means."

Chapter 24

We Aren't All Cuddly

Over the next few days, Cori learned as much as she could about zombies. It wasn't easy since Grayson didn't really want to talk about it. Cori understood—kind of. She couldn't imagine that being a walking dead man, undead—although she refused to think of him like that—was something to be happy about. But with Aiken's help and the little bits that Grayson told her, Cori had learned a few important details. She knew about their survival. What they ate, how they were killed, and how they aged.

She was surprised at how much Hollywood had gotten wrong. And at how many human qualities the zombies retained. In so many ways they weren't different at all—the way they required sleep and oxygen and sustenance. The way they had feelings and desires and needs. The way they used logical thinking. The way they cared.

That wasn't your stereotypical zombie characteristic, for sure.

But Cori wasn't stupid. She knew that, just like with humans, not all zombies were good ones. If they were, there wouldn't be a need for Reapers. When hydrated, they were stronger, faster, tougher than humans. Harder to kill. The most terrifying thing: they were invisible. Not literally and physically, but...*no one knew they existed.* No one knew to watch for them.

The thought that a zombie could attack and nobody would expect it left her cold with fear.

Even though she trusted Grayson completely, she was glad Aiken and his pretend parents were there. It felt right that someone was watching over the people of Asher.

One day when Cori and Grayson were picking up trash along the river, he brought up the subject for a change.

"We aren't all nice and cuddly, you know," he said as he stuffed another aluminum can into the half-full trash bag that swung between them. He'd said it out of the blue and Cori had to think a minute before she realized what he was talking about. "Some of us…well, you just shouldn't think that we're safe."

Cori eyed him. "You talking about someone in particular?"

He shook his head, staring at the bag. "It's just that not all risers value life. There are always rogues."

"Rogues?"

He nodded.

"You mean…"

He glanced away. "Live eaters." His voice was barely audible.

"They eat…"

"People," he huffed, his disturbed gaze meeting her shocked one.

Live eaters. She felt sick. Aiken hadn't told her about rogues. Maybe Hollywood was closer than she realized.

Grayson picked up a candy bar wrapper and jammed it in the trash bag with too much force.

"Are there many…live eaters?" God. Saying it gave her a chill that wouldn't go away.

"No. It isn't common. And Aiken assured me the Reapers keep on top of them."

Cori breathed deep the pine and floral scent of the cemetery, letting the information sink in. She eyed Grayson, the way his jaw clenched tight, the way his brow shaded his eyes. It hadn't been easy for him to tell her this. And again, his disgust with who he was made more sense. Even if it was misplaced.

"Okay," she said. "Call me careful."

"Good."

Cori counted seven more pieces of trash before he said, "I can only say for sure that Aiken is safe. Anyone else, you should stay away from."

"And you," Cori added.

He stopped walking and let out a huge sigh that seemed to take most of his tension with it.

"And me." He half-grinned. "That's a given. I could never hurt you, shrimp."

Grayson dropped the bag and pulled her close.

"You haven't called me that in a while," she murmured, a pout on her lips.

"Yeah, I've been thinking maybe I should come up with a better nickname for you." He pretended to think about it. "How about baby?"

"It's a start."

"Hmm…sweetie?"

"Better."

"Angel?"

"That one. I like that one."

Grayson swept a quick kiss along her jaw. "You really are my angel," he murmured against her skin.

She wasn't sure if he'd meant for her to hear it, but she answered anyway. "Mmm hmm."

He pulled back with a half grin—a Grayson grin. "Okay then. From now on I'll call you angel…shrimp."

Even with complications, they were disgustingly happy. Which of course meant that things couldn't stay that way.

It was two days before the dance and Cori still didn't have a dress. She'd never been shopping for a formal before and didn't have the first clue where to start. She figured a mall would be useful, but there wasn't one of those in Asher. So, she asked Peg.

Apparently there was exactly one dress shop in town. Peg had been there just the day before and swore she'd found the perfect dress for Cori. Cori had her doubts of course, since Peg's style was so flamboyant. Cori preferred to blend into the crowd, not be the centerpiece. The selling point though, was the fact that the dress in question was on sale. If it fit, Cori wouldn't even have to ask her mom for the money. This was a huge plus because if her mom found out about the dance, she'd want to go all out for it—dress, hair, makeup, shoes, jewelry. And well, Cori just didn't want to make a huge spectacle of it.

She met Peg at Judy's Formalwear that evening. They walked into the dressing room the saleslady had prepared for them and she spotted the dress. Her jaw dropped and her eyes bugged.

It. Was. Gorgeous. A pale teal that reminded her of tropical beaches, and elegantly simple. It had only one shoulder strap that swept down into a fitted bodice. A spattering of tiny jewels lined the waist before flaring slightly at the hips to a skirt that formed graceful lines perpendicular to the ground.

"What do you think?" Peg asked.

"I can't wear this."

"What? Why not?"

So many reasons, but…"I don't have the hips for this. It's…it's…"

Peg scoffed. "Perfect? Amazing? Everything you've been looking for? Try it on." She ducked out of the room before Cori could even begin another argument.

Quickly she slipped the dress on and winced when Peg came back in.

"Oh, Cori! It's perfect!" she squealed. "Look at how it brings out your eyes."

Cori was afraid to look. She probably seemed ridiculous in a dress way too fancy for her. Grumbling about how silly it was, her eyes floated to the mirror. Then did a double take. Was that really her? She looked so different. She looked…pretty. Could a dress really make that much of a difference?

"Now, tell me that dress isn't perfect." Peg was staring over Cori's shoulder in the mirror, her green eyes ablaze with excitement.

Peg was right. The dress *was* perfect. "Okay, maybe you're pretty good at this stuff," she admitted. Credit where credit was due.

"Of course I am." Her tone was certain. "What else were you expecting?"

Cori smoothed the front of the dress, turning from one side to the other. "It's a little long though."

Peg waved her off. "Nothing some four-inch heels won't fix."

"Are you sure?"

A firm nod. "Absolutely."

So Cori bought the dress. And the shoes.

Two days later she was pulling it on when she heard the front door open and her mom call for her.

No!

Cori froze with dread. How could she be home already? She was supposed to be working the night shift.

Before she could get the dress off and hide it, she heard footsteps climbing the stairs and then a brisk knock on the bedroom door. She glanced at the closet. The window. Under the bed. Oh, this was crazy. The ruse was up. She was busted. Besides, how much damage could her mom do at the last minute? It wasn't like she could schedule hair and makeup appointments now.

Cori flung the door open and was shocked to find her mom beaming.

"You knew."

"Of course I knew," she said simply. "Aiken's mom told me. So, it's a group date then?"

Aiken's mom who wasn't his mom.

Cori turned back to look at the mirror as her mom strolled into the room. "Yeah, five of us."

"I see. That dress is gorgeous, honey."

Cori straightened the skirt nervously. "Uh, thanks. I didn't, you know, want to make a big deal about this. That's why..."

"Sure. Why would your first dance be a big deal?" Mom said sarcastically. She smiled though, and Cori felt relieved. "I understand. Your daddy always told me I tried too hard to make you be like me. I figured I should listen to him this time," she said quietly. "That's why I didn't say anything."

Cori was shocked and had to look away. She knew what it cost her mom to say that sort of thing, even just to mention her daddy.

Finally she said, "It's not such a bad thing, really. Being like you."

"Thanks, I think." She bent and adjusted the hem of Cori's skirt. "I know things haven't been…right for a while. And I'm sorry for that."

"Things are okay, Mom. We both just need time."

"Yeah." She nodded, sadly, and ran a trembling hand down Cori's hair. "Well, I'll let you finish getting ready. I *am* going to take pictures though, Cori. And you cannot object."

"Fine."

As she watched her mom go back down the stairs she realized that they'd actually come a long ways since moving to Asher. Things weren't the same as they'd been when Daddy was around. But then, they never would be, would they? That was what happened when you lost someone so crucial; life changed. Eventually, you had to accept what was different about life in order to keep on living.

Grayson was surprised at how nervous he was as he pulled up to Cori's house. Even more so when he saw her mom's SUV parked in the driveway.

He looked at the clock on his dash. Right on time, if they were going to meet the others at the school for pictures. It might be a "group date" but he was determined to be the first one to lay eyes on Cori in her dress. If he couldn't have the night with her all to himself, at least he could have that one little advantage.

Grayson knocked on the door, anxious to see her.

But she wasn't the one who answered. It was her mother.

"Hello," she said easily. "You must be Grayson."

He nodded because he'd been caught off guard. His anti-social tendencies picked the worst time to show themselves.

She stuck her hand out. "I'm Elaina, Cori's mom."

Grayson shook her hand and tried to figure out what to say. How stupid that he was tongue-tied. "Uh, nice to meet you."

Just then, Cori came up behind Elaina and he was struck stupid all over again.

"Hi," she breathed just before her eyes flitted away shyly.

She was stunning. Beautiful beyond words. Her dress was just as he'd hoped. And her hair was down. Right then, she was lovelier than any angel could ever hope to be.

Annnnd he realized he hadn't said anything yet.

"I-I got you these," he said quickly just to fill the silence. Grayson held out the box to her. "They're flowers. For your hair. I asked the lady at the shop what kind I should get and she said those. They're uh, miniature roses or something…" He was babbling. Like, for the first time ever, he was babbling. He ground his teeth together to prevent more words from tumbling out.

Cori grinned and opened the box. "Mom?"

Elaina was grinning too. "Let's see what we got here."

Grayson waited patiently while she pinned the pink-tinged blooms into Cori's hair. When she finished, Elaina stood back and admired her work. The flowers were perfect.

Grayson just stared because he couldn't look away.

After a second, Cori's smile faded and her hand went up to her hair. "Umm, are they okay?"

"Perfect," he said softly.

"Okay, let's get some pictures," Elaina chirped. "Grayson, you stand right there. Yeah, in front of the mantle. Now, Cori, scoot in close. There you go. That looks good. On three…two…one…"

There were a lot of camera clicks. Grayson didn't think he was smiling really, and he kept looking over at Cori, but eventually Elaina seemed satisfied.

Soon, they were in the car heading toward the school. When they got there, Peg and Rex were already waiting but Aiken was nowhere to be found. Grayson thought since this was all Aiken's idea in the first place, he'd better show. But he kept the thought to himself.

"My, my, my. Don't you look marvelous," Rex exclaimed as Cori approached. "The flowers were a nice touch."

Cori glanced away, clearly not any good at taking a compliment. "Thanks. The flowers were Grayson's idea."

Rex looked at him suddenly, as if he'd just realized Grayson was there. "Hmm, how…sweet."

It was in that moment that Grayson realized he hadn't exactly told Cori how gorgeous she looked. He would have to fix that later since Peg was herding them all into the picture line.

After a few more camera clicks and some punch/water, Grayson finally had a chance to dance with her. The DJ played a song, nice and slow, and the dance floor filled up quickly.

"Dance with me," Grayson whispered in Cori's ear as soon as the song started.

She shook her head. "I told you, I don't dance."

Lucky for them, Raina had taught him. One of her many "gentleman lessons," none of which he'd taken seriously. Except for the dancing, and only then because it had been fun. It reminded him of sparring in a way. Only softer.

He took her hand and pulled. "It's easy. I'll teach you." This just made her head shake more aggressively.

"It's not that I *can't* dance, it's…I just don't."

"Why not?"

She pressed her lips together. Sighed. "It reminds me of my dad. We used to dance to the credits of Disney movies. When I was little he let me stand on his feet until I learned." Her smile was so sad there should be another name for it. "Just before…the accident we watched *Pirates of the Caribbean*. I didn't want to watch it and I was being a brat. So when the credits rolled and he asked me to dance—" Her voice cracked. Her eyes were filled with a mix of horror and grief. "I said no."

Talk about regrets. Grayson could only imagine how Cori felt. Her lip trembled and he squeezed her hand, tried to think of something to say. What could he do to make it better?

"I get it," he said.

She shook her head.

"I'm willing to bet your dad wasn't the type to hold grudges. Am I right?"

She laughed sadly. "You are. He was probably too forgiving at times."

Grayson nodded. "And I figure the number of dances versus the number of non-dances leans heavy to one side. Am I right?"

She nodded.

"I know what you need."

Her brow lifted.

"You need to dance again. For your dad. For the memory of the one who taught you. It'd be a shame to turn your back on what he started just because he's not here to do it with you, don't you think?"

He hoped he was right. Hoped he was saying the thing that would make her feel better. Grayson held his breath.

Finally she gave a slow nod. "This won't be easy."

He brought her hand to his lips and brushed the soft skin there. "It wouldn't mean anything if it was." He knew this was true because it was proven by their relationship. It wasn't easy but it was the most meaningful thing in his life.

Once he'd persuaded her to the dance floor, he pulled her close. His hand spanned her ribs perfectly. "All you have to do is go where I take you." He started to sway. "Loosen up. Yeah, like that."

Her breath hitched and her hand gripped his jacket so tight it looked painful.

"Grayson, this isn't working."

A distraction was needed.

"Shh. It's fine. You're doing it. Just relax." He hesitated, but went ahead and whispered, "I think your dad would want this, Cori."

"You're right." She eased a fraction.

"There you go. Perfect. Just try not to think about it too much."

"Don't think about it. okay. Yeah. Umm. So, where do you think Aiken is?"

Grayson frowned. That wasn't the kind of distraction he'd had in mind. "I don't know. I haven't heard from him. You?"

Cori shook her head.

He didn't want her thinking of the Reaper right now. If anyone was going to be a distraction it was going to be him. Not Aiken.

"I don't think I've ever told you this," he began. "But…um…" Why was he finding this hard to say when it was so plainly true? "You're beautiful," he blurted, sounding like an idiot.

She blinked and looked away, the same as she had with Rex. Her shyness urged him on.

"And tonight," he continued as they swayed together. "You're more gorgeous than the stars in the night sky." Yeah, it still sounded strange coming from him, but it was true so he shrugged inwardly. She needed to know.

Cori's flush was so bright he could see it even in the dim lighting. "Thanks," she mumbled, a small smile curving her lips.

Dancing was nearly effortless now. Most of her tension was gone and he hoped this memory could overshadow the bad one. Because after what she'd told him, he knew how important it was to her.

He pulled Cori closer, determined to make this dance count. She was the perfect height for her head to rest against his chest. Grayson frowned. She must be wearing some very high heels. Almost naturally, she let her head fall there and his hand went up to cradle it. Really, he just wanted an excuse to touch her hair again. For a moment he wondered what it would be like to tangle his hand in it, perhaps in a moment of passion.

Cori's head popped up. She had a dreamy little smile on her face. "Your heart just started beating faster."

Grayson felt like he'd been caught with his hand in a cookie jar. He wanted to correct her and remind her that he didn't actually have a heart anymore—at least not a normal heart. But he let it go.

"Are you…blushing?" she asked, astonished, perfect eyebrows arched.

"No. Zombies don't blush."

She giggled quietly. "Well, you're doing something."

His face felt cold. Which meant his mud had rushed to his cheeks. Not blushing exactly. More like…tanning.

"Come on, Cori," he said, to cover up that he was becoming flustered. He also managed to give her a dirty look.

"I like knowing that you react like that."

"Can we just drop it?"

She looked at him, her lips pursed. "Give me your hand."

"What?"

"Your hand." She placed his hand on her neck, his thumb resting on a pulse point. "Feel my heartbeat?"

Through her delicate skin he could feel the hard thump of her heart rushing blood through her veins. For a moment he was entranced by it.

"Now kiss me."

He looked at her, questioning. "Right here? Now?"

"Yes. Kiss me."

He figured it was a shame for her to have to ask a third time, so he wasted not a second more. As he kissed her, the pulse under his thumb increased its measure until it was a pounding staccato rhythm.

Grayson pulled back, staring at where his hand was on her neck, a slow smile spreading across his face. He did that. He'd made her heart beat faster with a simple kiss. Or maybe it wasn't quite so simple. Maybe it was a very complicated, yet awesome, kiss.

"See," she said, breathlessly.

He nodded, still amazed.

The song ended. "You wanna get out of here?"

Cori's eyes darted around to find Peg. "What about the others?"

Grayson spotted her and Rex on the other side of the dance floor, doing a decent rendition of the Dougie to whatever fast song was now playing. "They'll be fine."

Cori grinned as she spotted them too. "Okay, let's go."

Chapter 25

DARN HEELS

Westland Heights High backed up to a thick fringe of woods — the same woods that surrounded the cemetery and eventually led to the river. There was an extensive network of jogging and hiking trails, each ending in a different location of the city and many skirting the natural waterway. It was the kind of attraction the nature-loving people of Asher appreciated. Although Cori was a city girl, even she had to admit liking all the lush green things.

She wasn't at all surprised when Grayson led her down one of the more secluded trails. A little sign posted at the entrance said, RIVER AHEAD 2 MILES.

All she could think was *four-inch heels*. But she didn't say anything because she wanted to be alone with him. It was worth the aching feet.

When they were far enough down the path that the lights from the school could no longer be seen, she decided to say something before she developed blisters.

"How far are we going?"

He stopped and looked at her. "Do you want to go back?"

Cori bit her lip. "It's my shoes." She lifted up her dress to show him.

Grayson looked amused. "That explains a lot." He smirked.

"What does that mean?"

He shrugged, a grin tugging at his lips. "You were lagging behind. And you look a little less shrimpy tonight."

Cori rolled her eyes. "Ha. Ha. Very funny." She walked on, determined to show him she could keep up. Before she got very far though, she found herself with her feet off the ground. In a move that really shouldn't have been so easy, Grayson swept her up in his arms and started back down the trail.

"What are you doing?" she squealed.

"It's not that much farther."

"I can walk. Put me down."

"No way. We'll get there faster like this."

"What, are you in a hurry?" she huffed.

He stared into her eyes and she wondered if he should be watching where he was going. "Not at all," he whispered.

Cori was captivated for some reason. Maybe because of the intense way he spoke. Or maybe because his eyes seemed to dance. Like the day she'd pushed him in the river. He was happy.

She sighed in defeat and laid her head on his shoulder as he carried her.

It was dark out and the path was lit only by beams of moonlight that tangled between the branches of the trees. It should have been spooky, but Cori didn't feel spooked. Ironically, she felt like she was in exactly the right place, at exactly the right time.

Before long, they reached a large clearing that went right up to the bank of the river. With the trees giving way to the moon, Cori could see the landscape clearly. The river was different here than it was by the graveyard. For one, it was wider, more significant—and deeper, she guessed. Also, the lack of trees in this area was quite a departure from the norm. But the way the stars twinkled above and reflected on the swiftly moving water made everything seem fantastical. Almost magical.

"What do you think?" Grayson asked.

She said the first thing that came to her mind. "It's beautiful." And it was. The sounds of the water rushing and the tree frogs chirping, the scent of pine and spruce and night blooming flowers, the feel of the breeze on her face…all of it under the magic of the moonlight worked together to make the moment utterly beautiful.

Cori turned to look at Grayson and was surprised at his expression. "What is it?" she asked. The powerful way he was looking at her was nearly alarming.

"Nothing." He glanced quickly away, but she put a hand to his cheek to bring his gaze back to her.

"Tell me."

"I just…there are things I want to tell you but I don't know how."

"What things?"

He opened his mouth to say something and then closed it, his expression turning into a scowl. He looked back toward the trail they'd come from and then scanned his head left to right as though he was looking for something.

"Grayson?"

He didn't answer. Quickly, he set Cori back on her four-inch heels. With his nose in the air he turned in a complete circle. The look on his face was indescribable—part animal, part hunter.

"Grayson? What's wrong?"

He turned to face her again. "I don't know. There are zombies nearby. Several of them. At least three. I don't recognize them."

"What does that mean?" she whispered.

He put a finger to her lips and cocked his head to the side, listening. Cori couldn't hear anything. She listened hard, but heard nothing. And then she could. Barely, she could make out the sound of brush rustling but it was inconsistent, a crash here, a rustle there.

In a flash, Grayson picked her back up and ran through the clearing toward the trail.

"Grayson?" she whimpered, trying to get her bearings.

Just as suddenly, he stopped and set her on her feet so that she was closest to the trees that bordered the left side of the trail. Grayson stood between her and whatever was coming toward them, facing the opposite set of trees.

"Are we in trouble?" she whispered fiercely.

"I don't know. Something's off. Something's…not right. And they're coming from both directions." His voice was urgent.

Cori gripped the back of his suit jacket as the sound of stumbling through the brush came ever closer. But she could only hear it from one side. Branches cracking. Leaves crunching. And then it stopped. For a moment she was confused but then she realized the person — zombie — was standing in the middle of the clearing, staring at the river. She watched as he slowly turned away from the water, trying to decide on a different direction.

Grayson was right. Something was off about this guy. He didn't move right and he was too far away for her to get a good look but he seemed to be…deformed?

He took a slow, lumbering step toward the trail and then another. Soon he was close enough for Cori to see his face, and what she saw there was sure to give her nightmares for the rest of her natural life.

The zombie wasn't deformed. He was falling apart. Literally. Huge sores pocked his face and oozed a rusty brown liquid. His lips were a mangled mess and one of his eyes was hanging slightly out of its socket. His hair had fallen out in chunks leaving raw bald spots exposed…and that was just his face.

"Oh, God," Grayson whispered as he pushed Cori further behind him.

Instantly, the zombie's head snapped up looking for the sound. He shuffled closer to them, grunting as he went. The sight was grisly.

Cori was gripping Grayson's jacket so tight her knuckles ached. *This* was a monster. This was what her mind automatically went to when she thought of a zombie. This, she remembered from what little she'd learned, was a dangerous zombie. A very dangerous one…a *contagious one.*

Could they outrun him? He seemed to be struggling with his motor skills. Surely they could. Even with her god-awful heels.

The zombie stopped walking and sniffed the air. Suddenly, a gruesome smile spread the flesh that at one time used to be his lips. "Grayson…" he said in a voice that was a strange cross between a growl and a grunt.

Grayson went stock still. Cori wasn't even sure if he was breathing. Seconds passed, or maybe minutes before he spoke…

When he did, it rang of utter despair.

"Leiv?"

Grayson stared in horror at the sight before him. At the same time his mind was racing to figure out how to get Cori away from Leiv before he could infect her. It was clear he was contagious.

"I've…beeeen…looking for you…bro." The sound of his brother's distorted voice was like a blade through the heart.

Leiv was completely unrecognizable, his body deep in stages of decomposition—hard to believe since Grayson had seen him only eight hours ago. Even his scent had changed to something putrid. Not the typical dead smell that Grayson associated with zombies, but the rank smell of rotting flesh.

Leiv was a rotter, and as good as dead. But Grayson couldn't allow himself even a second to mourn the loss. He had to think. Get Cori away. They could run, but her shoes were an issue.

"Leiv, why are you here? Where is Raina?" Grayson was stalling.

"Rain, rain, go away. Come again another day," he sing-songed. "If you don't, I'll be sad…" A slow smile made him look even more hideous. "Maybe I'll do something really, really bad."

Grayson had never encountered a zombie who'd come of age. He knew, however, that their mind deteriorated as rapidly as their body did.

"Leiv, you should be at home. The Reapers…they will take care of you." Grayson couldn't help the sadness that seeped through his voice.

"Reaper…peeper…" Leiv stumbled another step forward. "…don't fear the Reaper…" he sang. Grayson recognized the lyrics from a song Leiv liked to blare in the mornings.

"Where is Raina? Does she know you're here?"

Leiv laughed at that, a resounding cackle. "No…she would kill me…or maybe not…who knows? I wasted too much time…"

Grayson kept hold of Cori, inching her backward toward the trees. "Why are you here, brother?"

"Oh…that's an easy one. I'ma going…to…hellllllp…you."

"Help me?"

The gruesome replica of his brother gave a jerky nod that resulted in his head being cocked sideways. "You…deserve to be happy…Grayson…"

This couldn't be good. "I am happy."

"No, you're no-ot!" Leiv gurgled and belched, then laughed. "You will be though…when I'm done."

"Leiv, I'm not sure what you're talking about but…I am happy. There is nothing you need to do. Except go home and call the Reapers."

Leiv stared blankly at him for a moment.

"Corinne, Corinne. Where oh, where have you…been? Hiding behind…your zombie friend?"

Grayson stiffened and a jolt of fury went through him. "Don't talk to her," he barked.

"If that's what you wish…I just thought we could get to know each other…before…" Leiv trailed off.

"Before what?"

"Oh, don't play dumb…You know." He staggered to the side, another step closer.

Grayson felt numb with fear. Fear for Cori. "Before what?" he demanded.

"Before I bite her, of course. Come on…bro…get with the program."

Grayson growled. He couldn't help it. Even when he felt Cori jump in surprise, he couldn't stop the animalistic sound coming from within him. He would fight his brother—kill his brother—if he had to. Cori would remain human, no matter the cost.

"I'll kill you first," Grayson snarled.

Leiv looked like he was going to start giggling again, but before he could, three zombies eased out from behind the trees. It was Aiken and two others who Grayson could only assume were Reapers. This was the approaching he'd zeroed in on earlier. They'd been so stealthy, he hadn't realized they were this close. Or maybe he'd been too distracted.

"You won't have to," Aiken said grimly while the other two—a man and a woman—went to the sides to form a more complete barrier between Cori and Leiv. The three of them were dressed in leather and *steels* and strapped all over with daggers. Each of them wore a short sword on their hip. One word came to mind. *Deadly.*

Grayson felt an overwhelming rush of relief, even as he dreaded the loss of his brother. At least now he wouldn't be allowed to infect anyone. That was most important.

Leiv scowled. Or at least Grayson thought he did. Who could really tell with his face all torn up like it was. "Reeeaperssss…" he hissed.

Aiken responded by drawing the sword from its place on his hip and holding it out in front of him.

"Leiv," Grayson started. "You have to go with them. You know it's the right thing—"

A familiar scent hit his nose right then and he watched as Leiv's head swung in the direction of the river.

"Raaaaaina…" he breathed.

A new sense of dread pounded through Grayson. His sister would be distraught to see Leiv like this.

There was only a second or two before she came through the edge of the forest, close to the bank of the river and when she saw the scene in front of her, she stopped cold. It was obvious by her tear-streaked face that she'd already known of Leiv's deterioration. But perhaps she hadn't known how bad it had gotten because the look on her face was pure agony.

"Oh, Leiv," she whispered, stepping cautiously toward him.

"Raaaina…have you come to—" he laughed a cruel sounding laugh "—saaave me?"

Raina pressed her lips together as tears welled in her eyes. She shook her head slowly which seemed to make Leiv angry.

"No? Well, what good are you for?" he growled. A sob escaped her lips and like a switch was thrown, Leiv was a different person. "I'm sorry, Raaaina…so sooorrry…I-I'm not myself…" He took a shuffling step toward her but stopped when Aiken cleared his throat. "Raaaina…forgive me. For all of it…the past…for everything."

She nodded but held her hand over her mouth, trying to contain herself. Grayson wanted to comfort her, but he couldn't move away from Cori.

"Why are you here?" Aiken asked Raina.

She swallowed hard before answering. "I was looking for Grayson." Raina's eyes went to Cori and then back to Aiken.

"It's time…to tell Gray the truth…Raina…" Leiv's distorted voice cut in.

She swung around to face him. "No," she breathed.

Leiv squeezed his eyes shut, seeming to have a moment of lucidity. "Yes, Raina…we've played this game long enough—"

"What are you talking about?" Grayson asked. "Truth about what?"

Raina was shaking her head, her eyes dancing frantically between Leiv and Grayson.

"Tell him, Raina. All of it. Now."

A strange foreboding swept over Grayson. He'd never seen his sister act like she was now, wringing her hands and shuffling her feet.

She stared at Grayson. "Have you decided to use your *Save?*"

His forehead wrinkled. "What? Of course not. I don't have the slightest clue how to go about doing that and besides, I could never let her *die*." It was hard to even say the word.

Raina glanced at Cori.

"What?" Cori asked. "Grayson, what is a 'save'?"

They both ignored her.

"What if I told you there was a way to use her…where Cori wouldn't have to die? Would you be interested then?"

"That's not—" Aiken started to say something until he was cut off by Leiv's feral growl.

But Grayson wasn't paying any attention to the Reaper. He was hanging on the words Raina had just spoken. *Was* there a way for him to be human again…and keep Cori? His heart soared at the prospects: He could be human for her, normal for her. They could stay together forever. Maybe she would even marry him someday…

"Grayson, what is she talking about?" Cori asked again.

He turned to look at her, so giddy he could hardly contain it. "For each zombie, there is one human who we are drawn to. We call them our *Save* because they can help us become human again. You are mine."

"That's not exactly—" Aiken tried again, but Leiv growled ferociously.

"The problem is," Grayson continued, ignoring them. "In order for the zombie to be saved, the human has to die." He put his hand to her soft cheek. Her eyes were wide. "For us, that simply wasn't an option." He turned back to Raina. "But if there really is another way…"

Raina eyed him before she spoke. "I know there is one thing you've wanted more than anything else, since the day of your rising… to be human again."

Grayson nodded. "Yes, of course." He wished she would just tell him what to do. He would do anything.

"But now, I believe there is one thing you want more than that." She hesitated. "Am I right?"

He was confused until he really thought about it. There *was* one thing he wanted more than anything.

"Yes," he told her.

Raina nodded. "It means more to you to be with her than to be human again…am I right?"

He nodded. Though it would be more accurate to say that Cori's *life*, her safety, was more important to him than his humanity.

"Then I will tell you how to use your *Save*."

"Yes, please. Tell me." He was anxious now. So much so that he wasn't expecting her next words.

"There are two things you must know. After that, it's simple." There was a pregnant pause where Grayson had the distinct feeling his life was about to change. "First, you can never be human again. Never. Accept it and move on. And second, you must, *must*, turn her."

Chapter 26

TURNING A LIE INTO TRUTH

Grayson hadn't realized how high he'd soared until he came crashing down in a disastrous heap. He thought this must be how Icarus felt on that day when he'd flown too close to the sun.

"What did you say?" he hissed at his sister.

"You heard me," she said flatly. "That is how you use your *Save*; you turn them into one of us, bring them into our family. Just like Leiv did…just like I did."

Grayson's head was shaking in disbelief. "You told me…I don't understand. You said it didn't work with you and Leiv, that no zombie had ever successfully used their *Save*."

"It was a lie. I was Leiv's *Save*. And you were mine. We call them *Save* not because they can actually save us but because they are saved, reserved, for us. To bring into our family."

"But what about the tests?"

"They aren't what we made them out to be. They're genetic. And Cori has already passed. You can tell by the pull. Only zombies and their *Saves* can feel it. It proves her biological line is compatible with the zombie virus, meaning she can easily be turned. No chance that she won't rise."

"A lie…" Grayson echoed.

Raina stared at him.

"So I never had a chance to be human? That was a lie too?"

She nodded.

But what about his message from the Oracle? *She alone has the ability to save you from your unhappiness, from the reality that you hate so badly, but know that it will come at a price: her life for yours.*

She'd never exactly said he could be human again. He'd just understood it that way. But she…she was talking about turning Cori.

Grayson had never truly felt betrayal before. But he knew it now and it was a sour knot in the pit of his stomach.

"We were trying to protect you," Raina explained. "You were so miserable, Gray." She raised her chin. "We gave you hope. A reason to live."

He stared at her like she was crazy. Did she really believe that?

"You gave me *false* hope. That's not the same." His voice was hard and heavy. It was like a Buick was parked on his shoulders. How could they—the only two people he'd loved until Cori—have lied to him?

"Grayson, really…it's not as bad as it seems. We were always going to tell you."

"When?" he bellowed.

"After…after you became attached to Cori and realized this was the best option."

Hearing those words made him fully understand what his brother and sister had expected from him. The hopefulness he'd seen so many times on their faces when they'd talked about his *Save*…It hadn't been there because they hoped he'd be the first zombie to succeed. It was there because they wanted him to accept their way of life—by bringing another human over to the dark side. They'd *hoped* he would murder her, make *her* into a monster.

"You—" he had to swallow the knot in his throat "—wanted me to *kill* her?"

Raina was shaking her head viciously. "No. Not kill her, *turn* her. Make her like us."

"It's the same thing!" he raged.

"It's not wrong, Grayson," she yelled back. "It's how we procreate. It's how our species survives. We must use our *Saves* and in return we have companionship, family, a reason to go on. *Happiness.*"

She was crazy. They were all crazy. If they thought this wasn't wrong, that there was nothing wrong with turning humans into zombies, they were nuts.

Grayson looked around. He was surrounded by them, by zombies. It didn't matter that he was one too. At that moment he hated them. All of them. Except for maybe…

"Aiken?" was all he could manage to get out.

The Reaper had a bewildered expression on his face. His head went back and forth in a helpless gesture. "I thought you knew…I had no idea you thought…"

Grayson's breath was coming in heaves, his head was pounding. He felt his skin tighten over his bones as he turned in a complete circle. All around him, they were all around him. And Cori, they surrounded her too.

"Grayson?" It was her voice that centered him. He looked at her. Her blue eyes were wide, worried, confused. Her bottom lip trembled. "Are you okay?"

She was fearful. But not for herself. She was encircled by zombies — zombies who could hurt her — and she was concerned about him. "Your eyes," she gasped.

Grayson didn't even notice when everything turned murky but he squeezed his eyes shut anyway. His hands went to grip the sides of his skull where it pounded as if it were being played like a drum.

"Grayson!"

Cori reached for him, but Aiken held her back.

Grayson struggled to focus on her and managed to succeed even if only for a second. "Angel. You're safe. It's all gonna be…okay."

He felt his mouth dry up, his eyelids seemed sticky, his lungs struggled to suck in air. He needed water. Fast.

He went as quickly as his dried up joints would allow, toward the river, flinging his jacket off along the way. Desperate, he knelt on the muddy bank. His knees were the first to touch liquid. As the fabric of his pants wicked moisture to his arid skin, he felt a tiny measure of relief. But not nearly enough. He bent and drank like an animal, straight from the stream, dunking his head all the way under the flow. But still, it wasn't enough. So he ripped open the front of his dress shirt, sending buttons flying everywhere, and delved into the water. He grasped armfuls of it as if to embrace it, soaking as much of his body as he could. When the pain barely started to let up, he drank more. Drank until he couldn't take another sip.

Grayson stood, breathing hard, trying to calm himself. When he finally gained some control, he turned back to the grisly sight. He didn't look at Cori. Couldn't. Neither did he look at Aiken or the other Reapers. He looked only at his tribe—at Leiv and Raina.

"If you thought that I would ever be okay with turning her…" he snarled as he marched back to where they stood. "If you thought that I would pass on a fate I so obviously and desperately hate…" Each word snapped from him like a whip. "If you thought even for a moment, that I would go along with this…" He looked directly at Leiv when he said his next words. "Then you never really knew me at all."

"Gray—"

Grayson threw his hand up to stop Raina from talking.

"From this moment on, I have no tribe," he spat. "You are both dead to me."

"Gray, you can't mean that—"

"I knew…you couldn't doooooo it…" Leiv grunted and twitched. "That's why I came…I know you better than you think, bro."

Grayson shook his head. He couldn't find the despair that had racked him earlier when he looked at Leiv. Now, he just wanted him gone. "You know nothing," he said, his voice a cold bark. "And I'm not, nor have I ever been, your brother."

Leiv looked longingly at Cori.

"Give me a reason to kill you, *bro*," he told Leiv. Grayson's temper was hanging on by a razor-fine thread.

What happened in the next few seconds would haunt Grayson for the rest of his morbid life. One day, he would look back on it and realize there was nothing he could've done to stop it, change it, or postpone it. It was fated. Destined to happen. But until then it would be pure undiluted guilt in his mutated zombie veins.

Not very far away in the forest, he could hear a voice—no, two.

"…I don't think they're out here…"

"Yes, they are…I saw them come this way…"

"You sure it was Aiken?"

"Pretty sure…"

There wasn't enough time to warn them. There was only enough time for Grayson's eyes to meet Aiken's before the voices were there…

And Leiv struck.

She wanted to run. She should have run.

Cori wasn't sure what happened. One minute her eyes were glued to Grayson, watching his every move, the next all hell broke loose. The air was filled with hideous, threatening snarls and bodies were being flung here and there.

Fighting. They were fighting.

Grayson, Aiken, Leiv…there seemed to be extra bodies in the fray but she couldn't tell who. The only people she could see clearly were the girl Reaper—who was hovering close to her—and Raina who was standing off to the side, looking worried. Everyone else was a tangle of limbs under the moonlight.

And then, as fast as it had begun…it was over. Gruesomely over.

"Noooo!" Raina screamed loud and long and painful, the sound echoing in the clearing. It was a sound Cori would never forget.

She didn't see what was about to happen until it was already done. With a swift and efficient motion, Aiken swung his sword in an arc bringing it cleanly across Leiv's neck.

For a micro-second everyone was still, all eyes fixed on the ghastly looking rotter as he went motionless. Then just like a scene from a horror movie…his head fell. Cori slapped a hand to her mouth to keep from crying out. Her eyes were peeled so wide she saw stars and the only sound coming from her was a panicked whimper.

No one moved.

Raina sobbed.

Grayson stared at the decapitated body with a void expression.

Aiken was breathing heavily, angrily.

That was when Cori noticed Peg and Rex. Both were on the ground. Leiv had lunged at something. Must have been them. They sat up, staring frantically at their surroundings.

"What. The. HELL?" Rex said, his voice rising with each word until he was screaming. "What is that…thing?"

No one answered him. He glanced around and noticed Cori. Gave her a strange look.

"Someone answer me!" he yelled again.

Cori knew what he felt like. Confused. Scared. Shocked. So she fessed up. "It was a z-zombie," she told him, her voice shaking so badly words were less like words and more like syllables without a home.

Rex got to his feet, though he seemed unsteady. Peg stayed on the ground, her mouth opening and closing but never finding words.

"A…zombie?"

Cori nodded. "A bad one."

Rex scoffed, eyes bulged. "As if there might be a good one?"

"There are," she said.

"Are you all right?" Aiken asked but he wasn't talking to Rex. He was talking to Peg. She nodded, her eyes wide and glassy.

"Well, isn't this just lovely," muttered the girl Reaper — Cori couldn't remember the name her mom had used…Coma…Cody…

Aiken flashed the girl a warning look.

Rex stumbled over and bent down to look at the corpse. "I'm sure this isn't a zombie, Cori. He was probably just…sick or something." He looked at Aiken. "Good God, did you really have to *kill* him? And why in the blazes do you have a *sword?*"

"Yes," was all Aiken said.

Rex straightened and pulled out his cell phone. "Well, I'm calling the police—"

"No!" Aiken snatched the phone from his hand. "You can't do that."

"Aiken, seriously. It was self-defense. You won't be in trouble."

Aiken shook his head. "You can't call the police, because he's not human."

To his credit, Rex didn't roll his eyes or laugh. He ran his tongue over his front teeth and Cori guessed he was grappling for patience. "Not human? Then what is he, and don't say he's a zombie."

"He *is* a zombie."

Rex blew out his breath and planted his hands on his hips. "Right. Okay. If you think—"

Cori glanced at Peg then, figuring she must be in shock or something since she wasn't talking. But no, it was worse than that. "Peg!" she exclaimed and rushed forward.

Peg's eyes rolled back in her head and she was convulsing, her body twisting in impossible directions.

"No, stay back!" Aiken shouted as Rex went to kneel next to Peg. "Rex, don't touch her. Cori, stay back."

Cori stopped short but Rex ignored him. Just before he went to touch Peg's face, the girl Reaper snatched his hand back. How she'd gotten there so fast, Cori wasn't sure.

"Don't touch her," she snarled.

Rex stared at her, his mouth hanging open.

Aiken dropped to his knees in the dirt and began pulling Peg's wrap aside, lifting her dress, looking for something…Then he found it. On her upper left arm was a set of vicious looking teeth marks.

"She's been bitten," Grayson said from somewhere behind Cori.

"No," Aiken whispered. Both of the other Reapers bent next to Peg. "This can't be…"

"What?" Rex asked. Panic dripping from his voice. "Tell me what's wrong with her."

"No, Peg!" Aiken's voice was broken, bleeding. He was holding her now, her body still seizing. "I never wanted this…God, I never wanted this for you…"

"Aiken! Somebody, call 9-1-1! She needs an ambulance." Rex was struggling to get to his phone.

"They can't help her," the girl Reaper said, her voice flat, lifeless.

"What do you mean they can't help her? Of course they can help her." He'd reached his phone by then. Cori knew she should try to explain things to him but she was confused herself.

"Grayson, what's happening?" she asked, desperate for some kind of explanation. If Leiv had bitten her…

When he didn't answer, she looked at him. He was staring with huge eyes at Peg, his head shaking back and forth. His expression… it made Cori want to scream in terror.

"She's turning into one of us," the guy Reaper said quietly.

"One of you?" Rex screamed. Any trace of the manners he usually possessed was long gone. "What the hell does that mean?"

"She's turning into a zombie," Cori said numbly. Oh Peg…how could this happen?

"Cori, just stop it! Zombies aren't real!" Rex was beyond frantic.

At that moment, Peg stopped moving. The seizure was over. She was perfectly still as Aiken held her close. Was she breathing? Cori couldn't tell. She saw Aiken's face though, and it was contorted with grief, the kind of misery most people never experience, even in a whole lifetime.

After several minutes, Aiken laid her back on the ground. "I'm sorry," came his tortured voice. "I'm so sorry, baby."

Baby? What had happened between those two, Cori wondered.

He was touching her face, her hair. "I'm so sorry. I'll never forgive myself for not protecting you…"

"She's not breathing," Rex said. "Oh, god. She's not breathing! Aiken, do something!"

"There is nothing to do," he ground out.

"What is *wrong* with you," Rex said angrily as he crawled over to Peg. The Reapers didn't try to stop him this time. "Haven't you ever heard of CPR?" He checked Peg's pulse. Checked her neck and then her wrist. After a minute his hand fell away and his butt hit the ground. "She's gone," he barely whispered. Tears rimmed his eyes. "She's…dead. How can she be *dead?*"

"She's not dead," Aiken murmured, still touching her face.

Rex looked at him like he'd lost his mind. "She's not breathing. Her heart isn't beating. She's dead."

"She's not dead!" Aiken said fiercely. "She's just…turning."

Rex shook his head and actually laughed. It was a slightly hysterical laugh, crazed. "You guys are all absolutely freaking psychotic."

"They aren't crazy, Rex," Cori tried. "It's true. They are zombies and now Peg will be one too."

He gave her a withering look. She wished someone else would back her up but they were all eerily quiet. "There is no such thing," he hissed. She'd never seen him like this. But of course he'd just watched his best friend die.

Cori had tears running down her face and all she could do was shake her head at him.

"There *is* such a thing," the girl Reaper finally muttered, never taking her eyes off of Peg and Aiken. "You're surrounded by four of them, this very minute." Rex's eyes jetted around. "That's right, everyone except you and Cori."

He didn't say anything for a long time. And then, "You can't prove it."

Slowly, she turned and looked at him. The expression on her face made Cori shiver. "Is that a challenge?"

He shrugged, narrowed his eyes, tension leaking from his pores. "Call it what you want," he bit out.

In a lightning quick move, the Reaper pulled her dagger and sliced open her palm. Then she shoved the gaping brown wound in Rex's face. "Does that look like human blood to you?" she asked through her teeth. "Does it?"

Rex glared at her hand and then at her face. "No," he said finally.

She closed her fist over the wound and turned back to Peg's body—which was rapidly losing color.

"Cota, head's up." The guy Reaper tossed her a bottle of water and she drank it.

At least now, Cori knew her name.

When Cota finished the water, she glanced at Rex. "Want more proof?" She didn't wait for him to answer, but flashed him her now nearly healed palm.

Rex simply gave her a nasty look.

"What happens now?" Cori asked. "With Peg?"

"Now, we wait," replied the guy Reaper.

"For what," Rex asked.

"For her to rise."

"Rise?"

The guy looked at Rex sympathetically. "From the dead."

"And when she does…then what?"

"She'll be one of us."

"But…" Rex hesitated. "She'll still be…Peg, right?"

The guy looked at Aiken while he spoke. "She won't remember much of her human life, but yes. She will still be herself."

Rex looked stricken. "She won't remember me? That…that…is impossible. We've been friends since, well, forever."

"I'm sorry," the guy told him, and he seemed to mean it.

"How? How could she not remember me?"

"It's just the way it is, Rex," Aiken finally spoke up. He sounded hoarse and Cori noticed he looked ill. "She likely won't remember any of you."

"Aiken, drink," Cota commanded. The other Reaper held out some water.

"I can't," he moaned.

"You have to."

He shook his head.

Aiken seemed more distraught than Rex. Strange. He'd only known Peg for a few months. But then she guessed it had something to do with being a Reaper. He must feel like he'd failed.

"Drink *now*, or I'm gonna shove it down your throat," Cota snarled.

Aiken gave her a look that should have killed her. But he drank. Not that the little bit of water did much to help his sickly appearance.

"Just because she's your *Save* doesn't mean you can give up," she told him more gently. "You have to be there for her when she rises."

"What did you call her?" Rex demanded.

"She is Aiken's *Save*," Cota told him.

"And that means…what?"

"It means she's his mate."

"That's not what it means," Grayson said suddenly. "I wasn't Raina's mate."

Cota looked at him like he was stupid. "In this case, it does. You and Cori too. Wise up, civie. You two are mated *Saves*. You and Raina were familial *Saves*."

"There are different kinds of *Saves?*"

"Yes. You're basically her son. Not by birth but by rising."

Grayson jerked his head back and a strange expression came over him. "More things I didn't know," he muttered.

Cori couldn't think about it now. She needed to know that Peg would be okay. She filed it all away to talk about later.

"We need to get her out of here, Aiken," Cota said.

He nodded, his movements jerky. "We'll take her to our place."

"Herrin, you stay and clean up," Cota told the guy Reaper. "Meet back at home." He nodded. Aiken was lifting Peg into his arms; her body hung limp.

"I'm staying with her," Rex warned.

Cota eyed him.

"Me too," Cori added.

"Very well, bring the humans."

"The humans have names," Rex sneered.

A grimace played at Cota's lips, but she followed Aiken into the forest without a word.

Grayson grabbed Cori's arm. "I'm going to stay with Herrin."

"I'll stay too then," she said.

"No. Go, be with Peg."

Tears kept falling even though Cori tried to stop them. She didn't want to be even an inch away from Grayson. "No—"

"Yes," he insisted. "I'll be there soon. I promise."

She bit her cheek to keep from sobbing. "Grayson, I lo—"

He cut her off with a quick hard kiss. "Go."

She went.

Chapter 27

LOVE IS SCARY

The waiting was the worst part. It seemed to go on forever, as endless as an ocean. But in reality, Cori knew it had only been a few hours.

They'd laid Peg's lifeless body on Aiken's bed and someone had brought in kitchen chairs. They were lined up around the bed, mostly unused. It seemed everyone wanted to pace, including Cori. Aiken occupied one chair, on one side of the bed, and Rex sat in one directly across from him. Both guys were holding one of Peg's limp hands. Cori watched Aiken closely. He hadn't taken his eyes from Peg's face since they'd gotten there.

She was his *Save*. Cori didn't fully understand the term. All she'd gotten from the bits and pieces earlier was that it was important to the survival of the zombie species. The word "mate" was thrown around, but Cori wasn't sure what that meant to a riser. That and something about turning them into zombies, except apparently Grayson and Aiken didn't agree with that part of it.

Good thing. She liked being human.

"I can't believe she won't remember anything," Rex muttered, dejectedly.

"She'll remember certain things," Aiken said.

"Like what?"

"There's no way to tell. She might recall bits and pieces but not whole memories. It'll be like she's in a thick fog. It will be hard to remember and soon, she won't try anymore." He sighed a shaky breath. "We won't know for sure until she wakes. The only thing for certain is…me."

Rex jerked his head back. "You? Why would she remember you and not me?"

"We shared a connection—"

"Yeah, well we shared seventeen years!"

Aiken stared at him. But only for a moment before he went back to her face.

"It's supernatural," he muttered. "The pull…it can't be undone. But still, she won't remember everything about me, either. We'll just have to wait and see."

Rex kept on glaring at him.

"Rex," Cori spoke up. "We all loved her."

He glanced at her. "Not them." He pointed to Cota and Herrin. "They didn't even know her."

"Okay. But Aiken did. And he's mourning too. Just take it easy, all right?" Cori said gently.

Rex didn't respond but at least he quit glaring.

How Cori wished Grayson would show up. Herrin had arrived an hour and a half earlier, saying Grayson would be there soon, that he had something to take care of. Cryptic, yet she hadn't questioned it. Maybe she should have.

She glanced at the clock on Aiken's bedside table. 3:37 a.m. Good thing her mom thought she was spending the night with Peg.

Twenty minutes later they were still pacing Aiken's ridiculously large bedroom, waiting for Peg, when Grayson came through the door. Cori's breath left her in a massive puff. She went to him, her arms locking around his waist. He squeezed her close and somehow it made her feel like things would be all right.

"How is she?" he asked over Cori's head.

"Still dead," Rex snapped.

Only Cori would've noticed the way Grayson flinched at Rex's angry words.

Two more hours passed in near silence. The only sounds were Aiken's whispered words to Peg and Rex's nervous shuffling feet. Eventually, the sun started to peak its head over the horizon. That's when it happened...a miracle.

It started with a tiny flutter of her eyelashes. Cori expected Peg's eyes to open right then, but they didn't. Instead, the movement switched to her fingers. Tiny twitches. The smallest of muscles coming to life.

"She's moving," Rex exclaimed. "Holy crap, she's moving!"

Aiken leaned forward, close to her ear. "Wake up, baby. Please wake up. I'm right here."

Then she didn't move again. Cori wondered if it had just been some sort of nervous response. But then it happened again. Fluttering of the eyes, spasming fingers...

And then a retching gasp, so loud Cori jumped and yelped.

Then more nothing.

The whole time Aiken kept whispering in Peg's ear and Rex kept squeezing her hand as if they could pump and prime her body into working.

Finally, after an eternity, her chest moved again and she sucked in a huge breath. This time her lungs kept going, taking air in and pushing it back out. Over and over.

Cori couldn't believe it. Only in that moment did she realize she never truly thought Peg would come back. But here she was breathing again. A real life miracle. She was *alive*.

"Peg, open your eyes," Rex urged. "Open your eyes and look at me, please."

She didn't. But she was trying; her lids seemed to be staging a protest.

"Baby, wake up," Aiken said again, his voice urgent and raw.

A few more tries and her eyes came open with a blank, glassy look.

Cori's heart sank. Would Peg still be the happy, caring friend she knew? She wasn't human anymore. How would that change her?

Peg looked around, seeming to panic, until her gaze landed on Rex.

"Rex...what...happened?" Her voice came out ragged and choppy.

Rex had tears in his eyes that he was clearly trying to stem but he let out a small laugh of relief. "You...you...well...how do you feel?"

She blinked her eyes, and her hand went to her forehead. "Like a crap-cicle. Where am I?" She looked around, clearly not recognizing the people around her. "Cori? Is that you? Where's Dracula?"

"Yeah, it's me," Cori said excitedly. Peg remembered her! She hadn't been expecting that at all.

"Oh, there he is," Peg muttered as Grayson came into view. "Will someone tell me where I am and how I got here?"

"You were hurt," Aiken started to explain. Even he sounded relieved that Peg remembered so much. But then she jumped as if she hadn't realized he was right next to her. She yanked her hand from his.

"Who are you?" she asked with narrowed eyes. Her expression was almost hostile. Very un-Peg-like.

Aiken's mouth opened to say something, but nothing came out. The hurt was obvious in his eyes, and Cori wanted to cry for him. How could she remember them all except for him?

"It's Aiken," Cori told her quickly. "You remember him, Peg. He came to school the day after I did. We eat lunch together every day. You remember, right?"

Peg was shaking her head slowly, staring at Aiken like he was a complete stranger. "No," she said and then turned to look at Rex. "Rex, what's going on? How come I don't remember him?"

Rex was speechless. He looked to Aiken for help, but he was useless; there was nothing there but anguish. "I...I don't know. You and Aiken are...were...close, Peg. Try harder."

She looked at Aiken's stricken face again, squinting. "I don't...I can't remember him at all." She shook her head. "There's just nothing."

Everything was silent for several awkward moments before Aiken smiled—or tried to. It was a sad, pain-filled thing that really wasn't a smile at all.

"It's okay," he whispered to Peg. "It's...okay." Cori noticed the way his lips trembled, the way he was breathing heavily. What little color he had, drained from his face. "I'm gonna..." He stood and pointed to the door. "If anyone needs me...I gotta go." He rushed toward the door.

"Aiken, wait," Cota tried. But he just shook his head and went past her.

When he was gone Peg just looked more confused. "I'm sorry," she said to no one in particular.

"It's not your fault," Cori told her.

It took a while to explain the situation to Peg. When it was all said and done, she still didn't seem like she believed it, that she was actually a zombie. There were no tears. No anger. No hysterical laughter. Cori figured it would take some time for it all to sink in. That's when Peg would need her friends the most. She wished Aiken could be included in that mix. Maybe Peg would remember him later. Like temporary amnesia or something.

Sometime that morning, Grayson took Cori home. She was exhausted and there was a saying…everything looks better after you've slept. She figured it would hold true this time too.

He walked her to the door. Neither of them seemed to have anything to say even though they had a lot to discuss. Right then, she was just too tired to think about it.

It was a quick goodbye, kiss on the cheek, tight hug, then he was getting in his car to leave. And she was climbing into bed.

Grayson went home. He didn't want to since Raina was there, but he didn't have anywhere else to go. She was in the living room, crying, when he arrived. He ignored her and went up to his room. He'd said all he had to say to her when he told her to go home, before he helped Herrin dispose of Leiv's body.

Part of him — a bigger part than he'd like to admit — didn't want to lose Raina. Even after all she'd done. Even after all the lies. But he could never trust her again and unless he found some way to get past that, they were through.

He got angry all over again as he remembered that Leiv and Raina would have readily taken Cori's life, that they *had* taken his. This whole time, he'd had no clue that his own "family" was to blame for him being a zombie. They'd killed him. Turned him. Made him this thing he hated.

It was too much.

And he had no clue what to do with the whole mated *Save* thing. He'd have to talk to Aiken about it — since he was apparently the only one of his kind Grayson could trust. But later, when things settled down. Right now, the guy had enough to deal with.

Grayson showered, hoping to somehow take his mind off the horrible events of the night. It didn't work. He was haunted by images of Peg on the cold muddy ground, jerking and seizing. Of her lying dead in Aiken's bed. Of Aiken as he waited for her to rise. Of how he looked after she woke. He couldn't imagine what the Reaper must be going through.

If it had been Cori…

He squeezed his eyes shut and leaned his head on the cool tile wall of the shower. He was so grateful she wasn't suffering Peg's fate. So very thankful she wasn't one of the Dead.

And to think, really it was all Grayson's fault. If he was truly honest with himself, he'd have to admit that Leiv had been acting strange the last few days. The limp. Needing excess water. Why hadn't he paid more attention? Been more vigilant? Now he was responsible for the misery Aiken was in, and worse than that, he was responsible for Peg's heinous death.

And there was no way for him to fix it. You can't undo dead.

He got out of the shower and collapsed onto his bed. He didn't think he'd be able to sleep, but his eyes only lasted a few minutes before sliding closed.

He couldn't tell how long he'd been asleep or even when the dream started, but at some point he rose from his bed, fear so thick it felt like lava weaving through him. He'd never felt like this before. He must be dreaming, but he couldn't be sure. He scanned his bedroom looking for the danger, but he couldn't find any threat. So he lay back down, tried to relax.

The next time he opened his eyes he was standing in front of Cori's house. It was dark and all the lights were off inside. That same feeling of terror washed over him, nearly crippling him.

What was this?

From the darkness of the house, there was a sudden terrified scream. His fear notched up a thousand levels because he recognized that scream. It was Cori.

Without thinking, Grayson tore open the front door and charged inside. There was another dreadful wail as he hit the stairs two at a time and more whimpering as he flung open the door to her bedroom. It took Grayson wasted seconds to piece together what was going on. There was Cori, lying on the bed, her eyes wide with fright. Raina was holding her down, not even fazed by her panicked struggle. A giant syringe full of a brown substance was jammed in Cori's left arm. Four more just like it sat empty on the wood floor.

"No!" Grayson screamed as Raina thrust the plunger on the syringe. He charged, knocking her into the opposite wall. Where she stayed.

"It's finished," she said. "She'll be like us now. It is as it should be."

Cori stared at him in horror.

"I'm so sorry," he whispered, anguished. Grayson knelt by her bed. She would be dead in a matter of minutes. "Angel…" His voice was throbbing. "I-I can't reverse it. You're going to turn."

"Turn?" she cried. "Like Peg?"

"I'm so sorry, Cori."

She reached for him, so many tears streaming down her pretty face. He held her desperately close. How could this have happened? How could he have let it?

"What if…what if I don't remember you?" She was crying so hard she could barely speak. He couldn't catch all the tears, but he tried. Just like that first time. These burned him all the more. They were sour, an angry acid.

"You will," he said, forcefully. "I won't leave you. I'll stay with you the whole time, I swear."

"I love you, Grayson."

He froze. He wanted to say it. So badly. He just couldn't.

"Tell me," she begged. "Please say you feel the same way."

His mouth opened, intending to say the words he felt, that he'd felt for so long…but they just wouldn't come no matter how hard he tried. It was as if something had a lock on his vocal cords.

Her face crumpled. And then she started seizing.

Suddenly, he could speak. "I love you too," he said. And then he screamed it. "I love you too, Cori. Do you hear me? Please hear me! I love you."

He squeezed his eyes shut because he couldn't stand to see her body convulsing against him the way it was. It meant she was dying. This couldn't be happening. He couldn't lose her.

When she went still, he opened them again. But he wasn't in Cori's bedroom. He was in his own. In his bed. Breathing hard and fast in a choking spasm.

It was a dream. A nightmare. Oh, thank god.

But he had to be sure.

Grayson jumped out of bed and ran downstairs. He checked the kitchen, the living room, the bedrooms, the computer room. Raina was nowhere to be found. He looked outside, in the den, and as a last ditch effort, Leiv's room. She was gone.

A ball of dread hit Grayson smack in the center of his chest. He had to check on Cori. After running upstairs to get his phone, he drove his car to her house as fast as it would go. On the way there, he called her. She didn't answer. He tried again and again, but nothing.

When he arrived and saw that the house was dark just like in his dream, the dread built in layers. In his mind all he could see was Raina jamming the syringe full of tainted blood into Cori's arm.

Grayson ran to the door and pounded on it with his fist. Fear pounded his temples with each second she didn't answer. He pounded more, harder, he even tried the handle, but it was actually locked.

Just when he'd decided to kick the door in, the faint click of the lock turning stopped him. And then she was there in front of him, yawning and looking sleepy…but alive.

Grayson couldn't stop the progression of panic that had started deep inside him, though. He stepped forward and caught her by the arms, yanking up the sleeves of her sweatshirt and checking for needle marks.

"Grayson? What are you doing?"

"I…I…"

He took her face in hands, inspecting everywhere he could see. She seemed fine but he still couldn't make his chest stop pounding.

"Hey," she said, seeming to wake up. "What's wrong with you?"

"Are you okay?" he asked fervently.

"Yeah, of course. Why?"

He shook his head because there was no way he could explain it to her. Instead, he wrapped her in a hug, squeezing too tight, but he couldn't help it.

"Are *you* okay?" she squeaked out.

No. No, he was not okay. He'd dreamed of her dying. Dying without knowing how he felt about her. Without knowing that she was his everything, that he needed her more than air to breathe. Even on her deathbed he hadn't been able to say it.

He had to say it now. She had to know.

"I have to tell you something," he said as he rubbed his cheek over the top of her head.

She was here. She was safe. She was his. Everything else was just details.

"What is it?"

He pulled away, just enough to look in her eyes, eyes that held him to the ground.

"I love you." It came out more easily than he'd anticipated. So he kept going. "I love you so much it scares me sometimes. I just wanted you to know."

Slowly, she smiled a sweet little smile. "I think love is supposed to be a bit scary."

Grayson relaxed. "You think so?"

Cori nodded. "Are you okay? After last night, I mean?"

"I'm fine."

She gazed at him, her eyes searching. "I'm so sorry about your brother. And your sister."

"I don't want to talk about them."

Her fingers traced his jaw. "Okay. For now." She laid her head against his chest and he wondered at how right it felt. "What do you think will happen with Peg? Will she be all right?"

He nodded and tamped down the shame that crept over him. "She's strong. It will take her some time to adjust, but she has her friends to help. It's lucky that she remembers so much."

"And what about Aiken? Will he be okay?"

Grayson fought a shiver. "They will work things out," he said with faith.

Huh. Faith. Another thing for him to wonder over.

Cori nodded. "Yeah. I suppose they will."

"We are okay though, right?" He hated having to ask, but he needed to know for sure.

Cori reached up and touched his face. Her gaze sparkled with emotion that made him warm inside. "Better than okay, I think."

He breathed a sigh of pure relief. He knew they still had so many things to sort out, but for now they were okay. She was alive. And human. And she loved him.

Better than okay.

He kissed her lips and realized that even though the worst had happened a mere twenty-four hours ago, right here, right now, with her…things really were better than okay.

Epilogue

He ran.

It was all he could think to do — to run. Just run.

Everything hurt. His whole body. His head. His eyes. His throat.

She was dead. No, she was one of the Dead. He knew the difference.

It was his fault. He hadn't protected her. He would have died to prevent what had happened, but in the end, he hadn't. He should die now, again. Yes, a life for a life. Seemed right.

The worst part was he'd almost been relieved. Almost. Because he wouldn't have to fight the pull anymore. While waiting for her to rise he'd envisioned their future. The future that only a few hours ago had seemed non-existent, was suddenly within reach. Even if it was at a ghastly expense. Things wouldn't have been easy for either of them, but none of that would matter because they could be together. They would've gotten through things *together*.

Peg hadn't woken the way he'd expected. She remembered more. But not him. She didn't remember *him*. which meant she didn't remember the time they'd shared. And she didn't remember the things he'd told her. She didn't remember the promises she'd made. What little they'd had together was wiped away as though it had never even existed.

Aiken remembered it *all*. Every little detail.

How would he get through this?

A horrid surge of physical pain broke through all the throbbing he was feeling on the inside and he realized he'd run too far. With no water. And the sun was shining.

He stopped. Had to. His joints were locking up like the Tin Man without oil. Glancing down at his hands he noticed his thin shriveled skin but couldn't find the will to care much.

Apparently he wouldn't have to wonder how he would get through anything. Peg's death, resurrection, and amnesia wouldn't affect him much longer.

In a lame last ditch effort to live, he raised his nose to the air, sniffing for a water source. There was nothing close enough.

Shame blanketed him anew. Not only had he failed to protect his *Save* in her first life, now he wouldn't be there for her second one either. But she had Rex. And Cori. She wasn't alone. And the way she'd looked at him when she woke…

When she found out what had happened to her, she wouldn't want him around anyway.

Yes, it was okay to go. Better, probably. For her. For him.

Over. It was finally over. This half-life, half-death he'd been living was finally finished.

He sank to the ground. Not even the leaves there were wet. The sun had stolen all their liquid too. Another cramp wracked him and he curled into a ball.

He thought of Peg, but it made the pain worse. No matter. She was the final thing he wanted on his mind when the end came. Green emerald eyes. Red bouncing curls. Chipped front tooth. But her smile…oh, her smile.

As he lay gazing at the fractured sunlight through the tree limbs he was suddenly doused with liquid. The force of the splash hit his tissue-paper fragile body like a wall of bricks. Then, just as quickly, his cells began absorbing, plumping, and reliving.

He glanced around but couldn't find the source of the water before another wall of liquid hit him in the face. Sitting up, he searched for the source and found a familiar face gazing passively at him.

"Get up," she said. Two now-empty buckets were at her feet.

"Why'd you do that?"

"Because. You have work to do. Now get up."

He just stared at her. Brown eyes that he knew weren't really brown narrowed into a glare. "I told you this would happen, fool."

Siam wasn't a patient Oracle. However, Aiken didn't care about that—or anything else—at the moment.

"You never told me this," he yelled.

Her rusty blond head cocked to the side. "Didn't I? 'If you refuse this information, you will be sorry, Reaper. More sorry than you can imagine.' I believe those were my exact words to you." She dug in her backpack and came out with a bottle of water.

Aiken shakily stood, glaring down at her and the water she was offering. "That was a threat, not a warning."

She shook her head in disagreement. "I also told you the best way to protect her was to know about her."

He scoffed. "What could I have known that would've prevented her from being bitten?"

Shrewd eyes bore into him and he swore he could almost feel the burn of the nearly white irises that were so expertly hidden behind contacts. "You could have known the extent of her inquisitive nature." She took a threatening step toward him. "You could have known how protective she is when it comes to those she cares for. You could have known and predicted how those two traits would've coupled together as she witnessed Grayson taking Cori into the woods. Then," the word snapped from her mouth, "maybe you could have prevented the turning of your mate."

Aiken swallowed hard. She was right. The Oracles were always right.

"There's nothing I can do now," he whispered, grief swamping him anew.

"Wrong," she huffed, shaking the bottled water at him. "There is plenty for you to do."

He finally took it but couldn't make himself drink. "Don't toy with me, Siam. There is no way to undo what has been done."

She crossed her gloved arms over her chest. He only just realized what she was wearing: black and pink striped leggings under jean shorts, a black T-shirt, and elbow length leather gloves. She had to be the only seven-thousand-year-old who could get away with dressing like that. Seriously.

"True," she agreed. "On both accounts."

He scowled at her. "Quit reading my mind and get to the point."

"You can't change what has happened to Peg. But there is still work for you to do."

Aiken shook his head. "I'm done. I don't want to be a Reaper any more."

"Why? Because you failed the one most important to you?" It was something he'd been thinking since Peg was first bitten, but to hear it out loud made it real, made it sting. "Well, too bad. She's still yours, Aiken. Still your responsibility. And besides, there's a bigger problem."

Her tone was enough to make him pay attention.

"Grayson and Cori," she said. "You know the law. They can't be together unless she is turned."

Aiken's heart sank even lower. Yeah, his plan to turn a blind eye on Cori and Grayson's relationship until he could leave town went out the window when Peg got bit.

"Grayson is like me," he told her. "He'll never turn her."

She nodded, gravely. "I know."

"There has to be a way, Si." He didn't even try to mask the desperation in his voice.

"There is no way around the law, Reaper. You know that." Even she couldn't keep the sadness from her tone.

"That's one rule I've never understood. Why? Why can't they be together?" he demanded.

Her face took on a frosty demeanor, her eyes becoming haunted, and was she trembling? One of the great Oracles, trembling?

"They simply can't," she said in a hard way that told him that was all she'd say on the subject. He should care more about what she was telling him, but all he could think about was what had happened to his *Save*.

"Why doesn't she remember me?" he croaked, not caring what she thought of his jumbled emotions.

"She does."

He almost laughed. Except it really, really wasn't funny. "No, she doesn't."

Siam let out an exasperated sigh. "She does. She just doesn't right now."

A tiny flutter of hope bloomed in his chest. "So, she will? Remember me?"

Siam nodded. "Yes. But it may not be to your advantage, Reaper."

"What? Why not?" If only Peg could remember, he knew everything would be all right. Knew it deep down.

"That is all I can say on the matter," she said, cryptically.

He stepped closer to her. "Si, tell me. What do you mean?"

Her lips parted to speak but then slammed shut, seemingly of their own accord. She appeared frustrated but finally she said, "Your instructions are to return to your mate, to help her as much as you can, as much as she will allow you. And one more thing, beware of the *carrier.*"

Carrier? There was a *carrier* in Asher?

"Who?" he rushed out. He must know who the *carrier* was. He *needed* to know.

She shook her head. "You will know soon enough."

And then, like an apparition, she was gone.

Acknowledgments

There are too many people whose influence culminated in the creation of, as a dear friend put it, "One of the strangest zombie stories I've ever read." Though I'll never be able to express my gratitude to all, I'd like to say thanks to some, without whom, *Fatal* would never have been published.

To my seventh grade English teacher, Mrs. Geneva, for being so infectious and making reading fun by playing the best of the seventies CDs during class. And for introducing me to *The Giver* and *The Outsiders*.

To my many writer friends on Twitter (yes, I'm talking about you!) for making me realize I'm not crazy, I'm just a writer.

To my critique partners and beta readers: Jennifer Brown, Maria Cope, Summer Wier, and Drew Hayes, for talking me down off the ledge when I was riddled with self-doubt, and for lending a virtual slap when my weirdness started to take over the manuscript.

To the wonderful team at Omnific for taking a chance on me. Jennifer Haren, Elizabeth Harper, Lisa O'Hara, Colleen Keough Wagner, Sean Riley, and Traci Olsen. I couldn't have asked for better people to work with.

To my mama, who always told me I could do anything I put my mind to. For reading my work over and over and over. For feeding me. For everything.

To my littles, Courtlyn and Ronan, for making me laugh when I wanted to cry. Love!

And last but definitely not least, to my husband, Johnathan. For reminding me that true love is nothing like fiction. But mostly for knowing how to make a really good cup of coffee and being willing to wash dishes.

About the Author

T.A. Brock lives in Oklahoma, where zombies do not thrive. When not immersed in the world of fantasy writing, she enjoys spending time with her big girl, baby boy, and hubs. Some of her favorite things are coffee (specifically with cream, sugar, and chocolate), music (especially something with a good beat), books (especially paranormal), and tennis. She despises raw meat and therefore is exceedingly glad she's human.

⟵ ⟶ New Adult ⟵ ⟶

Three Daves by Nicki Elson
Streamline by Jennifer Lane
Shades of Atlantis by Carol Oates
The Heart series: *Beside Your Heart* & *Disclosure of the Heart*
by Mary Whitney
Romancing the Bookworm by Kate Evangelista
Fighting Fate by Linda Kage
Flirting with Chaos by Kenya Wright
The Vice, Virtue & Video series: *Revealed* (book 1) by Bianca Giovanni

⟵ ⟶ Erotic Romance ⟵ ⟶

The Keyhole series: *Becoming sage* (book one) by Kasi Alexander
The Keyhole series: *Saving sunni* (book two) by Kasi & Reggie Alexander
The Winemaker's Dinner: *Appetizers* & *Entrée* by Dr. Ivan Rusilko & Everly Drummond
The Winemaker's Dinner: *Dessert* by Dr. Ivan Rusilko
Client N° 5 by Joy Fulcher

⟵ ⟶ Paranormal Romance ⟵ ⟶

The Light series: *Seers of Light, Whisper of Light* & *Circle of Light*
by Jennifer DeLucy
The Hanaford Park series: *Eve of Samhain* & *Pleasures Untold* by Lisa Sanchez
Immortal Awakening by KC Randall
The Seraphim series: *Crushed Seraphim* & *Bittersweet Seraphim*
by Debra Anastasia
The Guardian's Wild Child by Feather Stone
Grave Refrain by Sarah M. Glover
Divinity by Patricia Leever
Blood Vine series: *Blood Vine* & *Blood Entangled* & *Blood Reunited*
by Amber Belldene
Divine Temptation by Nicki Elson
Love in the Time of the Dead by Tera Shanley

⟵ ⟶ Historical Romance ⟵ ⟶

Cat O' Nine Tails by Patricia Leever
Burning Embers by Hannah Fielding
Good Ground by Tracy Winegar

Romantic Suspense

Whirlwind by Robin DeJarnett
The CONduct series: *With Good Behavior* & *Bad Behavior* &
On Best Behavior by Jennifer Lane
Indivisible by Jessica McQuinn
Between the Lies by Alison Oburia

Anthologies

A Valentine Anthology including short stories by
Alice Clayton ("With a Double Oven"),
Jennifer DeLucy ("Magnus of Pfelt, Conquering Viking Lord"),
Nicki Elson ("I Don't Do Valentine's Day"),
Jessica McQuinn ("Better Than One Dead Rose and a Monkey Card"),
Victoria Michaels ("Home to Jackson"), and
Alison Oburia ("The Bridge")

Singles and Novellas

It's Only Kinky the First Time (Keyhole series) by Kasi Alexander
Learning the Ropes (Keyhole series) by Kasi & Reggie Alexander
The Winemaker's Dinner: RSVP by Dr. Ivan Rusilko
The Winemaker's Dinner: No Reservations by Everly Drummond
Big Guns by Jessica McQuinn
Concessions by Robin DeJarnett
Starstruck by Lisa Sanchez
New Flame by BJ Thornton
Shackled by Debra Anastasia
Swim Recruit by Jennifer Lane
Sway by Nicki Elson
Full Speed Ahead by Susan Kaye Quinn
The Second Sunrise by Hannah Downing
The Summer Prince by Carol Oates
Whatever it Takes by Sarah M. Glover
Clarity (A *Divinity* prequel single) by Patricia Leever
A Christmas Wish (A *Cocktails & Dreams* single) by Autumn Markus
Late Night with Andres by Debra Anastasia

www.ingramcontent.com/pod-product-compliance
Lightning Source LLC
Chambersburg PA
CBHW020358120726
47904CB00002B/622